GREENLOCK FARM

BY

DERNBERGER SPENGLETON

Copyright © 2016 Dernberger Spengleton

All rights reserved.

ISBN-10: 069281678X
ISBN-13: 978-0692816783 (Spengleton DBA)
[Second Edition]

ACKNOWLEDGEMENTS

I acknowledge various things including the existence of gravity, the concept of neural plasticity, and the proofs of Gödel's incompleteness theorems. I also acknowledge the Surreal Times newspaper (surrealtimes.net) along with its editors and correspondents. Finally, I acknowledge my family.

DEDICATION

I hereby dedicate this fine story to the Castle, her Village, and all her Inhabitants gnarly or sweet. I'll see you inside the walls, my friends. We will cut firewood and sing songs and build our very own kingdom.

GREENLOCK FARM:

The Tale of Tomph and Yofim.

ONE

    Grand oak trees lined the fields at Greenlock Farm. It was morning, and two boys awaited the working hours that would soon come. One of these boys was lanky, tall, and awkward. He stood in direct sunlight despite the cool, mossy shade available just beside him. This was typical of him, being the type to strain in all his efforts mental or physical. This was the nature of Tomph.

    Tomph's friend, the second boy, was short and plump. Generally, he was aloof and playful. He was Yofim, the boy who kept things simple while Tomph, in contrast, would aggrandize even the smallest of troubles to enormous scale.

    Something caught Tomph's eye that made him question his sight. So he asked his friend, "There, on the rockside! Do you see that, Yofim?"

    Yofim shook his head. He responded, "I see nothing, Tomph. Why must you suggest so often the existence of nonexistent things?"

    "Because there are things, for you nonexistent, which are plenty real to me. I was inquiring as to if this was one of said things."

    Dawn had almost undeniably come. So, in lagging resolution of their time before work, the two boys loitered on their hillside. From there they could see long, tall rows of cornstocks that blended with silhouettes of mountains in the horizon. From the high end of the field, one had perspective over everything. The farm was beginning to grease its gears and dust its cobwebs, picking up speed. Yofim dug his bare toes into the cool moss. He sat with his legs crossed. Tomph remained standing, watching in awe of stallions carrying knights in shining armor, equipped with magnificent swords.

Concluding his morning daze, Tomph watched smoke belch and bellow from the bakery smokestack. He watched miscellaneous farmhands sputter into life, in general, he watched the farm spread its wings. But an acorn rolled in from somewhere into Tomph's tunnel of vision. This nut toppled and bounced through a tangle of exposed tree roots. It captivated our Tomph, and our Tomph followed it intensely as it first tumbled like a football then rolled like a frisbee. It meandered its way eventually into the lap of Tomph's big-boned friend who sat cross-legged on the ground. Yofim recruited the stray nut into his growing collection of things --- a collection composed of three subordinate collections: one stack of leaves, one pile of stones, and one tangle of barbed-together pine cones. Yofim mixed his sorted piles into one heterogeneous concoction. Until then he was careful in his efforts to segregate. He added the acorn into the mix, not unlike a leaf, stone, pine cone, or any other miscellaneous fragment of nature that might have been included.

Tomph blared, "What'd you do that for?!?!" He rushed over, slid to his knees, and delved into Yofim's pile of hay, searching for the needle that he knew was hidden someplace inside. He screamed, "What have you done?! You blind imbecile, void completely of foresight. What have you done?!! What have you done? What have you done?" His scrambling intensified. "Yofim, you invalent. Move here and assist me this instant!"

Goofy, good-hearted Yofim was keeled over giggling now. For, to outbursts such as this one, he had grown accustomed. In fact he had grown to take satisfaction in prodding at Tomph's instabilities.

The acorn, Tomph finally understood, laid out of his reach. Hence the boy shifted his attention to Yofim. He berated and begged him, asserting, "You are unable to be helped, fat one. Me, however, I must survive the week if I'm to be at the very least present for the invasion, let alone prepared. Therefore, I beg of you, Yofim. Retrieve the totem. It is imperative to my well-being as well as the community's in whole."

All these words and their tone did nothing but exacerbate the natural state of Yofim. He giggled and his giggling reverberated back, angering Tomph further and thereby winding Yofim's laughing box a few cycles more. Tomph sloshed Yofim's collection of items all around, flattening it, broadening it, digging until he hit ground. The totem... the totem.... it was nowhere to be found.. Tomph dug his nails into the virgin soil. Yofim erupted laughing, eventually with an intensity that Tomph could not ignore.

"What are you huffing about, you maniac?" Tomph asked. Only then did he find his unhelpful friend jabbering incomprehensibly, laughing off his head with an acorn between his fingers. Not a totem, but an acorn. Tomph saw this now, and he felt his friend's watering eyes burning through his skin.

So much anger surfaced in that moment, it seemed Tomph would implode. He cocked back his hand, preparing to deliver a powerful blow. A moment of clarity came, though, during the last instant possible. Our subject had lurched forward to strike Yofim, but ultimately, his hand fell only as a playful slap upside his friend's head. Playful as it was, it brought about an imperfect sense of relief.

Tomph said, "You jokester... Often I wonder why, for your jokiest of jokes, you choose the most sensitive situations."

"It's because you are my friend, Tomph. You love me indeed!"

"Oh, of course, yes, I am sure. I am sure," Tomph said.

Gradually the rising sun illuminated the northern fog that sloshed in, down and around the valley. 8:00am had come, and so, per usual, the boys began their journey across the fields. The cows were to be milked.

Tomph urged, "We must hurry, Yofim. We are running late."

Again, Yofim joked, "By any measure we aren't running at all! Ha! Haha!"

With that the playful Yofim broke into a belligerent, side-winding run. Tomph hesitated to follow with such carelessness into the precious cornstalks. Ultimately he did, though, but only via an awkward, half-run half-walk. His run, it was the result of giraffe legs combined with his trying to control consciously and precisely all his muscles at once. The boy, tottering, was fundamentally different than his friend Yofim, who taunted, "you were always the slowest!!!!", referencing back to their days pulling sleds of hay to the milkery. "Though I was the fattest!" Those days, the boys would race, pulling terrible hay-bail sleds. Tomph, awkward atop his legs, would fall behind each day, always, to find that the others had returned to the barn for sandwiches. Tomph would be left with the burden of returning the sleds to the utility shed. Tomph cared not about the sandwiches..., but their maker! - Mrs. Greenlock herself!!!! He desired so much to meet her... yet the other boys – they would be scrambling away the moment her hands were empty. No words would be said but:

"Hello, boys."

"Hello Mrs. Greenlock."

"Would you boys like some butter, bread, and milk?"

"Oh yes please, yes, I am hungry!" Tomph imagined the fat one saying.

An obligatory "thank you Mrs. Greenlock" would conclude the interaction.

"You were the fat one indeed.", Tomph told Yofim, who he still chased despite falling behind.

Yofim laughed maniacally. He turned back, but didn't rebut. Instead, he focused forward and quickened his pace, running a tad faster than Yofim's top speed, as to avoid allowing his friend lose hope.

Tomph called, "Run with care, Yofim. Avoid damaging the cornstocks!"

"Of course, not to worry", Yofim assured. In the same moment, he tore a corn stock from the dirt, roots and all. He tore up a second stock, and he swung these together as a double braided scythe which, if swung swiftly enough, would slice out the bottoms of cornstalks. Yofim went on smashing and slicing, and picking up new stalks when his broke.

This was the necessary impetus that brought Tomph to a full sprint. He pleaded to Yofim, "You mustn't do this to me. In one week, we will be harvesting the quarter. Time is scarce! We'll need every stock!"

Yofim stopped 30 yards ahead. From there he grinned a maniacal grin that drove Tomph into an ever-faster sprint. Tomph panicked. Would he swing now, with that cornstalk scythe? "No. Don't you dare! No. Please!"

It was not until the last moment, when Tomph was nearly in range to grab Yofim, when Yofim swung widely, wildly, chanting, "Down with the cornstalks! Down with you, and DOWN WITH YOUR COMMUNITY."

Tomph leveraged his shoulder into a tackle such that Yofim's final words were uttered in flight. Soon Yofim learned the ground was hard, and that Tomph was not as harmless as he seemed. Wrestling on the ground, they rolled into more cornstalks that toppled and crunched. The scramble left the boys tangled together under a heap of vegetation. It was dark underneath the greenery.

Light came only when Mr. Tomleson meandered about on his gopher rounds, and when the thick-framed man poked at the tumbling ruckus.

"Lord's nostrils, what is that?", he said.

He readied his pitchfork. But the beast before him seemed more lively than a gopher. So he was hesitant to prod it. He was rightfully hesitant, as it turned out. Because there were children there, not gophers.

Nonetheless the children were in a place where they ought not have been. So…

DONK.

Tomph fell by a heavy blow from Tomleson's pitchfork handle. Confused, Yofim squirmed under Tomph's limp weight. Having freed himself, he rose to his knees. He investigated. He thought, "What in the name of?" Then, a moment after, another DONK came, and there was darkness.

Barely hindered, Mr. Tomleson carried an unconscious hooligan in each of his arms. He muttered, "God-damned hooligans," shaking his head, blowing cigar smoke into the early morning fog, and continuing his gopher hunt.

Not long after, a hog peeped from its hole. It was a snoop. Too curious. Too eager for its own good. Mr. Tomleson took a deep, savorous drag of his cigar. He exhaled all he had and he watched this hog. It was paralyzed. So Tomleson took his careful time setting the boys down, setting his cigar down, and tightening his belt all the while his pitchfork stayed leaning against his leg. He balanced his cigar in an armpit of a ripe green cornstalk. It remained smoldering. From his satchel, Mr. Tomleson retrieved some warm kernels of corn, and he tossed them down. The hog scurried from its hole, only to be stabbed through the torso. Soon, Tomleson was peeling the carcass from his pitchfork with his foot. He left the twitching creature jammed sideways in its hole.

Tomleson put down his pitchfork. He groaned as he squatted awkwardly, reaching for his cigar that had fallen down. He was careful to avoid dropping the boys, who he had balanced upon his shoulders. He got the cigar between the tips of his fingers. And he stood up, and he grumbled, "on to the next one," before putting the cigar between his lips.

This freed up one of his arms, which he now used to carry his pitchfork. Mr. Tomleson got on walking. Upon an inward breath, his cigar re-ignited. He took a deep drag, and he exhaled through the corner of his mouth, spawning a swirling eddy of hot smoke which began to rise, cooled, then fell intermixing with the surrounding fog.

TWO

Books lined grand shelves in the Master's library. On the center desk, various papers and things laid illuminated by the skylight. The architect had oriented this skylight precisely as to enable reading and writing at the desk despite darkness pervading the remainder of the room.

From the shadows behind his desk, Master Greenlock said with conviction, "I can't have you boys causing such ruckus 'round here. Not on this day. Not on any day henceforth. And so I've decided..."

Tomph pleaded, "Do not banish me, Master!"

"Do not interrupt me, boy. Not in my house, not on my farm. I have decided. Tomph, you are to mend the North fences with Omnious. Begin in the morning. And you, Foolish One, I'll have you by my side henceforth. There is no work in a thousand miles I could entrust you with."

Yofim joked, "Have you no mind sir?! Tomph cannot mend his toe-nails let alone a fence. Let me fix the fences. Keep the loon by your side. He is a loon."

"Pipe down. Pipe down, I say. My reasons are my reasons, of which you needn't be aware. Furthermore I know of only one winged-idiot around these parts," the Master said.

The master was stern. Yet Yofim found reason to grin. "Who, master?" he asked.

"I stare into his eyes. The boy who, even with wings, could not fly."

Tomph had been sitting cross-legged on the floor. Now he stood, bowed his head, and made his way. Yofim followed him out.

The Master called, "Where are you going, boy!"

Without turning back, Tomph answered, "to do my duty."

"Do not bother. The cows have been milked."

To these words, Tomph did turn. And he asked, "By whom, master!?" But the Master spun his chair to face the wall, leaving Tomph to wallow and eventually depart. That night, the boys did not speak.

THREE

Tomph got up early to prepare for his first day with Omnious. His boots needed to be waterproofed; therefore, a hike to The River Round would be necessary. This "River Round" is a sharp curve in the river 2 miles southwest of the barn. Clay deposited there is fine enough to be water resistant. Tomph would line his boots with it.

Climbing down from he and Yofim's shared hay-barn loft, he stopped beside the second-floor utility area. Instead of stepping off his ladder and entering the utility area, he leaned sidewards and reached outward a long but manageable reach. After a brief struggle, he was climbing down again, now with pale in hand.

Typically he wouldn't rise so early. The morning darkness felt foreign. It was frightening. Equally, it was enlightening. Free of pecking signals from his eyes, his mind could breath. The wind, the rustling trees, the forest. It all meandered into Tomph's consciousness with a lucidity he hadn't experienced in a long while. The water, though miles away, felt ever near. With his feet Tomph could feel the trail's natural guardrail. It guided him through the darkness. The sounds from the river grew all-encompassing. A storm seemed to be just beside him. With each step forward, the sound of the current grew nearer, so near, he feared that, in darkness, he would stumble upon the riverbank unexpectedly.

Soon, as envisioned, he found himself trapped in the cold,

powerful eddy currents. One step past the edge left him wallowing, this time with water and fishes in place of the Master's gaze.

While underwater he pondered his early days on the farm. As a child, he was a vagabond. The Master told him this once (Tomph didn't remember the fact himself). But the community embraced him as the promising young boy he was. There was work to be done. But the work was not excruciating. And more importantly, it felt necessary. One felt hunger often enough, in those days, for labor and togetherness to feel necessary. Life was not easy. But it was good. Each morning, before work, Tomph would wake up his fried Yofim, the boy who'd wandered into the farm on the same day he had. And together, they'd climb down the ladder from their bedroom in the barn (that was once a hay storage room), and they'd push and shove as kids do, crossing the apple fields. They'd make it just in time for morning song with their community of friends and mentors and neighbors.

Their first morning set a precedent for the rest. The community watched, seeing the boys poke and prod each other as they raced to the meeting place where they'd been told to meet. Not a single note sounded until the boys arrived. That was the unspoken rule. People observed excitedly but quietly, because the written rule, SPEAK NOT BEFORE THE FAMILY SINGS, in that time, stood in full effect. So people stood smiling, looking at each other silently with open arms. In time, the boys would skid to a stop, leaving mud scrapes in the grass, and the orchestra would lift off, Omnious carrying the rhythm, The Master singing gallantly, and a slew of others contributing in every which way. Afterwards, Mr. Tomleson would approach the boys. "There's work to be done!" he'd say. And the boys would get excited. "But first!" Mr. Tomleson would stop, pointing toward the boys' skid marks. "Fix your mess."

Songs were improvised because, as Tomph remembered… or absurdly, as he did not remember. The reason why they improvised their songs escaped him. For him, the community was the world. How could he forget?

The community! It had gone so gray. Everything felt tedious now. Tedious, tedious ugliness everywhere. There was no morning song or afternoon embrace. People felt nothing for each other. And only a minority of farmhands would remember things differently. It had been so long...

"What has happened to us?" Tomph wondered.

Then he remembered Granger saying, "We sing not from mind, but from the soul, which possesses no memory." Tomph remembered Granger, and his love, and the love he seeded in those around him. Where had Granger gone?

The bucket! Tomph, lacking air, came to realize his position in the world: under rushing water, soon to drown, and soon to lose the horses' apples that he'd scavenged during the journey to the river. Losing those apples would leave the horses hungry for the day. He hadn't the time to scavenge another bucket. Omnious awaited him. Tardiness would preface doom for him and the community at large, for not a soul on the farm knew of the immanence of which he knew. To be late would be to be banished, and to be banished would be to leave those who he loved helpless against those monsters! Tomph imagined what he'd seen -- heavily greased, smoke-machine driving, churning convoys popping and cracking, crawling along, swinging scythes geared to hands-off destroy all its path. decapitation on wheels MOWING DOWN THE COUNTRYSIDE - A MACHINE MOVING ITSELF, UNPULLED, UNPUSHED, CRAWLING, CARRYING WINGED DEMONS WITHIN ITS HULL.

The apples, the apples, the apples! Scrambling for air on the water's surface, Tomph hitched the bucket with his toe. It was half-full. Floating nearby were two stray fruits. He grabbed these. They were made heavy, saturated by water. Quickly, then, Tomph was on his way, climbing out from the river, galloping back to the horses, back to the day.

One apple was made particularly water-filled and useless by the many earthworm pathways through its core. Tomph wound up and tossed the thing into the trees. On came a most satisfying SPWACK that tempted Tomph to toss another and another apple. Before long, his bucket was empty. He was full of angst running the remainder of the way home.

FOUR

Morning hadn't yet come for the common folk, but Tomph had already conquered death on this day. He was wide awake charging back into the barn and climbing the ladder. A rung snapped on his way up, leaving two sequential rungs in need of repair. This was but a small puddle in his path.

"The time has come," Tomph said to the sleeping Yofim, evoking little response.

The fat one rolled away when Tomph barged in dripping both water and urgency. Yofim grumbled, and he avowed, "The Master will seek me out if he requires me".

Tomph said, "I'm sure he will. As he did with Alfredo, the man unwilling to run. Surely Master awaited him as he would the world's tallest, most beautiful broad. Certainly it wasn't the case that fat man was pushed and rolled off the face of our earth to never eat or live again. Certainly, Yofim. You are undoubtedly correct."

"AHHHHH, WHERE HAS MY FRIEND GONE?" Yofim whined at the seriousness of Tomph and everything in the days of late.

"It is not your friend who has forsaken you but your mind", Tomph said. "Open your eyes, Yofim. The community has decayed to plantation life -- slaves selling their lives to live. Ever since Granger went... wherever he went... Things have been never the same."

"Gahhh, what are you going on about now...", Yofim whined.

"The COMMUNITY, Yofim!"

"May the wasps have your community! That myth, Granger, he is a fairy tale. He is as here as he ever was. He never was. You are leaving me, I'm afraid. You are deluding yourself again."

Tomph winced, preparing to speak of the destruction machine and the winged demons from the west, but he became frustrated and cut toward the door without speaking. The noise of the door slamming and then opening again was a prequel to the noise of Tomph's bucket smashing against the wall just above Yofim's head.

"Gather some apples for the horses", Tomph said, having barged back in. "I must meet with Omnious." The door was left swinging on its hinges.

FIVE

In the East, a great storm terrorized the morning hours. Bodies littered the fields, displacing crops and tearing at the hearts of those who out-climbed the floods. Few souls remained. Fewer souls expected to remain much longer. By their choice or nature's, something would give.

So Master Greenlock spoke of "The bridges.." He told the prestigious son of Mr. Tomleson, "we must raise them, Jack."

But Mrs. Greenlock exploded at this thought. "Dare not suggest such a thing!", she said. "Allow the workers to flee as you would allow the horses to. Unlatch their gates. Damnit! Let them run."

"They won't make it a quarter ways across the canal," the Master explained. "These people, they are buffalo herding toward the cliffside."

Mrs. Greenlock slapped her husband in his face. "How dare you!" she said. "How dare you reduce the human form, handsome as it is, to that of the animal."

The Master rotated his head unflustered back to its natural orientation. "It is not a truth I am glad of," he admitted, "but it is the economical truth."

"You best keep those bridges crossable," Mrs. Greenlock said, "I won't speak to you again until the storm clears. That's it. I'll be where you won't."

"Now where's that?", Master Greenlock asked his wife.

"MY bedroom", she told him.

Jack Tomleson interjected when he shouldn't have, patronizing a woman he clearly underestimated. "Madame, you ought to have more faith in the Master's judgement. When it comes to matters such as these, involving... complications, per se. He understands, you see."

"As to say I do not understand? Shoe, Jack. Be away, you fool. Go immediately."

Soon after Jack made his way, Mrs. Greenlock slammed the heavy oak doors behind her as she retreated to the master bedroom. The Master kept still, awaiting time to confer with Mr. Tomleson, Jack's father and the subduer of the boys, who had stood quietly through all this, knowing better than to engage between matters of Master and Mistress.

Once alone, Mr. Tomleson said, "My apologies, Leo. Jack is young, learned by books but unattuned to the world."

"Quite sharp, too," The Master affirmed.

"That is kind of you to say, my friend."

"It is true," Master Leo said.

The two rejoiced in most attuned rapport. Since their early days, it had been as so. Their interactions were characterized by minimalism, diplomacy, and absence of ego. They understood the importance of composure, and how oftentimes it is necessary to keep mind and mouth separate until thoughts are properly wholesome. But also how it is sometimes necessary to share premature thoughts in order to see if they'll grow better in another mind. Mr. Greenlock and Mr. Tomleson confided in each other on the highest level.

Mr. Tomleson suggested that they make their way to the library.

The Master smiled. It had been years since such a conference with his friend had been necessary. To some degree, he felt opportune under the thunder clouds. Finally, he felt necessary and therefore wholesome. He led Mr. Tomleson around one corner, then another, and through a door. They entered quietly, making certain of their privacy. Then they latched the door shut and begun their discussion.

SIX

In the South, things were normal. The high waters of the East hadn't yet permeated the flatlands characteristic of the region — of slow-flowing, side-winding rivers which divided rolling fields, ranch houses, and cotton farmers. --- cotton farmers bred to be cotton farmers: short, with small hands, and dexterous fingertips, fit for their task. In this place, Uncle Edward and family tended mainline plants, as he and they always had, recruiting help from the miner people of the southern west. These miners were not fit for cotton picking. Still, they picked; for the mines had been dry for forty years, and a worker needs his task. The burly fur-balls found solace at their uncle's side.

Scanning the horizon, one sees sombrero-wearing silhouettes dotting the river's edge. Their shadows stretch long with the morning sun. The sun shines gently from its low angle. A rooster makes its call. Over time, the heat of the day intensifies. Shadows shorten. Silhouettes crawl into the distance. One notices how the smaller figures grow distant more quickly than the larger figures. As a result, the small appear smaller at a faster rate than the large. In the time a miner crosses the cotton field, a cotton farmer might circle back three times over. But when the sun lowers again and everything turns orange, shadows lengthen so long that everyone looks the same.

Rarely would a cotton-picker speak on the cotton field. Because words were made unnecessary long ago. One day, Uncle Edward emerged from his hut wearing a cowbell that the Master had fitted him. From this day onward, Uncle Edward wore this bell. It was not long before the other cotton pickers learned to follow him and his passive jingling. It is rumored that, approaching his hut, one hears him jingling late into the night and also during the early morning hours. It is rumored that he has never slept in his whole life. But it is also rumored that he does nothing but sleep.

In this place, gazing into the distance brings a sense of eternity in the moment. People grow older, having already grown old. Their gray beards continue being gray. Born short, these people remain short. Just the same, every cotton picker stands sun-browned and thin as one can be; for they are born this way. And with this cotton-picking breed alongside the furball miner men, who differ greatly in appearance but look similarly eternal, time flattens into a single dimension. Approaching close enough to see the size of their ears and the age of their noses, is the only way to gauge time. Because these extremities grow even during old age. But from a distance such that the ears and the nose cannot be seen, the steady, crawling silhouettes work, working away always always working as they always work.

Late into one particular day, the silent, diligent silhouettes began catching glimpses of the sky. A profound uneasiness brewed. Gradually, a crowd congregated around Uncle Edward, who kept on picking his cotton strictly as his schedule required. His subjects told him: "Look up, Uncle. Look at the sky," pointing to a great, swirling storm cloud. But despite this urging from his subjects, Uncle Edward kept his head down, picking cotton as he always had, as he always would. He did not wanting to pollute his mind with dreams or fears.

So he told his subjects, "Let the plants stare into the clouds. I will work."

SEVEN

Omnious put a leash on Tomph - because, he explained, water in the marshes sometimes rises. From stillness comes a current that in just seconds renders you one with the fishes. Best be it if the unfortunate souls who plummet down the rapids do so with company and while chained to the cross-logged raft. At least this way you will have someone to talk to when your bones are broken and when you find yourself concussed and washed ashore somewhere you've never been before.

Tomph and Omnious and two more fellows toured the marshes together with their raft. Their task was to repair the walls. These walls towered high over the marshes and they rooted deeply in the muck. They stood as defense against The Tree Swingers of The North.

Greenlock Farm was once the site of grand, mythological battles in which Tree People swung down on rope swings and launched themselves into the air. In the air, they would release spider-web parachutes and use these to float with the wind. They would slingshot meteorites down at the people of Greenlock. The people of Greenlock would reply with bows and flaming arrows.

"We fought back honorably," Omnious said. "But the Tree People control the wind and the water. So we were forced to manufacture a treaty and a wall."

"They are deplorable sometimes", Omnious explained. "They're crafty buggers, though. They live now and will live forever in the trees, by my hammer! Born there, like vines they grow, molding to the way of the wood over time. Eventually they grow sufficient girth to host vines themselves -- to host wood, whose growth they mold into any shape for any function. As such, they are master builders of things -- ladders, catapults, contraptions of all sorts. That is why we barricade here, in the flooded marsh. No tall tree can grow here."

Following Omnious's cue, Tomph scanned his putrid surroundings. Nothing taller than a stump stood for a dozen miles. There were weeds and a strange, white-flowered fungus. Nothing reached taller than the white flowers. Tomph also noticed, pressing his boot into the mud, that the pool's floor was terribly unpredictable: deep then shallow, then deep then deeper, shallow again, and so on.

Tomph said, "I imagine their ladders have trouble here."

"You imagine right," Omnious said, "permitting that the walls are not graspable. So let us smooth out these crevices in which the Trees might clamp their wretched claws. I will prepare the mix."

Omnious directed attention to a small cauldron balanced upon his massive palm. Removing the lid, he unveiled an a priori mixed concoction. When he sprinkled salt into the mix, it spouted a hot cloud of steam. A powerful odor tagged along, but this passed as quick as it came.

Omnious jumped to. He said, "Quickly, Muunsha Mix dries quickly. Take my hand, boy. I am sinking. Pull me up. There. Thank you. Okay. Now, each of you, find yourself a quality green." He told them this, referencing the leaves of the strange white flowers which, in families of threes, caressed their mother blossoms. Omnious plucked one for himself. Then he instructed, "With your green, cup your hands as a chipmunk would, eating its acorn. Boys, do as I do. See. Scoop some Muunsha."

A leaf was plucked from some arbitrary blossom. The next was pulled from the flower that Omnious had pulled his from. This taking of two from three left a lone leaf sentry guarding its flower. Tomph focused on this. He moved to take the final leaf from this flower's stem. But Omnious stopped him before he could.

Omnious said, "no," and he blocked Tomph's hand with

his own. "That won't do. Find a different green."

Omnious blew into his leaf-tube. The pressure belched poignant guck through the tube and onto the wall. "Quickly, boys", Omnious said. "We must hastily apply the Muunsha. It dries quickly. Soon I will make another mix."

And so they worked. Tomph struggled finding a leaf that Omnious would consider proper. Falling behind the others, he worried. He feared Omnious more than the master himself, because Omnious had been since the beginning, perhaps not a founder but a founding member certainly. And he was critical to the sustenance of the community, building contraptions and walls, fighting when necessary, and doing whatever needed to be done in general. He was a backbone of The Community. And it was he who originally retrieved Tomph from the mush, years ago. It was Omnious, he who is a father to few, a duty-bound recluse to all else. Tomph hoped to be a son to him one day.

The wall menders excluding Tomph and Omnious were two: an elderly useless man, trying to make himself worthwhile, and another boy, young, apparently new to the farm. Both of these individuals were foreign to Tomph.

Soon they were racing along, applying Muunsha to cracks in the wall. The elderly man asked Omnious, nervously, "Sir... um, I am applying dees correctly? Seems loose.. Maybe poosh harder?"

"You are fine, Thom. You are doing fine," Omnious reassured him. "Continue as you are."

Thom returned to his work. Either he hadn't been as nervous as he'd pretended to be, or his nervousness faded. Tomph noted that this man's work was pristine. He worked swiftly and effectively.

The younger boy's work, however, was rubbish. He could barely reach even the lowest cracks in the wall. Tomph tried to help him do better. He tried to hold him safely above the water and likewise Omnious's disapproving eyes. Unfortunately Tomph was drowning himself by doing this. He couldn't handle the extra load without falling behind.

The older man, Thom, confronted the boy, and he said, "I sees your trick'ry boy. No need for it. Ask a hand and I'al giv ye one. Good 'ol Thom. Good 'ol Thom on da good 'ol farm."

As they worked, Thom alternated: two leaf's worth of Muunsha mix for his section, one for the boy's. Two for his, one for the boys, and so on. Omnious lent Tomph a leaf's worth every fifth or sixth measure. When Omnious did this for the first time was when a sense of commonality emerged. No longer were they mere laborers serving their master. Instead, they were willing collaborators. Together they pursued what was best for each of them individually as well as the farm in whole.

It wasn't long before they fell into the most sensible arrangement: The boy mixed Muunsha as the others continued mending the wall.

"Like da good 'ol days," Thom said, "ay?".

"Yup, I'd say." Omnious harrrred a laugh, revealing he was capable. Then he suggested to Thom, "Now how about you secure that there flotation device? It's pulling at my leg with the river's strength.

"Yessssir not aproblum." Thom crossed leashes with the boy. A tangle occurred between his and someone else's leash. He had to unlatch himself to manage this. He stored his leaf and various other tools in the raft. Then he tied himself directly to the raft. He got ahold of the main leash, with which he trudged toward the nearest thick stump. He looked at the others because his leash wouldn't quite reach. So he unlatched again, and he trudged toward the stump where he would tie off the main leash.

To Omnious, Tomph said, "May I ask: what are the ingredients to Muunsha Mix? Knowledge of them would be valuable to me in the case a wall elsewhere might require mending."

"That knowledge would be valuable," Omnious said. "Ohhh. harrr. harr. But that is my secret, boy."

"But what if a wall requires mending?"

"Then you ought to holler for me!" Omnious said.

The dismissal hurt Tomph. By consequence he realized water in his boots. The waterproofing! He'd forgotten, during his ordeal at the river, to retrieve clay for his boots. He wouldn't dare tell Omnious of this error, though.

"Loosen your britches boy!" Omnious said. "I play. Harrr Harrr. I play. The ingredients are salt and... listen carefully, boy, for I will say only once. I suppose these are important for all those wishing to serve this land..."

"Of course, of course, of course. I am listening, sir."

Omnious corrected. "Omnious! Not sir."

"Sorry. Yes sir.. I mean yes, Omnious. Yes."

"The ingredients are salt...... and"--- A rumbling polluted the sound space, interrupting Omnious.

Tomph smiled, anticipating minor enlightenment only, but minor enlightenment as a symbol of future teachings and a life lived under the wing of this wise man, who would often converse with him in light of the community, sustenance and life in whole. So much valuable knowledge rested on this man's tongue, and so much more in his memories, heart and mind.

"Okay." Omnious restarted. "My apologies, the ingredients are... well. Rest assured, they can be found under the shoe of Good 'ol Thom. Harr Harr Harr"

Omnious returned to work. Tomph stood disappointed, looking at Thom who, when the currents strengthened, was thrown against the anchor stump, knocked silly, and swept down the marshes that had transformed to rushing, rising white waters. Omnious held hold of the boys with one arm while clinging to the barricade with his other. He redirected water with his back, shielding the boys. Simultaneously he lifted them up. The water lifted him, and he lifted the boys. Eventually the younger boy sat atop one of the wall's columns safely. Tomph climbed up behind him.

Omnious commanded, "Boys! DO NOT MOVE," And he detached himself into the rapids. He went off, searching for Thom, searching for this man --- who was he? Omnious risked his own to save Thom, the strange wanderer, as though he was a childhood friend. But that was Omnious, one moment there, the next: gone, tumbling down the howling rapids to save a stranger.

The boys sat jaws dropped under pounding rain, beside the raft which flailed flag-like in the rapids. They were trapped atop a 5-foot diameter column. It was an island in an endless string of identical islands, connected by untraversably narrow walls. Birds were darting frantically in all directions. In the rapids, logs and garbage of all sorts — jagged, pain-inflicting types of horrid things — rushed into the same horizon that Omnious and Thom had disappeared into.

Tomph thought: without Omnious there would be no wall and no backbone to Greenlock Farm. The farm would go flaccid and unprotected, vulnerable, not only to the winged demons and oil-spitting-death-machines, but to the Tree people of the North and other lurking foes. Without Omnious, all that was once good would never rehabilitate, and all things reasonable could never maintain. This once-wondrous place would be rummaged and burned. Yofim and Mr. Tomleson and the Master. His wife. The boy, if he remains. Noone would escape the question: to grill meat for the winged demons in their dastardly machine, or to hang bound by one's feet from the trees as a hell-employed scare crow for all eternity? Drowning would be a pleasantry compared to a life of worms eating out one's eyes.

"Breath. Breath, just breath", the boy said as Tomph hyperventilated. The boy explained, "You are stuck in a breath loop."

"I'm trying. Jesus I'm trying," Tomph said.. "What are you doing? Help!!! Helppp, why must you be still when I am in need?" Tomph, keeled over dying, wondered why the boy remained so calm.

"Because, impatient one,. When I was a boy, more so than I am now, I was nervous many times. Mother would say, 'little one, be calm.' 'Be calm,' she told me. She was good as a mother. I would listened to her. And, soon, everything would be okay. 'Breath, just breath,' my mother would say.

And I would breath, knowing that things would be okay

soon, as they had been before. Suddenly my breaths would feel full again, as yours soon will."

Clouds made way for a beam of sunlight to touch down. The rapids calmed moderately. Still, they were powerful enough to demoralize any hope of escape. They were calmer, though. And, with it being closer to midday now, visibility had improved. In the flow, Tomph spotted a tree-trunk cross-section similar to those used for the construction of countertops in the barn. It floated with the current. On its face, there were carvings. Tomph's chest tightened seeing these indecipherable patterns whose style he recognized. He reached for them... he reached... he reached for them.......

"You idiot", the boy squeaked, grabbing Tomph's arm as Tomph leaned precariously over the waters. "What do you intend, idiot boy? You will fall."

Tomph quivered, eyes darting back and forth between the boy's eyes and the river-turned marsh. "Damn you, boy. I've lost it now, because of you."

Tomph scanned his memory and the river for remnants of those a-million-times-desirable etchings. They were etchings of such unique style. They possessed a square, smiling form. They were dense, comprising no excess. The etchings were fetid as the smell of a lover's love-making scent -- aggressive, animalistic, foul, almost shit-like, but distinctly erotic and evoking a sort of primitive attraction.

EIGHT

Yofim awoke to the moonlight well-rested and with the world to himself. A walk was in order. Possibly to the marshes, to see about Tomph's hell fires? Possibly not. Perhaps along the way of the sea turtle? Possibly yes. Yofim followed the tortoise migration path, having never done so so resolutely before. On this day, he would learn of the creatures' destination, and he would make their destination his own destination.

Creeping, creeping, he crept along, careful to avoid turning wrong. The morning was dark but not black. People were scattered about, focused on their respective tasks. They were silhouettes in the distance. Yofim kept his space from these silhouettes. In turn, the silhouettes kept their space from him as well, being as weary of him as he was of them. So the silhouettes remained silhouettes. Keep calm. Walk on. You'll be in the trees soon.

Soon Yofim was under the green-glazed moonlight that came to be by passing through semi-translucent leaves. He walked casually, picking flowers from beside the migration pathway. It was all a spectacle. The tortoises, tobogganing together like a great river, over many years, had etched a deep, smooth crevice into the mountain rubble. In doing so they pushed aside sticks and stones, depositing them on the path's border. So there was a long, winding canyon with accumulating mountain moisture lubricating it like a slide. And beautiful stone walkways lined this canyon on either side. It extended miles long, two feet wide, a byproduct of the natural way of the tortoise.

Yofim brisked along these rocks, following a stray young tortoise who scurried along having fallen behind his family. Yofim would accompany the young pup. He would see to it that the little guy make it home safe. Because it was dark, cold, and this fellow was young.

The forest thickened. Still, the luge and its stepping stone brim remained consistent, attesting to the power of consistency multiplied by time. But bamboo guardrails did encroach, though they never interfered with the luge itself, and this encroachment made rounding corners difficult for those on foot who wished to keep up with the turtles. But, aha, the brush! Accidentally, Yofim realized that, approaching a leftward corner, he could cut sharply rightward, directly into the dense wall of bamboo brush. Timed properly, this would catapult him perfectly around the leftward corner in a backwards sort of way.

So he went on doing this, matching the pace of Little Alphonse, sloshing down the path that, by consequence of the nature of things, entailed two complementary, inseparable and mutually-dependent luges: a yin for Little Alphonse, enabling him to make his turtle journey, and a yang, the stone path, for Yofim, the turtle's curious protector. Without the stones and the forest providing structure and shelter from the weather, the crevice would flatten. Without the crevice having been formed, the stones would never have been placed, and the bordering bamboo would not have been watered and enabled to grow so thickly.

Suddenly an irregularity blocked Yofim's way. Noticing this, the boy skidded to halt, didn't halt quickly enough, and needed to jump over the impeding shadow. He tripped over the thing.. Falling, he latched his hand to a bamboo stock, which bent down and rebounded him back up and further, lowering him backwards face-to-face with a purple, bloated, water-logged corpse. The corpse's eyes were open wide and bulging. "Help me," they seemed to scream. But they were frozen lifeless.

Yofim froze, staring into those eyes. From their pupils, death flooded the world and Yofim's heart so engulfingly, it seemed he would drown in it. Fortunately the bamboo rebound tugged him out from the water. It launched him running at a speed that a fat boy should never know. He ran and he squealed, "Where are you, Little Alphonse? Waiiiit for meeee." He scrambled to find his little friend. Anything for companionship! For the first time in a long while, Yofim experienced pure instinct. FEAR. He felt it so completely pervadingly, engulfingly... And he ran... and he ran and he luged at a dangerous pace.

Footsteps behinds... no those are mine; those are my echoes. Is that a torch-fire? Lights! No. Are they? Should I abandon this little guy, leaving him and my self to fend for ourselves. Possibly I have no choice. But there is no choice! To be alone in this place would be unthinkable. Where are you

Alphonse!?!?!?!

    Yofim slowed, wanting to hear the woods clear of his own footsteps, breaths, and whimpers. Calm to the senses brought calm to his mind. And there they were!: a multitude of turtles swimming along, weaving amongst one another, playing yet always moving forward. It was so majestic; they gave off this sensation of stillness, despite their swift pace. The turtles were so smooth in their movement, as at rest as a person sitting down. Because true stillness leaves migrationists feeling uneasy. So Alphonse and family swam along aloof or apathetic to the impetus of Yofim's fear.

    They led Yofim to the Eastern Inlet, where the small turtles waited on the waterside looking to find mates. Possibly it was not the mate itself they sought out for. Perhaps instead, mating was a small contingent step in a larger process, that is, the migration. Necessary it was to find a benevolent partner, or protector, who'd permit you to join ranks with the reams of larger, older, wiser tortoises, who could show you the way --- until you learn the way and become capable of traversing it yourself, at which point, you would show others the way. How awestrikingly beautiful it was, the glowing, flowing river of green flowing within a deep, calm blue. The small turtles experiencing their respective individual struggles, attempting to highway merge with the large, faster-moving tortoises. Occasionally an antsy little one would jump out early and be rejected by the stream. Down, down the river, these failures would go. Unable to be helped, never mourned for — that was the way.

    Yofim watched Alfonse. The turtle had a very particular personality. It was so recognizable — almost gravitational for the eyes — how Alphonse scanned the horizon of green tortoises flowing with the current. The turtle was tranquil, knowing that his time would come if it would come. What he awaited was eye contact of some sort - some confirmation of his right to entry - some fleeting interest, at least, that might spark flame once he leaped helplessly into the treacherous waters to compel an adult tortoise to be his savior. And there it was!! Little Alphonse braced himself then launched himself into the currents. He launched himself into God's hands to be gripped by the mandible of a stranger who by nature's way would be his guardian for now and forever. Yofim watched, by that river side, as Mrs. Alphonse positioned Little Alphonse atop her shell. With his beak, Alphonse latched onto his guardian's thick neck leather with all his might. At first he was afraid to cause her harm. Soon the Mrs. raised her head to shield Alphonse from the currents. They sailed into the horizon, so smoothly, so naturally.

But the movement of this green glow created, behind it, a low pressure zone that suctioned in a trail of corpses upon corpses upon rotting corpses. Bodies flowing head-first as though exiting the womb. They weren't exiting, though; they moved toward the farm, Westward, via the inlet. Soon the entire plantation would lay eyes upon this gift from Lucifer. What was the cause?

Yofim thought to fish the bodies from the stream. Possibly with a branch, he could redirect them into this river eddy here, and there they would stay to decompose, at least until he returned with more help.

One corpse, he left it trapped in the eddy. The others passed by before he finished dealing with the first. And so they flowed along, racing with the turtles toward wherever they were going.

"I must find Tomph", Yofim thought. Just as suddenly, he was running upstream into the bamboo trees, slipping, sliding, looking for his brother who might evidently not be as loony as he'd thought. What was he on about the oil machine? The demons?

AHhhhhhhhhhhhhhhhhhhhh......

NINE

Mr. Greenlock tapped softly on the hardwood door to his master bedroom. Upon no answer, he entered. Inside he found wife sound asleep, her lips so peacefully resting upon on one another. They were as the pedals on early spring flowers, chilled but hydrated by morning dew; some soon to die and others to blossom. For a moment he appreciated his lady as one appreciates a sunset or the stars or another beautiful, otherworldly thing that one might appreciate.

Whispering in her ear, he explained "My love, I've brought you tea and chocolate. May I join you in slumber?"

Yet she continued to sleep. So he circumnavigated the bed and put his offerings on the lady's nightstand. Then he circled back to his own side. He set his spectacles on his personal nightstand. He wiped his face with a silk cloth. Carefully, then, he crawled atop the bed, lifted the comforter and slid himself underneath. A small distance separated the arranged couple. A small distance would remain, for if the Master were to close this gap, certain death would come to him. Because no daughter of Elsedorwn would tolerate such an unwelcomed advance. The Master understood this. His wife was in many ways like her mother, Elsedorwn herself, the birther of all this - the community --, who ruled as birds do, with not a fist, but with precisely directed whistles and tweets, which guided people into the woods when they needed woods and out into the sunshine when they needed light. This woman would have things as she wanted them, however she may want them. As such, the Goddess laid there sleeping, and Mr. Greenlock, being unexpecting in his husbandry, he gave her her space.

But Mrs. Greenlock moaned just slightly, adjusting for comfort, and her husband, lying on his back, staring at the ceiling, asked, "Remember your Mother, Gloria?".

Gloria Greenlock grumbled and complained, "Why must you lie beside me despite my commanding you otherwise?"

"Because I am not at your command. We are lovers, are we not? on equal field," Mr. Greenlock observed. "And your mother alone, in her beauty, floats above us."

"My mother was beautiful, wasn't she. How beautiful she was."

Gloria smiled and a glow came over her. Somehow she was possessed be her sacred holy Mother, the mother of all, here on Simanru, the rock on which Greenlock Farm stands. And as the master laid staring at the ceiling, reminding of Elsedorwn, her gracious mixing of stew, loving of all; Gloria, daughter of Elsedorwn, crawled into his frame of vision. She straddled his waist. She raised her arms blissful as an angel levitating from above. Time went viscous. It was as though Mr. Greenlock couldn't...-- Even if needed to, he could not escape that which shimmered divinely above him, her hair and cloths moving freely, beautifully - but soon, with strands of her hair CHURNING as SERPENTS dragging a wake of BLACKENING RIPPLING AIR ENGULFING THE PEACE. She, IT! The THING transformed into a POWERFUL, manipulating DEMON FORCE towering ABOVE.

Only when she leaned down from shadows did she retract her serpents and transform back into the gracious Elsedorwn again. She was beautiful again. She caressed her dearest husband Leo's cheek. She rested her left arm upon his chest. And she leaned in, straddling him tightly with her legs. She leaned in and kissed the Master on his limp lips, imparting on them warmth and perk. She kissed him again and he kissed back, having not reacted quickly enough for the first. On the third or fourth, wrapping his large hands about the rear of her skull, he kissed her, and they eloped into powerful pressing love between God Rorrick and Goddess Elsedorwn.

TEN

    Yofim ran the whole way home. By the time he reached the barn, he was soaking, dripping wet. It rained, and the rain muffled the sound. The world in whole turned into a sanctuarial library where people might go to focus. And through humid air and blurred whispers, Yofim charged in, up the ladder. He pounded on the utility closet-turned-bunkroom door.

    He yelled, "Tomph!!! Tomph!!!!! Get up! We must seek the Master at once. God, do not delay. Fetch your raincoat. The rain is DRENCHING, but we must go. We must!"

    Yofim left the barn, expecting Tomph to follow. But it became evident that those were not Tomph's beholden footsteps trailing behind him, but many a horse's bellowing, that caught his attention. Yofim went back to investigate. As it turned out, one horse alone was inciting the ruckus. The other horses didn't have anything to holler about except for each other's hollering.

    "Calm yourself, horse. Calm. Please calm yourself." Yofim massaged the horses mane. "It's okay," he assured, "it's okay." The hollering of the masses died down as this one horse internalized its panic. It piped down, but it continued heavily. But everything seemed stable enough. So Yofim called for Tomph.

    "Where are you, loon?"

    Suddenly the horse reared up again and NAAAAYYED. It slopped saliva across Yofim's cheek. "What's the matter, girl?" NAYYYYYYYY. She kept jerking her head toward the window like a maniac. It seemed she was hinting at something. Realizing this, Yofim followed the horse's hint to find a small, soaking-wet girl cowering in the stall corner, hiding behind dilapidated hay bales. She wore a dress which, before being mud soaked, was imaginably pure white and seraphic. And she was beautiful, so beautiful. Born of good stock, cherished throughout her years, but now cold, scared, and vulnerable.

This girl cowered as Yofim approached her. The horse got out of the way. Yofim peered into the stall. Getting closer, when he rounded the girl's hay bale barrier, she pulled a bail to her chest and hid behind it, like a child from her father who just wanted her to get ready for school, the girl hoping hopelessly that he hadn't seen her even though he certainly did. She hoped he'd leave. Just leave. But he eased further. By reflex she twisted, letting out a yell and tossing hay strands into the air.

So scared, so jumpy, she yelled, "It's raining out there!"

"Of course it is," Yofim said. "Look at me?" He pointed to his soaking, dripping overalls. "Certainly I'm dry and dandy, ay? Yourself, how are you?"

The hope was that she'd laugh. She didn't. Fortunately there was a crash outside. It was muffled by the pounding rain, but still loud. "Tomph!" he yelled. "You clumsy loon. Where are you?"

Outside, a fallen horse laid covered by staging brackets. It was struggling, groaning. Water splattered down from the roof, causing the poor thing to whine and breath dirty water washed down from the shingles. Such utter discomfort... To the dropping of water, directly onto its side, the horse's skin went raw. Yofim rushed to lift the staging brackets. Poor choice. Scared, the horse jumped and kicked. It nearly kicked off Yofim's head. Then it darted a safe distance away. A crack of thunder sent it a distance further. Yofim instinctively chased after the horse, but his chasing only worsened the situation.

He found the girl's hand on his shoulder. "Wait," she said, "let me lure him in."

She approached the beast, and in doing so, she passed by Yofim, allowing her arm to skirt across the boy's. The girl, she was so perfectly harmless, recognizably so by both man and beast. In just a moment, the beast had lowered his head for her. She brushed its mane. Tomph awed at the sight.

She found herself caught as the subject of Yofim's staring eyes. There was a moment when the rain seemed to halt. The thunder simmered down. All the while these lost kids felt found. In that time Yofim imagined a million things: this girl, her beauty in this place and that, and everything that she was. Then came the suggestion that he ought to search for Tomph. The girl said, "I'll take care of this one," before leaving Yofim alone in the dewy aftermath of rain - alone, free to think the best and worst of thoughts. Thoughts of this mystery girl and her mysterious soaking, dripping beauty, pale skin and white cloth. An angel in the rainstorm. The worst of thoughts, of Tomph and his seeing things. Of the oil machine ramblings and the bodies flowing strictly in line, logs of a logging stream, optimally arranged for speed.

"Where is my friend?" is all he could wonder.

ELEVEN

Tomph was sitting cross legged beside the garden trail when, through a spectacular transparent leaf, he spied the inside of what appeared castle-like, but smaller, like a hobbit's home made of stone. Behind its brownness, this leaf-embodied a window to another world. There were stones and pots and pans, a freshly eaten-off-of home-made picnic table, and goodies and knickknacks all around. A fire fizzled in the fireplace. Beside the fireplace, a sturdy, sturdier-than-the-house rocking chair rocked, and from said chair a knarly bearded giant uttered the words:

"He was hypnotized by the scripture..., the scripture of the Galagna tribe. He was cast under that which many were cast under before him, and to which many are destined to fall prey hence. I myself fell under once. It is easy as so."

The boy from the marshes was in this room inside the leaf. This boy sat cross-legged on the carpet. And he asked, "How so? How so were you cast under?"

"It was before a long while. I could not say how or when. For me to say would be to entrap you as I was entrapped," the man explained.

The boy stayed silent.

"Now what did the words say, my son. What did they sayyyyyyyyyyy." The man, his eyes remained closed, but his words slithered about the ether, endlessly reverberating, inquiring as to what Tomph had seen and as to the shape of the boy's head and inquiring as to everything that could be inquired of. The boy from the marshes recalled in precise detail, describing the properties of Tomph and the marshes so perfectly — more perfectly than Tomph remembered them himself. The boy could not recall the scripture, however, because he had never known it. So he admitted, "Even if I had seen it, sir, I could not comprehend..."

But the man persisted, his eyes still closed. "You did not see? I do not believe you did not see... I believe you did see, my son, though you may not have seen. Be faithful, my son, and you will have seeeeeeeeeeeen....."

The ether churning indicated that the storm had returned. The storm had returned. Churning, growling, churning, "BURNING in the eyes of the world!!! The eyes of the world the eyes of the world the eyes of the world the eyes of the world the eyes of the world the eyes of the world".

Tomph rubbed his eyes. It was so bright. Now there were horses trotting by. He was on the garden trails again, talking groggily as one talks after waking sometimes. He hid behind a tree, leaning against its base. Soon, from the direction behind him, a caravan of horses and two carriages corralled onward leaving scattered fires of leaves in their tracks.

Tomph scrambled to stomp out these fires. In doing so, he lost sight of the caravan. Alone, he was left confused, in the woods, unsure of where he was or how he'd arrived there. He rubbed his eyes, hoping his mind and his vision would clear in along with his lenses. In the end there was darkness. Cold, wet darkness.

He thought of his friend Yofim, who had likely woken up for the day just a short while earlier. Tomph wished he were by Yofim's side.

TWELVE

Despite dreaming he'd been dreaming elsewhere, Tomph found himself again atop a column of the North wall. He awoke to find The Boy crawling across a narrow connecting wall between two columns, high water flowing beneath him. He straddled the connector, inch-worming across on his bottom.

"You will fall!" Tomph warned.

The boy snarked, "Says he who sleeps atop a tree... Come here. Do not cherry my risks when it is in your power to lessen them."

Tomph helped the boy to his feet and steadied him. The crossing was not difficult with two. Safely across, the boy reached back to help Tomph, who crossed also. They inch-wormed together, carefully, along the infinite wall of the North. On the way the boy spoke of his life.

"In my village people lived small lives. Jon was the bread man. Gomas tended to the chickens. I was just a boy. To learn was my job."

And he spoke of his Mother.

"When my knee was scraped, Mother was there," he said. "And when I panicked, she taught me to breath. The village loved her so much...."

"She was a woman you loved," Tomph knew it. "She loved you also."

"Yes but the village loved her so…"

Over and over, the boy repeated this, "they loved her so... they loved her so... they loved her so..."

"She was my mother secondly, the village mother first. She made herself responsible for those in need. No one asked her to do that.... But those in more need than me, she gave them her love first.. I was angry one day because of this. I left the village... Too many people loved her.... She loved too many...."

Tomph worried that, while telling such whole-hearted a story, the boy might lose his focus. So he asked, "What is your name?" hoping to simplify things.

..... "I am Little One," the boy said.

On the upcoming connector, a large chunk of wood had gone rotten. The top edge was uneven, mushy, and coated in slippery rotten algae slime. This made the traverse especially difficult. One had to step down and into the rot crevice while balancing, then fall across to grab the nearest firm, healthy wood.

"Careful," Tomph said, holding the boy's hand.

But the distance was too large -- the boy had to let go from Tomph's hand. So for a while the boy focused on his task alone. His task: to traverse the section of rotten wood barricade. And his ultimate task: to find Omnious and that man, Thom.

Tomph could not help Little One for fear of knocking him off balance or shaking the boards.

Little One kept talking, telling his story. Tomph helplessly pondered it all.

"My mother... This once, Mrs. Ruth's dog had become sick. We didn't have enough supplies. The elders said we couldn't help the dog. It was very sad... So all of us, my friends — we visited the dog every day. We petted him and loved him. He was going to die. Mrs. Ruth was very sad. We hugged her too, and we told her Little Joey would be going to a better place. One day the dog ————"

Little One slipped and nearly fell. He recovered and

continued as though death by drowning hadn't come as near as it had.

"One day, the dog was in great pain. I could see in his eyes... Mr. Ruth whispered to me.. he said, 'little one, there are times when it is okay to give up. But sometimes it takes so much strength... Sometimes one doesn't have that strength.' Mr. Ruth looked to the weak dog, and he looked to himself, and he patted his hand on a cloth covering an item on the small table. He left me alone, in the room, with the sleeping Mrs. Ruth in her recliner, and her suffering, whimpering dog on the floor beside her. Under Mr. Ruth's cloth I found kitchen knife, which I grasped. The dog gave me these eyes... He jumped, he was scared. Then he realized, and..."

Whoa!!!

Little one slipped and landed on his bottom, nearly fell backwards, but held on, balanced in the slippery, rotten connector crevice. He continued talking as though he had never been in any danger.

"These encouraging, understanding eyes eased my fears. They said, 'it's okay, Little One, I am ready. Please, suffer me no longer.' So I took the knife from its sheath."

THIRTEEN

In the barn, The Mystery Girl comforted the horse in its stall. "I'm sorry love," she said. "You can be calm now. See, the rain is slowing already. Everything is calming... Be like Everything. Be calm." She said this and soon the horse seemed comforted enough for the girl to leave and to latch the door behind her.

A dank odor filled the interior of the barn. Just outside the horse's stall, the Girl stopped to look around. She inhaled deeply, then she exhaled. Then she embarked on an exploration of youthful curiosity in a muddy white dress, rummaging around, finding things, fiddling with them. She made rounds through the horse stalls, reading the horses' names from carvings on their stalls.

"Gina, you are elegant, tall, healthy, though somewhat thin... Respectable."

"Tom, oh why must you appear so exhausted... you burden my eyes.."

"Honeycomb, how distinct you are, white with burnt orange-brown spots. My sister would stick by your side day and night, had she the opportunity to."

"And you, Pigtails, where is your hair?"

The girl had reached the barn's end. She turned around and traced her steps back past each of the horses - Honeycomb, Tom, Gina, and the problematic one, Harald. It was there where she stopped: in front of Harald's stall. It seemed he was sleeping inside. If he wasn't, he nearly was.

"To think I didn't know your name through all we've been through... Hope all is well, Harald."

Tom whimpered from two stalls back.

"Leave me live, Tom," the girl said, not bothering to look.

She'd crossed isles to the long side of the barn, where the entire length consisted of horse stalls. Jerry and Lisa were nearest to the front, having almost forever been there, bonding through their duty of guarding the others, warning of unwarranted entry.

The next stall hadn't a nametag carving. Nor did the subsequent three. No. The final stall did have a carving, although lightly carved, which read: "Albany." That was the name of a midget horse, which bore a full size torso atop cursedly short legs.

"Christ, Albany, you're worse than Tom," the Girl said.

Moving along now... "Hi Harald," the Girl said, passing by. Up the ladder. To the second floor. Not much to see here.... The girl kicked a few hay bales. Soon came the idea to roll one from the loft. When it hit, it made an under-satisfying clack. The girl pouted and chased it down via the fire pole. Now up she climbed with hay in arms. To the top floor! It was difficult to climb with this large-sized loaf, though, so she hopped back down from the third step. A few times, she tossed the thing to no avail hoping to land it on floor two. Hmmmm. She pouted again. Then a lightbulb went off. Aha!!!

"Tom!!!! Oh Tom, you oaf, I have a use for you! Would you mind if I borrowed your collar?" "You would? I suppose I'll ask Harald then. Good day, Tom."

"Harald, how handsome you are! Have you been well? Oh good. Good."

Harald, sharp as he was, approached the Girl and lowered his head. He allowed her to lift his mane and find the button on his collar. And she wowed and she remarked, "Oh, you've overheard Tom and I.. What an oaf he is, ayy! Thank you so much, Harald. Know that I will return the favor someday."

Harald nodded and The Girl grinned gently. She bowed her head and said, "Good day, Harald," before strapping the hay bale to her shoulder and beginning to climb. On the third floor the ladder stopped. One had to cross a farmer's bridge to access the next ladder. But the bridge had been pulled, to the side opposite to where she stood. She thought to climb through the overhead post and beam structures. That would be unwise, she thought. And considering the rain had upstarted yet again, there was plenty-a time for patience. So she dropped down a floor, to the second, and looked about there. There were all sorts of cutting devices laying about: handsaws, both singly and doubly ended, and sledge axes —— things of every sort and some of sorts never sorted before. They were all man-sized or bigger.

Amidst rough pine finish, there were dozens of oddly sized and shaped shelves lining the walls. Some had cabinet doors, others did not. Some had solid bottoms. Others were latticed. There was no pattern, it seemed, to the containers nor their contents.

In one open-faced cubby there was a series of turtle shells increasing in size. That was beside the nickel-plated wood stove of fantastic symmetry. Going rightward, the shelves doubled in size. Then they halved. Then the rotated and whirled. Another shorter compartment held all sorts of colored bottles, some broken, some mud coated, some clean. And there were two long scythes pinned like a multiplication sign high on the wall, beneath the dormer peak. Then there was a monstrous mill saw, a 6-feet-in diameter trophy leaned against the wall, along with a million other trophies and utilities and one in the same. The girl fiddled with a flag-overdraped combination lock safe briefly before moving along, back to the 3rd floor, where she found an overhead conveyer hook slide.

"Aha!"

She looped the horse's collar that Harald had lent her over the hanging hook. It took a mere push to send the hay bale reeling across. Finally free of her burden, the girl monkeyed across leisurely, while whistling a tune. There was a balcony in the barn. Under it hung another flag, the same flag. Ducking under this, and around a narrow, nearly too narrow staircase, brought our mystery girl to the drawing room. There were 45-degree-angled drafting tables all around, made of glass. Drawings overlapped one another, some finished, most not. There were floor plans, blue prints, and sketches of beautiful women. Also, a few pictures of people, coated thickly with saw dust; the pictures themselves were coated in dust. The sole clue that anyone had been in this room in years was the cushioned rotation chair, which framed an imprint of someone's rear, a snow angel in dust.

One final ladder led from the drawing room to the cupola, where bird feces matted the floor, and where there were triangular built-in seats in each corner, and where the windows opened outward, needing to be propped with two-by-fours. She propped open the two of four windows that weren't already as so. And she felt the breeze. The sounds of rain and wind-blowing and trees creaking overwhelmed her, so down she went, back inside, back to comfortable, playful isolation.

"I'm back honey. Tom, tell Harald if you would." Harald nayed to this, alerting the girl he'd heard.

Then she was looking down, sitting down, in that recently-sat-on-chair, looking at blueprints and concept sketches of cabins and churches, and she'd walk over to the indoor balcony again, and she'd look down again. Touching the crusty, yellowing books left displayed the balcony railing, she smiled softly.

Then she ran over to the ladder and scaled the thing, grabbed her forgotten hay bale and scurried back to the balcony. She balanced it on the railing, reeled back, and paused.... With a forceful poke, she toppled it over, down the many flights she'd climbed. It crashed beautifully. She jumped! as a kid might after having seen a rock break through the pesty neighbor's window. Looking down, there was nothing to be seen. The hay had flattened and scattered so completely, it blended to the floor that was already glazed with entropic hay.

"I've got to tell Harald!!!" the girl said. And she ran off to do so.

FOURTEEN

Mrs. Greenlock awoke to the feel of cool, comfortable sheets -- the kind more home-like than the home itself, which in the morning becomes so external. Sliding skin on skin, skin on sheet, sheet on sheet, with a column of sunlight crossing her legs — that was the beauty that was the mistress of Greenlock. As she layed in bed, the veranda doorway had been left a crack open, somehow. It didn't much concern our lady, but that was the way it was. The veranda doorway let out a column of light.

Mrs. Greenlock tossed, turned in ecstasy, dreaming intermittently of a mountain-top valley, with a field, a tree at its edge, and a swing extending far off into the sunset. A sole horse scampered about the field, chasing a bumble-bee, losing sight of it, then being calm. Then another or the same bug would come about. Cut two and the horse would be off snapping its teeth, snackering around again, all the while that swing swung uninhabited, swinging at the edge of the world.

A breeze came along that gave Hwen Greenlock the impetus to slide out from her bed and gravitate to the heavenly veranda. The light! The wind, or seemingly the light, swung the doors to and fro. The curtains danced. It all opened before Hwen. So she strolled into the sunlight, out-stretching her arms, yawning. The birds were chirping, and the sun so warmly complemented the cool breeze. Horses, like slaves, were being guided about a meandering path on the hillside below Greenlock house. They were linked together with chain lengths so short between each pair of horses, that it became impossible for any one horse to stray or turn sideways. So the horses were locked in line. For this reason, only two guides were needed to keep the whole lot of horses in line. One guide led by the front. Another followed behind with the task of whipping the caboose periodically, conscripting him to communicate the message forward via push and shove and kick to the ass.

The cupola windows were open. Hwen noticed this from the veranda, standing with her hands resting atop her head, her lower back arched as lower backs desire to arch in the morning. Also, she noticed: she was entirely nude. The farmhands, young and old, had gathered around for a gander. Hwen lowered her arms. Her smile faded awkwardly. She backed away from the onlooking coyotes. Cautiously, she retreated inside, shutting the door tight, locking her troubles away, and laying back to continue her slumber.

FIFTEEN

Because night had come, Mr. Tomleson embarked on his kind of rounds unspoken of by even the most complicit of farm hands. These were the kind of dark clothing and his arrow pouch. The kind of boots and binoculars..

West of the marshes, to a meadow in the Garnering Forest. That was the location of Jack Tomleson's home. It was a hut like any other, a mix of stone and wood, dark, windows yellowed by the fire inside. The sight of it straightened Mr. Tomleson's path. "Jack, do you have a moment?" he asked, having peeked in the unlocked door. It was a familiar place. Before Mr. Tomleson moved into the mines, he had lived in this hut himself. He had crafted this it with the help of his friends and neighbors during the early days of the farm. And he helped them build their huts.

Mr. Tomleson reminisced of the time before these scattered huts lined the trees. He remembered the clearing of the field. And he imagined the huts' order of sprouting. That was Garl's hut. That was Granger's. That was Sharon's. Oh, Sharon. She had many cats, and a library. Men would visit her, sometimes for the calm that petting a cat brings, and sometimes for what a book brings. Sometimes for both and more. She'd have her bon-fire. And she'd wait there, reading and petting her cats, deep into the night until someone would come along to talk with her. Or a group would approach. To sit on Sharon's sofa. To speak with her. To relax. To think. If the visitors were few enough and of a certain chemistry, then she would invite them to retreat inside.

Leaning into his son's home, Mr. Tomleson asked "Jack, do you have a moment? It's your pops."

"Of course Father, of course. How are you? What is it?" he

asked with concern for his father. It was supper time. Jack's home smelled of stew being cooked over an open wood-fueled flame. Mr. Tomleson glanced at the shimmering smoke, which scattered yellow light from the oil lamps. Jack held a spoon in his hands. Mr. Tomleson gestured toward it.

Jack registered the notion. "Oh, would you like some supper, Father? Come sit. Delilah would enjoy seeing her Grandfather, I'm sure. And her mother is home tonight as well."

"I see your door is unlatched," Mr. Tomleson pointed out.

"Yes Father, I haven't had the chance to ———"

"You should latch your door, Son."

"Yes father ———"

"Come for a walk, Son, and we can talk. Bring your boots."

Jack recognized the immediacy in his Father's tone. Not expecting that it could, he asked if the talking could occur over dinner.

Mr. Tomleson admitted, "No, not this."

"Alright. I'll need a moment," Jack said. Then he retreated inside to confer with his family. When he returned, he returned with juice and two sandwiches. "For the road," he said. And they were off.

Passing the huts, and the garden trellises, and the stars illuminating the mist… Jack asked his father, "Where are we heading, Father?"

"You will see," was the reply.

That agitated Jack. And he asked "Why must you keep me in the dark even now. I am fully grown. I tend to my family. And I tend to Mr. Greenlock, as you once did. I am a man, Father."

In the near pitch black, Mr. Tomleson trudged on as though nothing had been said. They moved westward, deep into the Garnering Forest, then Southward and across the ridge of hilltops behind Greenlock House. Soon, southwestward going, they neared the River Round, where Tomph had gone to acquire clay. Its current flowed heavy. It was not their destination, though. Rather, it was a checkpoint. Rather, a

GREENLOCK FARM

decoy. Upon reaching the River Round Valley, Mr. Tomleson laid on his stomach flat.

As well, he commanded to Jack, "Get down."

"Tell me our business, Father. Or I will return home."

"I'm warning you, kid."

"I'm not your kid, Father! That is it. That's it, see!" Jack whined in more child-like a fashion than he ever had before. "You treat me like a child."

In the time a scorpion takes to strike, Mr. Tomleson was atop his boy. His thumpy fingers wrapped around Jack's neck. "Shut the fuck up," Mr. Tomleson said. "Don't you understand." With one hand he grasped his son's throat. With his other, he muffled his son's mouth. "You are a child. You are a child," he said. "YOU ARE A CHILD YOU ARE A CHILD YOU ARE A CHILD YOU ARE A CHILD YOU ARE A CHILD YOU ARE A CHILD YOU ARE A CHILD." He repeated himself like an alligator snapping uncontrollably. Mr. Tomleson's mind had broken. His son bloodied his nose with a head-butt. Only then did Mr. Tomleson reposition his hand off Jack's neck and onto reality.

"Let me go you madman!" Jack pleaded, disgusted and scared by his father.

But again Mr. Tomleson manhandled Jack, covering his mouth with both hands. The boy squirmed and whined but could not combat his father's strength. For a while Mr. Tomleson held Jack in place. "We must be silent," he expounded. Eventually Jack became calm. Out of necessity he took breaths through his nose. Meanwhile, Mr. Tomleson swiveled his head, following what appeared to be a wandering lamplight in the distance. It was weak being so distant. Still, it was present albeit slightly. And its presence grounded Jack, telling him of the severity of it all.

When Tomleson released his son, his son did not speak. Instead he bowed his head and eased his palms, as to say "whoa there" to a horse. "Don't tear my arms off; I'm not going to hurt you." At this point Mr. Tomleson strode down the path where he had come from originally. Quickly, Jack caught up. But Mr. Tomleson would speed up each time his son neared his side. So Jack trailed behind as a trailer does, being pulled along.

They romped over the hills to the forest, where Mr. Tomleson led his son and their shadow lurkers in loops and figure-eights and over nonsensical, chaotic paths of all kinds, zigzagging through the trees, thick and thin, crawling under deep brush, jogging down trails, only to jump in the bushes again. Upon one such jump into the bushes, Mr. Tomleson put his hand on Jacks shoulder and said:

"Jack, things ain't well here."

"What do you mean Father?" Jack asked.

"Ja————————"

Jack interrupted his dad. "I know of the floods. What I can't grasp is why we play like children in the forest in the dark."

"Hush, Son. Please listen. Please listen. Please listen. Aggggg, I can't explain. Read... read this:"

It was then Mr. Tomleson brought out an envelope. Inside was a map. It was old, hand-drawn with ink. One could make out the River Round. You could see a warped sketch of the barn and Master Greenlock's house. And there was a rough depiction of the cranberry fields (modern-day swamps, due to beavers). The forest in particular had been drawn with such incredible detail. Everything was pristine, from branch structures to bark patterns and a small monastery hut. All that went missing were the structures that were built after the time of the map's making. There was more, though. Between the barn and Greenlock House, there was a dastardly sight: tentacles marking a wrath of evil, sprawling widely and towering higher than anything for miles, suctioning the blood of farmhands who themselves toiled to feed their captors. This map was not a map, but a blueprint, and Greenlock farm was to become a farm milking not cows but farmers, their children, and their wives.

"It's a child's tale," Jack scoffed.

"Maybe so. Maybe so, Jack. How about you read the letter."

Deeper in the envelope, Jack found a small paper, folded a million times over, which when unfolded instructed Mr. Tomleson to investigate the origins of this map and others of its kind. Supposedly a great volume of them had been found — so great a volume, the master thought it wise to consider the matter seriously.

"This is absurd," Jack said.

"Read to the last word."

One line remained; it read: Bring along your son. I cannot have him here without you.

SIXTEEN

On the North fences, Little One was crying… trapped above the rapids on that narrow northern wall. Tomph notices a light in the distance. It originates from the flooded marshes outside of the walls. The light, it is approaching. It makes Tomph nervous, but he doesn't dare warn the boy because doing so might induce panic and thereby cause the boy to plummet into the currents.

Little one continued the story he had been telling earlier. "So I took the knife," he said. "It felt so slimy warm. I didn't know how to …. I….. And then my mom.. There was so much blood. Mrs. Ruth's dog laid there. I stared. And mother came upon me staring. She gasped and she dropped the supplies she'd somehow retrieved. Medicine bottles were breaking. I could feel the time. Mother dropped to her knees on blood and shattered glass. I was crying. She cried. Mrs. Ruth snored and gargled and belched. Mother went to speak, but there was no air; her lungs had emptied. But her mind still tried to pull air, but there was no air to pull. So she convulsed. Waving her hands, saying but unable to say, help me, Little One, help me! —— she hyperventilated, and all I did was panic myself, made her scared, and attract a swarm of loving friends to truly did suffocate mumma. Oh, momma.... When she needed air most, we loved her so intently, we couldn't help ourselves from swarming, selfishly, to be close to her, for ourselves!!! Momma suffocated beside Mrs. Ruth's dog... all because we stole her air."

SEVENTEEN

Meanwhile currents slicked across Alphonse's shell. The currents were strong although the turtle was small. Clinging to his caretaker, Alphonse was a leaf on a tree in the wind. But the turtle's caretaker, she had isolated him from her interactions, pinching his ventricles if he dared venture into the open. He was to remain hidden behind her head.

At random the caretaker tortoise would release bits of food into the current. Like spit from the bow of a great ship, these food particles would fall backwards for Little Alphonse to eat. Sometimes, being unprepared, our hero would miss his catch and have no choice but to watch the food bits flutter away irretrievably, irreplaceably. Alphonse was but a pocketed mouse, fed only upon convenience.

On Alphonse's left, in the migration heard, there was a smaller little turtle, smaller than Alphonse, whose relationship with his personal caretaker blossomed beautifully. Many relationships blossomed beautifully. So a large portion of our hero's surroundings bloomed garden-like, with various colors and shapes and smells growing and wafting. Leaders of the tortoise school would toss back fish. Those trailing would catch these fish and pass them onward backwards. In the process they'd save a chunk for themselves and their companion turtles.

Once, Alphonse's neighbor crawled on his savior's shoulder

after a meal. He nibbled crumbs left over on her lips. She would let him clean her teeth. They would kiss and they would eat. They would swim in the glowing green water together, straying from the school and playing out in the pitch-black emptiness. So carelessly... So joyously... until a small barracuda surfaced from the deep. Reacting to this, the caretaker nudged her passenger behind her head. She roared while re-integrating into heard of sea tortoises.

EIGHTEEN

Mr. Tomleson weaved through trees and crawled under bushes and so on. Jack trailed him, doing the same. They stopped. Mr. Tomleson gestured to his son, as to say: do as I do. Toss rocks as I do, along the valley trail, as to give the illusion that we are in that place or in that place or anyplace but here. Jack did so. Following his father, he tossed rocks from the bushes toward the far side of Thom's meadow.

His dad was as anxious as Jack had ever seen him - his dad, a man of men. He was scanning the meadow horizon, muttering. "Shadows, Shadows, show yourselves." Oh, where were the shadows? Jack's dad eyed for them intensely. Jack followed his dad's gaze. For this reason the two noticed simultaneously when a crack of light peeked from a door. A jittery young women peeked her head out from the tee-pee. She was suspiciously cautious, looking every which way, being sure the coast was clear. Then she darted out, all at once with a basket in her arms. She weaved through tee-pees frantically, certain that her destination was a tee-pee but uncertain which of many tee-pees it was. She approached some to examine them more closely. No, not that one. Not this. Oh, there it is! There!

Her haste was captivating, so captivating, neither of the

Tomleson's gazes strayed as this mystery member of an underground railroad, she peeked her head into a particular tee-pee only to be shoved onto her bottom in the dirt. For a man to stupor out ranting whispering angry. When this girl regained her footing, the man slapped her, knocking her down again. Then he grabbed the basket that she had been holding. He brought it inside, emptied it inside, and tossed it at the girl's feet before shoeing her away.

So she scurried back to her home not before entering the tee-pee home occupied by none other than Master Greenlock himself, who poked his head out and shoed the girl.

For what reason was he there? in a tent when his wife sits idly at Greenlock House? The girl scurried back, scurry scurry scurry. Mr. Tomleson snatched his son, knowing such gossip fodder was not safe in his hands. Unfortunately another multitude of fodder launched up for the taking when a concerned female voice called out from inside:

"What is it, Leo?"

And when a similarly flamboyant different female voice, in unison with another less familiar voice, echoed :

"Yes Leo!! What is it!!!" "Yaaasss Leeeooo!"

and when Leo Greenlock dropped his robe, raised his arms and skipped inside bare-bottomed.

Anticipating an outburst, Mr. Tomleson clocked Jack with his binoculars. Then he was off, unconscious son in arms, navigating the darkness. Jack didn't have the chance to hear the Master yelling, or to see the mystery girl making another run, or to contact eyes with the shadow men across meadow who'd realized the centroid of misdirection during the time Jack and his Father had been distracted from their rock-throwing plot. The shadow people, they were alerted when, with his binoculars, Mr. Tomleson sent booming echo across the hillside, down, and into the valley trail, by striking his son.

Jack slept as his father carried him west of the Garnering forest. Mr. Tomleson's eyes were distant, frantic, eying something further - outside the borders of Greenlock Farm.

NINETEEN

In their wake, Omnious clung to the erosion-exposed roots, the salt content of the marshes eroding his skin. The flooding had thrown the plants off balance. As a result, they leeched for nutrients.

Fairly quickly, the rapids receded into a stream. Omnious sat strung-out as a torn-shirt fraction of the man he'd used to be, void of strength, void of his friend, Thom.

"Thom!! Thom!!! Where are you!" he called. He was directionless, limping and yelling circles in the mud.

Shhhhhhhhhhhhhh came a hush. "Get in de mud," Thom whispered from a tree someplace nearby. But instead of heeding Thom's word, Omnious searched to pinpoint his friend's place in the trees. But Thom called again, "Omnious!" He threw a stick. He waved his arms, shedding light on incoming boats. Thick fog flowed where the water once did. The boats seemed to be buoyant atop that fog. The boats, they approached as though they were part of the ether, parting the fog, sloshing with it, swarming with it. Omnious laid back in the mud. His arm hurt badly. His ankle too. He squirmed in order to sink deeper into the mud. He covered his legs and torso and arms with guck. Meanwhile, these mysterious figures encroached from the waters.

Once reasonably hidden, Omnious whispered, "Are you alright Thom?"

"Shut your mouth!! Idiot!" Thom said.

Moments later a wooden rudder skimmed Omnious's nose. A whole army of vessels followed. They passed, leaving Omnious stiffening in the cool, drying mud. Thom stayed in his tree, having not a reason to lower himself. Omnious hobbled over to sit at the tree's base below where Thom was sitting. Together, they enjoyed the air, the calm breeze. Trapped in a desert state of irreparable chaos, a sense of relieve in helplessness pervaded.

Are you alright Thom?" Omnious asked.
"I'm alright enoof. And you, Omnious?"
"I'm alright too."

Thom climbed down from the tree. He sunk his knees into the mud beside Omnious. They sat shoulder-to-shoulder. Thom was at Omnious's sitting height while kneeling. They watched the sun go down. It seemed like the sun cleared the fog by going down. So there was one final period of clarity before the darkness came.

TWENTY

As the world went dark, Yofim took post in the Barn. He climbed the ladder, then he resolved to climb further: To the coop! Tomph hadn't yet returned. So, alone, from the high point of the farm, Yofim watched the day fade, and he thought of his friend. He sat where many times the two had sat together. He wondered how Tomph's day had gone, working with Omnious. He wondered about all sorts of things, such as why the Greenlocks hadn't been home. In this most absurd of times, nobody of importance could be found. Why?

It was odd, sitting idly while aware that something was terribly wrong. Nothing could be done for now, though. So Yofim resolved that the cupola, of all places, was the logical choice. Upon the Master's return, Yofim would rush down, beating the Master's horse to its stall, and he would tell someone about the corpses in the river. He would do something about all this.

But for the time being there was nothing to be done. So Yofim sat, fiddling with his fingers and later fiddling with an old wooden doll he stumbled upon underneath his chair. The doll was uglier than ugly. Yofim reached out the window with this ugly thing. He propped it up to straddle the rooftop so it could stand guard as the lookout.

"Keep an eye out for the Master," Yofim said to the doll, "And Tomph. Look for Tomph."

Yofim sturdied her (the doll). Once satisfied, he strained to pull himself back inside the window.

In that moment, a figure on the ground caught his eye. It was the Girl. She moved closer, waving up toward the cupola, saying, "Hello hello there, could you let me in? I haven't anywhere else to go... the door is locked!"

"Of course!! of course!!!"

Yofim barreled down the ladder and the fireman's pole and the stairs. He feared, opening the door, he would find that the girl had disappeared, or that she hadn't been there in the first place. Possibly he'd caught Tomph's disease. Possibly this was all a dream. For a while Yofim stood before the barn door, fearing what the truth could be.

KNOCK KNOCK KNOCK KNOCK!

Yofim unlatched the door allowing it to be pushed open wide. The sun shined so blindingly bright. Emerging from Yofim's blindness, in strode the Girl whose shine dulled the sun. She had bathed and changed clothes somehow. Before, her beauty had shined deep, but only through the pollution of her muddied clothes and ruffled temperament. Now she glistened pure as the water in the River Round, pure and fine enough to grind mulch to clay.

"How do I look?" she asked.

Fat Yofim stumbled trying to answer. At first he was unable to see, and likewise unable to think. The Girl was breathtaking as the sky was blue.

"I found it in the stalls." She said, referring to her new sundress. "Some poor lady is stuck without her clothes! Can you imagine!"

"I can, yes," Yofim said awkwardly.

But can you imagine!" she exclaimed, indicating something more. "Follow me," she said, taking Yofim's hand and leading him to the stalls. "You must meet Tom! His is a slouch, but he is mine. Oh!!! And Harald, you must meet Harald. You simply must."

They interacted one by one with each of the horses, giving time to each. That was, until Yofim pointed out, "you are introducing me to my own horses?"

"Oh!!! So you've already met!!!" the girl exclaimed.

"Indeed we have," Yofim said. "In fact, we are roommates!!! I live here."

"Oh that is wonderful!!!" the Girl exclaimed. Shifting her attention to the horse, she remarked sarcastically, "I am sorry for wasting your time, Tom. I realize your time is very important to you," before turning her head to Yofim and asking "are you fond of Tom?" while resting her hand on the fat one's chest, as to express concern and a desire for honesty. "I find him to be quite the... he is quite potato-like, see. Do you agree?"

"I'd say. Quite potato like," Yofim agreed.

While the two went on to brush Harald's mane, Yofim transitioned from his love-at-first-sight type of blissful awestruck staring to a deeper stare, through the Girl's bubbly facade and deeper into her nature. She was something special, he thought. Undoubtedly I am in love with this girl, he thought. Then a familiar-sounding sound sounded, triggering both of their attentions. The girl threw up her arm and commanded, "To the stern!!!" And so they went: up the ladder, across the posts and the beams, up some stairs and up another ladder. From the cupola they could see people scattered about the center area of the farm. Most stood still. Everyone seemed confused about what they'd heard, or if they'd heard anything.

But, while seeing others simultaneously questioning, an individual infers how something must have been heard. So people gathered and more people gathered. A consensus broiled. Yofim knew he ought to join the gathering too, but the Girl in her sundress sat plump on his lap; her presence argued against his movement as she sat there munching on popcorn, "watching television" out the cupola windows, and squirming around for comfort here and there, but only passively. Her attention was on the gathering. Yofim's attention was on the Girl. He wouldn't move. He couldn't.

The gathering culminated under the willow tree. When gatherings were more common, they would always culminate under the willow tree. The farmhands would await stragglers and the Greenlock's in complete silence. But many stragglers would not straggle in on this day, and many would not straggle in at any time. Yofim thought this while remembering the purple corpses buoyant in the water. There were so many in that endless stream. Yofim daydreamed nightmares of death and more death. For miles and miles and miles… The turtles somehow knew to migrate far, far from all of this.

The Girl reminisced, "I had a swim today. In a little hidden pool in the trees!! Oh, it was so wonderful. We must go together sometime." After suggesting this, she noticed Yofim staring into the distance. "Silly, what are you looking at?" she asked, interrupting his daze.

Yofim returned to life and the Girl answered for him. "Nothing!" she said, "You are looking at exactly, precisely nothing!" Then she told him "Look at me!! Look at me, Yofim." And when he contacted her eyes, she pecked him a kiss. Off he went day-dreaming again, and the Girl ran off to see Harald. She was gone before Yofim realized that she was going. "See you soon!!!" she called.

The Master's gathering had concluded. The farmhands were scattering, returning to work or to play. Few words were said during this particular gathering. Master Greenlock departed only breaths after he'd arrived. He left the group partially scattered, partially standing around discussing arbitrary things in small groups.

TWENTY-ONE

Little One, shivering, shaking, he froze overlooking the rushing water. Tomph couldn't save him. A narrating voice reverberated through the marshes. It said: it is in your power, little one, to save yourself, and to save the everything. Likewise, by your own doing, you may tumble into the rushing waters, and you may be swept to die in Omnious's wake —— to die by flesh-tearing log and bone-crushing stone. Little One, compose yourself. Rise! Trek to the next column. And remember Tomph. Do not leave him to the elements. He is your friend. He is your friend. Stand! Be sure that Tomph is near always. Please, cease your crying. Calm your shivers. Do not look up. Do not look down... Step forward."

The narrator narrated. The fog made way for the Galagna scouting boat whispering in. The boat weaved, bobbed, levitated, uninhibited by the laws of our world. The narrating voice triangulated to under the boat paddler's hood, from his mouth of razor-sharp beaver teeth and his darkened green, bark-like lips. His face, but for his teeth and lips, hid behind shadow. Little One, beware of the nearing boats, the nearing boats... the nearing boats... Don't dare acknowledge the ghostly outreached hand. It is before your eyes. Don't look. Don't dare.

Tomph imagined that he had only imagined these words. He imagined Little One standing and walking with perfect balance, and that the boy would soon be sitting safely on the next column with his legs crossed. Tomph imagined walking across himself, and sitting with the boy, talking with him. He imagined such a timid boy would never stand, as this boy did, only to be charmed by this encroaching vine-like green-man who levitated a person's height above the rushing waters. Tomph imagined such a timid boy would never relinquish himself unconscious into the arms of a strange creature who swiftly lifted the boy into the boat, and who paddled away, paddling himself, leaving Little One hunched over a vertical spiral braid of roots at the rear of the vessel. Little One hunched over The Book, enamored by scripture, in a trance, drooling over The Book which sat open-always prepared to be glimpsed by passersby.

That Galagna bishop paddled a vessel. His vessel carried The Book. It was dangerous to venture outside the forest with The Book. So quickly, the bishop hailed into the fog. He uttered his hymns which echoed for miles over the desolate northern lands.

Left was Tomph, alone and direction-less, trapped in the eye of the dissipating storm. Thanks to the fog's clearing, he could see for miles. He could see that there was nothing. He could see the nothingness -- uninterrupted horizons visible in all directions from the northern high ground. The marshes sat oddly atop a plateau. It was warming, but Tomph's hands were cold. Bluer were the skies in every direction but directly above, where a gray held hold.

TWENTY-TWO

It was morning on Greenlock Farm. The storm had cleared. People gathered outside the main house. There, an absolute, gripping silence took hold. In old times, a passive, meditative quiet would initiate the day. But in this silence, there was no meditation. Jabber sizzled and popped and froze. Gerald, the carriage mender, admired his two-story double-long horse carriage from a distance of 30 meters or so. It was glorious. As such, he had parked it centered affront the big house, in prime view of the crowd. He watched people in hopes of catching someone staring at the carriage. In the case that he did catch someone staring, Gerald would be opportune in speaking to them of this and of that and of his new technique for binding metal rims around their wheels using thick, cool mud to slow the temperature change process and thereby avoid cracking the wood.

Now Gerald spoke to a girl, Sherri - fifteen years young, youthful, humble, composed. Very sharp-minded. She had been born into the life at Greenlock farm. But somehow, she knew of realms outside the farm experience. She was attuned to her situation in the world, aware of her destiny, and aware of what ought to be said and what oughtn't.

She told Gerald, "Yes, yes. Of course. That is truly brilliant, Gerald. And curious!"

Like a pinball, Gerald went on bouncing, explaining…, "See, because today's convention is to heat the metal directly, to make it expand. But when you've got hot metal. Real hot. It touches the wood, the wood expands. It cracks! CRRRRACK! Then whadaya got? Broken wheels. They don't ride smooth. You want a smooth ride, like my double-tall will give yuh. But your daddy won't let you in there. So you 'gotta take some cold mortar, take your hot metal. Pack in cold mortar around your wooden wheel. It contracts, see. Then put your hot, expanded metal around it all. Snug fit, but not too snug. Dip it all in some water and it'll snug right up. In no time you'll have a double tall for yourself, you will."

Sherri played along, asking if "the mud will insulate the wood?" She enjoyed listening to Gerald. So she did what she could to keep him going.

"Correct-o-mundo!!! No more cracks. Smart girl you've got here, Earnie", Gerald said, patting the girl's father -- who had just walked over -- on the back. "Perhaps she'll apprentice me and my expansive wisdom someday."

"Not in my day, Gerald.", Earnie said.

"Now why is that, ya old grump!?"

"C'mon Sherri, let's go." Earnie said to his daughter. "This guy is a loon."

Gerald whined, "Awwwww, c'monnnnnn.. Why don't we chat a bit longer?"

Sherri looked back. Her dad held her hand, leading her away, but she turned back and caught Gerald's eye.

"Goodbye Gerald," she said. "I hope I will see you soon."

That's what she said. Then she winked a seductive wink that froze the unhumble craftsman. In her wake, she strutted barefoot through the mud, flicking with her hips the cherished, crimson sundress that her father had so pridefully mended for her on the anniversary of her mother's passing.

"Oh no no no!" Gerald thought. He jumped and shivered. "No no no NO," he said. "That girl has the devil in her eyes."

A while later, a beer-bellied, beer-drinking man who Gerald didn't recognize approached him. This man puffed out his belly, and he lifted his chin, and he asked, "Whatareya on about now Gerald?"

"That girl there...." Gerald pointed at her walking away, wagging her bottom. "She is... " -- Gerald cut himself off, realizing it was dangerous even to reveal his awareness of the danger. "She's trouble," he said. "Too smart. Too…——— — aware…."

"Who's that, Earnie's girl? Ha! My daughter said she was a good girl. Always 'gettin good marks in school better 'den any of the other students. Good for Earnie, lucky bastard."

During this time the crowd had been polarizing. Finally Yofim strutted in. A great many eyed his approach. Anyone who remembered the boys was surprised to see him without Tomph by his side. One women carrying child expressed concern.

She asked, "where is your brother, Yofim?" Asking this made for confusion.

"My brother? I don't have a brother," Yofim answered, making the women sad, and inciting her to whimper away caressing her baby. A great many people asked about Tomph. Yofim lied, claiming to know that Tomph would be coming along soon. Reality was that he didn't have a clue of his friend's whereabouts. He did hope the gathering would bring his friend home.

On the grand stone wall that bordered Master Greenlock's farmer's porch, two fellas sat having coffee and cigars, waiting around in a particularly approachable fashion. Yofim approached them and talked. One of the fellas was introspecting on the whole crowd-polarization ordeal. "See," he said. "We've got the silent farmhands and tenants, respecting the wishes of the Greenlock's -- those are, that this meeting will run smoothly. These people, call them compliant, respectful, sharp; whatever. On the other hand, we got guys like us, who don't give a nut about togetherness and community and all that. We're here for the food." The two hummed a bit. "That's right," the other fella said. "The food. But I'm here for something else also." "What's that". "I'm here for some of that right there," he said, pointing. "Mrs. Greenlock," he said. "She's a wild one." Harrr harrrr harrrrr.

Attention moved to Yofim, who stood below the wall on which these fellas sat.

One fella asked Yofim, "What's up boy?"

Yofim mentioned he'd been craving a smoke. "I've got my own matches," he hinted.

But one of the fellas said, "I've been craving one as well. Hey, that's why I bought these here tobacco leaves." And that was that.

Yofim moved on, muttering "I'd have lent you some if I had some, you know."

And as Yofim made his way, the other fella remarked, "but you don't have none, do you, boy?"

"I don't," Yofim admitted.

On his way to the other part of the crowd, Yofim took a gander at Gerald's carriage. It was something grand. He asked a man named Stan what was all the ruckus. Stan was another smoking man, and he wasn't much else. There were stories of him sitting around, riding high atop his Mrs. Stan's wealth, giving her what she needed, and spending the rest of his time polishing theories and hypothesizing new ones. The guy was a chef of a fellow, cooking shit up however he could.

Yofim knew Stan would have words about all this. So he probed the man, saying "It's been forever since we've had a gathering. And this doesn't feel like much of one. What a shame, huh?"

And Stan agreed. He admitted that he'd "smelled some fish in the morning" and how "the smell... ooo is it 'feelin strong right 'bout now." Stan went on mangling his fingers with his other fingers. He was nervous, fidgeting, frightened by everything in the world. This guy was a wreck, sucking on a home-rolled cigarette. He'd been raising his flask every half hour since the fourth grade. His cigarette wasn't even lit. Just soggy, sitting between his lips, soon to break off.

Yofim joked half not-jokingly. "I bet the psychosis set in 20 years prior, ay? Or 30?"

Stan agreed. "Yup yes it did young fella. Matter of fact, I met her in a urinal stall. When I got in there she asked me what I was 'doin. I says, "you, 'lil lady". I gave 'er a good 'fuckin. She never asked me again. She wouldn't ask me 'anythin as long as I stayed inside and gave 'er her daily fucking. Hold on. I must ask!" Stan leaned in. He put his hand on Yofim's shoulder. His eyes bulged, as though this was more important, in this instant, than anything. He asked, "What is your name?"

"Stan, you're losing it," Yofim said.

"I know Yofim. But what have you lost?"

It was then Stan's eyes wandered to the land of stars and dreams. Yofim found himself alone when the master Greenlock commanded, "SILENCE," silencing all but one women, an aristocrat who dressed nice and talked her head off, oblivious to everything but her own words.

"SILENCE." Master Greenlock clenched every muscle in his face. It seemed he was physically pained by the women's voice.

Still, she continued, having never slowed. She explained, "See, honey, because my youngest - he is in the prosperous field of medicine! But my oldest, on the other hand, he" ——

It was then, in booming monotone, Master Greenlock yelled, "WILL SOMEONE MUFFLE THE HAG.?!"

The circle of women huddling around this aristocrat lady seemed eager to pipe her down. One said, "Nancy.. Nancy! Shut your trap... Jesus, you are such a pest." The other women giggled.

Silently, the Master waited with his hands folded, his head bowed. He nodded. Then he looked to his wife, cuing her to begin. And she begun the ceremony as Yofim remembered the children of the farm once beginning ceremonies, and as Tomph had explained how Elsedorwn used to begin the ceremonies. "That was before there were any children at the community," Tomph had said. "There were very few members of the community in that time."

Mrs. Greenlock made her place at the head of the crowd. She reached down to untie her shoes which she abandoned shortly thereafter. The master followed in her step. At this, Gerald hollered a complaint, "Oh what is this?... are we singing again?"

In response, Master Greenlock pointed to Gerald's shoes, implying that he ought to remove them.

"Ahhhh what is this," Gerald whined. Reluctantly, he followed in step, removing his shoes. Everyone took off their shoes. Shortly thereafter, Mrs. Greenlock uttered the following verse:

> *A mist surrounding Rorrick.;*
> *Elsedorwn nearing eyes;*
> *Find us swiftly, do your deeds;*
> *Reep your reepings; sew some seeds;*
> *rid us of our unholy ties.*

The Master waved his hands like a conductor. But the response he expected, it did not come. Even he stumbled when adults nudged their kids to sing, when off-key chimes screeched in, and when canons and arpeggiations fell flat or clashed with the lead. Or when, in absence of a relay-singer offering to continue the lead, a collective directionlessness ensued.

Mrs. Greenlock eventually continued the lead herself, having realized no one else would. Her verse was smooth, and her rhythmic and metrical structure, precise. It was as though she had long prepared for this day. Nonetheless her prowess, if anything, exacerbated the disjointness of it all. Many people quit entirely, and that left those remaining even more obviously out of key or rhythm or both. Soon the drunks, who at first had been enjoying themselves, lost interest. Gerald got thinking of his wheels and of Earnie's daughter. Most people sputtered out. Everyone but Mrs. Greenlock, her husband, and some kids, had stopped singing. The kids were just having fun making noise. None of them had been alive long enough to know of the sanctity of morning song.

Despite the chaos, Mrs. Greenlock continued passionately as ever. She stared at her feet while she sung. The Master brewed angry at the disharmony of his farmhands. His face reddened. But dare he not interrupt his wife.

Rorrrrrick!
Elsedorwnnnnnnnn..
Among us today.
Time runs quickly; trim your needs;
Keep no reepings; do no greed.
Find us swiftly, for we are in need.

Concluding, the master pounded his gavel on the stump podium over which he stood. He commanded, "Gather 'round. This instant, Gather 'round. Henceforth Greenlock Farm will return to its roots: of love, function, togetherness. The Gods are unhappy. And be warned, they will remain as such if we sit idly. We must work, and we must love, in order for any hope of regaining their sanction. Do not expect forgiveness. Now off to work with you all. Love each other. Work. Mind your words..."

His wife continued, "for no word goes unheard in this

land."

She was a madwoman, sweeping her hands outward, scoping North and South, left and right, and supinating her palms, looking to the heavens.... "as we thrive under God Rorrick and Goddess Elsedorwn!!!"

She erupted into contorting spirit-possessed standing seizures, her limbs shivering, the chains dangling from her neck shaking and jittering against one another, foam dispensing from her purpling lips.

"OFF TO WORK," the Master commanded. "Off to work, all of you," he said while being rushed by his wife. Yofim watched as he calmed her, sat her down in Gerald's double tall. With haste, Gerald dislodged the wheel-wedges and got up front. As they reeled off in the carriage, Yofim witnessed Mrs. Greenlock grab her husband's head and pull him into her foaming, purpled lips.

The double-tall cornered around the Master's house. Yofim lost his line of sight. Soonafter, he felt a tap on his shoulder. It was the Girl.

"What are you doing?" she asked. "We must go!"

As the farmhands dispersed, Yofim stayed staring at this girl. She rescued him. Pushed him along, whispering in his ear, "Faster faster... Not too fast! There is a surprise! But we mustn't look too excited, or else the others will find the surprise too, and it won't be as exciting... will it?".

"I suppose," Yofim agreed, sticking by her side.

TWENTY-THREE

Yofim and the girl dodged carriages and people and plows and horses as they ran. Behind the barn, they came across two fellas huddled together talking to some third fella in an alleyway indent in the barn. The indent allowed a water well to be accessed from inside and outside the barn simultaneously. These guys were jabbering away quickly as ever, just beside the well. The third individual, the stranger, was jabbering the most. The two fellas mostly listened to him while smoking their cigars.

The rambling stranger was old, raggedy, rangly, talking of the old days —— talking about how he "came upon the place that Greenlock once was".

"Do you wanna hear 'somethin, newboys.. I know yous guys. I know. Yous guys came here for the work. Built some houses. Got a roof over yuh head. Got some food. You sung some songs because 'dat's what peoples did."

"Yea yea yea, so what's the point, old man!" said one of the fellas.

The ragged old man shook his head. He was flustered. These fellas weren't as excited to hear what he had to say as he was excited to say it.

So he said, "I'll tell yuh, yea I'll tell yuh. Now why don't you pull back that hair and show me your ears."

One of the fellas swiped at the other's hair. In return he got a heavy fist to the meat of his shoulder. The old man put his head as a blockade between the two fellas and he said "stop it, yous guys. Whadahya gonna do, punch through my head?" He craned his neck and looked the punching fella in the eye.

"Okay now... Here we go...", the old man said. *"It all began when I was eighteen. Some frens 'an I, we was fresh into university. Freshmen year. Summaaa tiiime, right. 'Couple weeks earlier I told my buddy Billy. Let's go on a trip. He said yea, and we thought of who else would be all for the journey. Colston maybe. We asked our buddy Colston: wanna go to Nilewood!? Sancho wanted in as well. That's a carriage-full.*

Billy and Colston and Sancho. They were from Winchendon. I lived in Capran Town, see. We were gownna go straight from the University, but I needed to see my brutha back home. Billy needed his huggy anyway. So we all taxied home for a night. And in the 'mornin, those three met up at Billy's house. Colston's brutha dropped him off there and Sancho got there somehow. Benjamin delivered him, maybe, or he was supposed to. We thought that Benjamin might end up joining the circus because he was quite the clown 'himself. Anyways they had breakfast. Billy's mother made eggs and fruit. His dad got out the map, showing it to Colston, and Sancho in his nice sweater (the nicest!). Meanwhile Billy barfed up 'is guts downstairs while his less-hungover brothers did some cleaning' up.

Billy's dad said you ought to avoid Wickholm. You don't want to get caught up in there. We all agreed, and we talked about roads and shortcuts and other things. Billy's mom asked what everyone was studying and so on. For two hours, Billy was 'looking for 'is belt, God Damn...

It was sunny and beautiful and the tumor-having dog wanted petting and Billy's brother shot some hoops. Colston's brother took off whistling a tune.

They took off a million freaking hours after they meant to. Hours later they were in the outskirts of Capran Town, 'looking for me. I was gonna meet them there so they wouldn't have to venture into the heart of the city. But my ride broke down a bit early, leaving them alone in that park with all the opium dealers on the playground intermixed with kids and moms and that piss-soaked outhouse, and that give-a-book-take-a-book that had nothing but a Spanish bible with a dedication to someone with the same name as Billy written inside.

They found me up in china town chaos in the hot sun. Traffic, it was bad. And these guys had a trailer full of goodies: guitars, bongos, stuff of all kinds. I had to keep watch. And these hooligans, they didn't give a damn. I wasn't gonna do nothing. At the intersection, we got stuck. And this feller here, he's eying Billy's guitar. So I tell him "I see you, you hooligan. Reach over that side-bar and I'll take your arm for myself. I'll 'ave your leg too God damnit, and I'll boil some soup." We got away shortly after that. Then we went down through the shithole they call New Grumlo, and we went through a million other places.

I remember. We met some fella at a diner. "What are you guys up to?" he asked. Colston told him we were going on a trip to New Nile-wood. "Where's that?" the guy asked.

"You know the place with the music and the hurricanes and all that?" Colston said.

"Oooo you're going to Nil-wood?"

"Yup, that's the pace".

"Have fun you fellas, not too much fun though. I been there before. Careful now. And don't ever say Nile-wood, never if you wanna make any connections."

See that's a little, ahhh, heuristic they got for recognizing outsiders..Not if they couldn't tell from the look of us, white fellas, equipped with soccer moms and clean shoes. TOURIST TOURIST TOURIST haha ooo man we were out of place down there, when Colston called out that local for his bullshit directions, got 'im angry, with those voo-doo fellas 'wanderin around, and in the midst of all those homeless people and drunks and homeless goons paying dollars to touch old ladies' titties.

GREENLOCK FARM

Anyways, it was our first night on the road and we didn't wanna pay for 'nuthin. Sancho said something like why don't we tie the horses in line. Then we can take shifts on the bow. We'll ride through the night. Be there in no time. That was the plan for a while until Jennyland.

In Jennyland, we were getting tired. Everyone was. No one felt like manning the reigns. So what were we to do?

Billy told us a story of making his way back home from some other place he'd hiked to. Mount Canterboro. Two guys with beards picked 'im up. He said they looked like orthodox Jews, bearded 'n all. They asked him what he was doing. Just visiting some friends. And he asked them. They told him that they were "delivering some rice to [their] sister community. They've had a tough year." Of course, Billy didn't know what that meant. For this reason, he inquired further. Turns out these bearded fellows had a religious community. And we were welcome there! And Billy had the address! Bluemington, Jennyland, here we come. Get the map!

We were nervous, real nervous, for fear of 'gettin stuck in the middle of some cult thing —- I suppose, righteously so. But we were also crossing miles upon miles for no reason at all, and we were itching for something, anything —— an experience, you know —- a touch of reality. So we went to Bluemington, Jennyland.

Pitch black. It was pitch black when we made it there. 'Man it was creepy over there. We creeped down this unlit road, speculated as to what we'd got ourselves into. We passed by what looked like the house we were looking for. There was a lamp on. Then a guy came out, all weary of us watching him from darkness, so we booked it. 'Turns out that it was a bar or some'thin. We didn't really know what we were looking for. A church? A house? A fucking tent? We had a weird, 5-digit address. Colston thought maybe the community had their own weird numbering system. I'm not sure if it did.

Turns out that the place we were looking for had been the first house on the road. We'd gone right passed it. Turns out that was the meeting place, and it was the bar that we'd past, and the cemetery, and all those creepy plantation-like houses ——— they were all part 'a the community.

So we pull in. I see some shadows 'movin around. The fucking cows scared the shit outa me. Fuck, I look over and Colston's leaned against the window, listening in. His face is Ghost White. "What is it?" I ask.

"They're singing!",

Fuck, we were walking straight into Charles Manson's backyard. Billy's all excited. Sancho's smiling his smile. Everything in me is saying fuck this. Let's get a motel. But we walk right into the screened porch anyways. And the door is wide open, swinging with the wind. It's dark but for a few dim lamps. I could see, through the open door, that just inside was the kitchen, and across the kitchen, there was another door, left open to reveal a downward staircase. Flickering light and shadows told me that the singing was coming from down there. I suppose we could have walked right in. But we knocked and waited and knocked and waited. Eventually a spooky pale-faced girl came running by, noticed us, and stopped light a deer. She ran off as quickly as she'd come. Not to long after, she returned with a wise-looking' bearded man who said:

"Hello!"

He was wide-eyed. Excited but confused by our presence. "Ummm, how can I help you guys?" he asked

We hadn't prepared anything to say, and so... Well, no one said much for a moment. I wasn't gonna say anything. Billy stepped up and broke the silence, him being the one who'd had an invitation, if he did have one.

Billy started from the beginning. "I was hiking near Mount Canterboro. These two guys.. Caleb and Yacob, they gave me some help. Caleb told me about your community. And the 12 Tribes."

"Oh did he now...," The man said. This guy he was wacky. I mean, wide-eyed, drooling, absurdly interested in what we had to say. I mean, we knew it was a cult. We knew they'd do what they could to bait us in. But this man was so absurdly interested in us! I mean...

He told us he'd be right back. In the meanwhile we looked at eachother. We were a buncha kids conditioned to look to adults in times of indecision. But the man was back, and he talked to us like adults.

"I'm Yacob," he said (a different Yacob from the one Billy had met while hiking). He shook Billy's hand. "This is Luke, and this is Paul."

Luke took over, and Billy told him what he'd told Yacob earlier. Luke seemed very important. In his early-thirties, probably. Bearded. He was careful with his words. Also, he wasn't blindly excited about our presence like the others were.

Mostly every man there was bearded and curious to interact. Every women wore conservative dress and walked cautiously with her hands folded over each other. Typically the wives stood behind their husbands.

Billy explained how Caleb had mentioned this, if we needed a place to stay, this community could help us.

"Did he now?" Luke inquired.

"Yea," Billy said, "I was hiking. He said we could some work and, in exchange, have a place to sleep."

Luke was cautious, but the others looked excited, albeit a bit scared. As Luke deliberated, more people gathered 'round. Fuck I rememba this one particular kid who stood out to me. Looked like he fucked dogs for fun, just sitting in the back of the room, watching us, grinning. I thought to myself, then, that if I died in my sleep at this place, it would be by that kids hands.

*Luke told us, "Yea, I think we can help you out. Come in, come in."
Suddenly he was comfortable, though extremely tired, and he apologized. "You know," he said, "y'all are a bit intimidating showing up here, four strangers in the middle of the night."*

He brought us in the kitchen. We says hello to everybody. They says hello. All the kids are filing up from the basement. Caleb said that on Saturday nights they have a celebration. We'd just missed it, unfortunately. Now it was tea time. We were invited. So we followed these people around the corner to the 'livin room. There were two-dozen wide-eyed maniacs in that room, sipping tea sitting in a candle-lit circle with ceremonial placemats. Everybody seemed wacked. They were far out, man. Drooling over us and asking a million questions, fascinated with each little mundane answer we gave them. Billy and Sancho took a seat on one couch. An excited old woman sat next to them. We didn't wanna cramp her, so we, me and Colston, we grabbed the couch just inside the living room entrance. Colston was at my right.

The freaks were going around, asking us each how old we were, what we studied - all that. Where we came from. Billy answered most of the questions, saying how We'd all come from Winchendon but for me. It took 'em a while to understand that. I don't think they cared much to understand, because their eyes glowed and never once blinked, but they kept asking the same questions.

Anyways Billy and Sancho are over there talking to the lady. A fat man expert tea-maker man brings us some of his mysterious tea. He called it tea. We'd come in there planning not to eat or drink anything, or at least to ensure one or two of us didn't, but here we are, gulping down funky tea in this room full of kooks and candles. One muscular, upper-middle age kook is telling me and Colston about his navy days. Dishonorable discharge. How all he'd wanted was to be a part of something. That's why he joined the navy. But having joined, he found no love in it. And so he hit the road, wound up here.

"This place is love," he said, before going on about how, every year, they would stake out the Appleton trail, baiting in hikers to come stay for a while-- to sleep, eat, drink some tea, and to work if they're up for it. This guy was waaaacky. And Colston's just sitting there, silently observing, analyzing everything, looking suspicious as you can look. Meanwhile, in the shadows behind the sofa, there's a hypnotized 4-year-old-girl walking scales on a stand-up bass. I notice, there's a young boy matching her notes on the grand piano in the dark corner of the room

So it's getting late. Luke comes in with another guy. He's talking about baking bread and needing to be up all night. He's asking what's been done and what hasn't. Then he asks us if we've seen our cabin yet. We say no. He says we'll go see in just a minute. A bunch of people start filtering out of the meeting house, to their respective places of 'livin, bringing their kids to bed. Some of the older, wiser leader-types, as I saw them. They said they weren't leaders. They said everyone just did what they felt they should, and it worked out. This one guy, Jerry Garcia, sitting beside his wife, massaging her shoulders. He told us about their morning giving of thanks, and how at 7:00am we would meet and they would sing. He didn't ask; he told. Billy asked if we could sing with them. They said it'd be hard. "We're trying to build a community," Jerry Garcia said, "and our songs, you wouldn't know them." We were unsure of what he meant. 'Tryin to explain 'imself, he pointed at Billy - "you seem to be the leader of this group, am I right?" We all looked at each other. "Well," Jerry Garcia said, "you might understand that, to have a community, you need culture. We're trying to develop some culture here."

That was that. We talked about the community, their farm, and all their properties on the road: a chapel, some fields, the brewery, and the Yellow Deli. We offered to help out in the 'mornin. Jerry Garcia said that he was sure they could find 'somethin for us to do. Great. So we said our goodbyes and followed Luke to the cabins.

He shows us out the door, around behind the house, over an enormous cobblestone mosaic, then down a hundred steps. Cross a ditch, and there's the house that he says we can use for bath and shower. Cross back over the ditch and there we have it: A bunch of cabins -- twelve or so of them. Luke brings us to our cabin. Inside there are wo bunkbeds, a lamp, and a nicely hand-woven basket filled with four apples and four cream sodas. Luke offers to walk our horses to the barn. I tell him that would be great.

We're all inside the cabin, smiling at each other, realizing we hadn't been drugged and that these people, wacked as they were, were good at heart. Colston said "Good call Billy." We all laughed. Then it was time to grab our stuff - to lock it up inside. So we head outside. And just then, this kid comes bolting down the hill, hops over the ditch. The chants he was yelling scared the shit outa us. It was that weirdo kid from inside. Turns out he lives in the house where we were told to do our washing. I know this because he's doing his chants later in his kitchen and I'm trapped on the shitter in his house, afraid to answer when he's knocking, looking to take a shit.

Alright. So me and Sancho are going to sleep. There's some ruckus on outside. I dunno. I guess we got there on a busy day. Eryone was 'workin through the night. Sancho says to me "Gabe, I like this place. It's just.. it's so beautiful how they work together and live together and love each other. What do you think?" I tell 'im it's a fucking cult. He agrees, "yea, it is," and he giggles. I laugh too. Then he's quiet for a while. I hear some weird sounds and I realize - our cabin's just next to where the cows were grazing. But then Sancho starts fucking with me, making sounds, freakin' me out. I tell him to shut the fuck up. He says to me, what the fuck, I swear I'm not doing anything. So now were both

on our toes. And this dog starts barking right next to us. Then the thing pisses on
the outside of the wall behind me and Sancho's bunk. I think he pissed through
the vertical barn boards and onto my 'fuckin sheets. Then all around there's this
wild howling. We're in the middle of the mountains, down some uncharted roads,
and these cult freaks are surrounding our cabin making noises and pounding on
the walls. The cow's mooing like the world's coming to an end.

Suddenly Colston and Billy come rushing in, all discombobbled. They're
scrambling. We ask 'em what's going on. Now we're totally wacked. We get up,
light the lamp, stand up from bed. We start conspiring to sneak out, but there are
people out and about everywhere and our horses are in the stalls. We didn't even
know where the stalls were. That's why we decided to wait it out 'till morning.

Colston and Billy decided to go out for a walk. I put up my hands as to say
"What the fuck?" And they're 'lookin at me funny, like we were at school again,
just 'foolin around. Sancho asks "what are you guys doing?" The others just
laugh and they're off. We go to bed. Fuck those guys, right. We locked the door,
only to have to open it for them two hours later when again they're ranting and
raving about some wonderful, horrifying playground and a school. Colston draws
some wacky picture. It was his interpretation of the scene of us walking in on all
those wide-eyed wackos at their celebration.

Morning wafted in. None of us had gotten much sleep. It was five or six
a.m., and this ethereal, angelic guitar sound is echoing around the valley, waking
up the rooster's. All I could hear or think about were those words, so unabashed,
so mystical.:

> 'Somethin 'somthin on a mountain top heyyyy.
> Boots and all but the lord forgot...
> I feel my toes freezing although I'm plenty clothed.
> I'm young and lost, lord knows why I'm cold.
> Yoshua came 'a 'callin now,
> and I felt the warmth inside.
> I looked to the west,
> Then to the east,
> and I made my way home.

We were exhausted and thinking again that maybe we would sneak away
before morning gathering. It was either then or never though. Time was running
short.

"I say we go to the gathering," Colston says. And he thinks we should do
some work too. Billy's like, of course, why would we do anything else. And
Sancho agrees; he's up for some work. So we climb those steps; we cross the divine
cobblestone mosaic; and we make our way into the house. It's awkward. We greet

some of the wives who were cooking. They don't say anything, but instead nod their heads and give us some tea. The tea is warm this time. Hot, actually. And we're ditraled into that same living room from the night before. Nobody sits. Instead everyone is just standing, looking down piously at their folded hands. They're waiting for someone. I noticed, we were the only ones drinking tea.

A girl and her kids come rushing into the living room. She says she's sorry; then she says she's sorry for saying sorry. Pretty quickly, they start singing a song. Everyone joins in. Everyone individual stands in the same place they were sitting the night before. Jerry Garcia closed his eyes while he sung.

Now I can't remember what they were singing about. I can't remember what they said. But I do remember: it was the most beautifullest, bizarre thing I'd ever seen or heard. It was the responsibility of the children to provide ethereal chorus, while the deeper-voiced men arpeggiated and canonized the lead. Women confident enough would improvise with polyphonic melodies, and others would snap their fingers and add to the song however they could. Then the lead would switch and bounce around according to the randomness of ideas sprouted into people's minds.

After a few songs were sung — each volunteered by a community member —, there was a moment of silence. A long, patient moment, during which the community reflected on its previous day, its previous week, and their general feelings of things.

Morning discussion began gently when one women spoke of how she had been feeling uneasy recently and how she'd been having a hard time. Her kids were keeping her up at night. But she knew Yoshua would give her strength. "It doesn't seem that way sometimes," she said. "But look at me! I'm standing here after it all. I always will be, as will you."

A young man took stage next. He was young, seemingly new to the tribe. It seemed the elders were letting the youngsters go first. This one spoke simply. "I just wanted to give thanks," he said. "Thank you all, for being who you are, and for loving me, and for giving me a home. A year ago, I didn't know who I was, or what I was looking for. Now I see the path. I see Yoshua's way. I have a long road ahead of me, yes. But I am certain that I'm heading the right direction. Thank you all."

A few others spoke, not by any pattern, but by whoever felt they needed to speak, or by whoever felt they had something valuable to say. Most words were fairly docile. Also, it seemed that people had us on their mind. Us as young men looking for something in this tumultuous world, we reminded the elders of their younger days. We were the same, they said. Young people looking for beauty in the world. Looking for purpose. One day they had been the same. From the wince-inducing Navy man snagging hikers, to the farmer man vagabond-gone-lonely-

and-empty, to Yonathon, the boy our age, whose mother had brought him to the community when he was a kid because she was poor and drug-addicted and incapable of loving him the way the community could. They'd all been searching for something. Some found things which turned out to be nothings, or worse, black holes sucking goodness from the world. Each of these kindred souls went about their path and by fate wound up in this place, full of love for one another, full of love for this "Yoshua".

Even the children shared their stories. One little girl spoke of a dream she had the night before involving a piece of cake that she'd stolen. This girl confessed her sins and accepted her punishment. "I'm sorry Yoshua," she said. "I have done wrong."

Then the women who had arrived late stepped forward. And she did so frantically, clearly in a tumultuous mental state. She apologized for being late.

"My kids, we were troubled this morning by an unspeakable force. It was powerful, so powerful, made up of a million million little things." The woman cried. It was so hard not to say anything or to console her somehow. She was an individual, though. These were her words and her thoughts, not meant to be walked in upon prematurely.

"The path of Yoshua is difficult sometimes. And sometimes you stray. But when you do, it is important you don't let straying be.. don't let being off the path excuse further straying. Or else you will burn alive in the hell fires." It was like she was convincing herself right there, that there is only one path. What was truly troubling was how the kids and the adults and everyone solemnly nodded their heads in agreement with her. It was simple; if you stray, you burn. No question. This woman had a torsion in her eyes, almost unbearable to see. This torsion was unusual for the people of the community. Most of them were full and wholesome. Blissful.

Me, Sancho, Colston, Billy. We're all looking at each other, wondering what comes next. Breakfast came next, alongside some socializing over tea. Yonathon, the kid about our age, talks about one of the sister communities. See, because they've got these things all over the place. "This one specializes in music, while this here is a farming community. Over there I was building instruments, and I was learning from them. Now I'm here sharing what I've learned."

Jerry Garcia told us about his youth. We ask him questions while we were eating some disgusting porridge at the long table. That ebullient German kid came over all excited about what he'd cooked, waiting anxiously for me to sink my teeth into his disgusting shit. Jerry talked about all sorts of things. Books, music, stuff from the real-world that he hadn't spoken of in years. Colston asked him if anyone's parents ever come around all angry about their supposedly indoctrinated kids. "Oh sometimes.." he says. "But we talk to them, and we show them our ways. We show them the love in our hearts. And almost always, they eat porridge *with us and drink tea with us. And eventually, they go home. Some of them visit occasionally for more porridge and to see their children."*

Jerry Garcia's farmer friend said he would find us some work to do. That was after Colston and Sancho insisted that the community make use of us somehow. Meet at 9:00am in the rain. Will do. Our job is to till up some dirt and thereby do two things. One: feed the chickens exposed worms. And two: fertilize the dirt for farming. Yonathon, the kid whose mom dropped him at the community, joins us. Colston won't stop talking about how this kid is some mysterious divine figure destined to be a centerpiece of the tribe someday.

Now we're moving along. Here's how we do it. Okay. We take these tormenting huge pitchfork-like things, and we stab 'em in the ground. We jump on 'em with our feet, to dig 'em deeper, you know. Then we push down real hard, with all our weight -- it's tough! -- and you have to flip the ground upside-down. A bunch'a worms come out and all these chickens come swarming like vultures. The chickens don't even care when the pitchfork comes stabbing at their feet. These farmers just let 'em roam free.

The farmer guy told us that the chickens won't wander far. He said they always straggle back. And he said he would execute the chickens in the order they wander back. It's crazy man, I tell ya. They're free but they're too homesick to avoid the knife.

Then some rats go running in all directions. Fucking things. Yonathon's chasing the fucking rats, 'stabbin at 'em 'with his pitchfork. He's 'tellin us to do the same. Oh man. It was hilarious. But it was grotesque, too, seeing these ginormous holes through the rat carcasses. Squirming rats bleeding from their bellies, twitching off their feet while trying to get away.

The young man, Yonathon, was enjoying himself, working, 'talkin to us about regular life, pushing chickens around, killing rats. Then...

Anyways, we finished up and said our goodbyes. Colston told Jerry Garcia that it was inevitable our paths would cross in the future. Farmer guy let us wash up in his man-made pond. It was a tiny pond with a canoe in it. We jumped in in our undergarments. It was cold. Colston jumped in a second time.

Pretty soon, we were on the road again. One bread-maker fellow gave us a letter to deliver to his friend in Chattanooga Tennessee.

I donno why I told yous alls that...."

The old man said "thanks for listening, fellas," to the fellas and unknowingly to Yofim and the mysterious girl also. With the fellas having finished their cigars, and time having passed, one of them acknowledged "I best be 'gettin to work," and made his way.

The other fella hung around, talking to the old man in a more serious tone, asking "so what's going on here now?"

"I dunno," says the old man. "Figure it out, why don't ya." He'd gotten tired of talking, it seemed, and he was off trailing behind the other fella.

Mystery girl grabs Yofim by the arm and pulls him into the barn, into the barn... into the barn.

TWENTY-FOUR

Yofim's love has herself laid back on a hay bail in Tom's stall. Her legs are crossed and her hands are behind her back. She's staring at Yofim. She's rocking to and fro, giggling and grinning like she was waiting for Yofim to notice something that she'd done. The boy was clueless, though, standing there, brushing Tom's mane to pass time. The horsed leaned over, resting his weight on the stallside. It was only mildly interested in what Yofim had to offer. The girl smiled and giggled, knowing that Yofim was only petting the horse to avoid awkwardly doing nothing.

Eventually Yofim gave in and asked, "What are you on about?"

"'Nothin!" the Girl exclaimed, giggling some more.

"I don't know where Tomph is. I'm sorry, I'm worried."

"Come here, Yofim!!" the Girl said. And she bounced to her feet. From behind her back, she presented a figure. It was the doll Yofim came across earlier while in the cupola.

"Where'd you find that?" he asked, stepping toward her.

"It wandered somehow from you to me, to bring me to you, and now I am here."

Yofim reached to caress the doll. But this mystery girl swept his legs. Cut two and she's sitting on top of his belly on the hay bales beside Tom.

"I've never felt this way before," she admitted while playing with his hair. Yofim couldn't speak. He trembled as the girl meandered her hands from caressing his hair, down and around his cheeks and his neck, and as she leaned in to kiss his lips, and as she balled up his t-shirt at his sides, brimming his jeans. Yofim looked up to find The Girl's eyes — her deep, gravitational eyes.

He said to her: "You have beautiful eyes".

She leaned in, bringing her face close to his. She looked into his eyes, and asked him, "do I?" It was the most powerful, potent, but perplexing moment.

Yofim looked deep into the girl's eyes where he found browns and greens and hints of blue inside of which there was a spiderweb of yellow golden fibers.

And he told her, "yes, you do."

She smiled and kept there smiling and looking into his eyes.

He leaned up awkwardly for a kiss himself. She responded, leaning his way also. And Yofim didn't know what he was doing, but he leaned up anyway, only to be blocked by a finger on his lips which tossed him back into the hay bales.

"No, no," she wagged her finger. Yofim froze. It would be her on this day. It would be her, excitedly whispering to Tom, teasing him, saying, "what are you looking at?!", playing with Yofim's hair, his lust, his paralyzed glare, fiddling with his belt buckle and watching him squirm, kissing him passively as minutes and hours past. Then darting out the stall in a cloud of hay, leaving the boy ravished, his belt undone, graced by the presence of the old horse Tom.

TWENTY-FIVE

Little One sat cross legged under a forest haze. Below him, a round stone tablet was embedded into the earth. Thick roots from the Galagna trees encroached onto this stone. Father Galagna sat against the grandfather tree; he became one with the grandfather tree, interwoven with its owl hole, supporting and supported by the grandfather tree, preaching to his people, echoing through the northern forests, waving his hands. The tree slowly enveloped him while he uttered his sermon. Soon, only his hands and lips remained unsurrendered to the tree; but with these alone, he directed armies.

The Tree lowered his attention from his people and his world to Little One. He spoke words only the boy could hear. He spoke in a language only the boy knew, though the boy did not know he knew.

"In the realms of Galagna one is dwarfed by trees thicker than houses, taller than vision itself. A soul is made feel small even while beside the ants, for the ants here are crocodilic. And the roots of these trees, strong as horses' legs, can be seen interweaving, churning eternities in the horizon. The roots, they border deep, narrow canals inspired by the waterways of Rome. Treehouses are our villas. The infinitely interwoven fabric of roots is our foundation which isolates water from land and thereby connects and heals the people and allows them to grow. A vast irrigation and transportation network, stretching from the sun to the hellfires. The trees farm the water, and the trees farm us, Galagna people, who farm the trees and utilize the waters."

"We are one," he said.

The waters were high-rushing, providing a world-fluidifying white noise that united Little One and the Galagna people with the forest. As the tides lowered, the trees' roots swelled, conserving moisture like bears preparing for hibernation season. The swelling roots encapsulated Little One. And they encroached upon the canals, tightening, heightening the flow, giving the scarce water less room to breathe and less time to conspire plans to make its way elsewhere.

"The noise is present always, reminding us of our togetherness with the world, and of our togetherness with the atmosphere."

Father Galagna raised his palms, embracing the brewing storm. For a long while, his graciousness held this pose.

"Always," he said, "we must be thankful for The Way."

In that moment, the Grandfather tree creaked and arched its back. A hundred years past as Little One lost himself in the scriptured hearthstone. In this time, the magnificent roots tangled around Little One's legs. Squeezed him like a snake... And in this time, Father Galagna's arm and his head disappeared beneath rugged blue-veined bark. Only one of his hands remained visible, but it was petrified into stone.

Little One heard a voice. Then many voices — voices of passersby. A passing series of canoe-paddlers continued each others' sentences. As one approached, he would speak some words as part of a larger whole. This paddler would pass, and the next canoe-man in line would continue the previous's words. Then another canoe-man would come along. Then another. And so on. They explained to Little One that:

"Galagna is a tribe of tenders to the elements. Not the elements of material — gold, silver, and the like — but of the fundamental forces of life: mutual dependence and the worldly way. We worship the tree and cultivate the storm. We tend to the rivers and ride their currents. When a man dies, we birth another. When a flower bush grows, we set fire to a garden somewhere else."

"To read the scripture is to know of the knots untie-able (these are the axiomatic irreducibles of our world), and to realize how all things decompose into these units of unknowability and no further. To read the scripture is to flatten tangles of lines and curves and worldly chaos, and to realize all and everything as the single chain of untiable links that it is. And then observe the forces at work. Then you will know. You might also add links to history's chain."

The last of the canoe-rowing figures passed. Little One, with his legs trapped by the roots, laid on his back. From that position on his back, he feasted his eyes on the tremendous, infinitely parallel trunks of trees that extended into the heavens above. And rain rained down everywhere but atop the 10-foot radius circle that surrounded the boy. It rained everywhere but atop the hearthstone with which Little One was becoming One. The roots climbed up his torso. Water fed the trees, and it fed the streams; and the streams overflowed, feeding the roots, making them swell. Little One was further entrapped.

The marshes churned, and rain fell. Tomph, like Little One, had a unique calm centered about his position. As the world flooded, he remained dry in a spot where no rain fell. This prompted visions of laughter on swing-sets, small gray birds sliding down children's aluminum playground slides, and Yofim somersaulting down the old hill into piles of leaves. Visions of dogs came. Vicious, brutal things, chomping at their bits as their masters trudged on through snow and mud and ice, starving their slaves into a primality -- dogs so hungry and ferocious, so willing to bleed.

Yofim thought of his friend. He imagined Tomph hunting rabbits in the wilderness with hand-sharpened stick spears that he carried so proudly. He was always so glad to be of use to his community.

The girl reassured Yofim, suggesting that "Tomph is probably on the rounds with Omnious." She said, "they're perfect for each other, perfect complements," caressing Yofim's chin. Then she ran off into the sun that shined across the fields. Yofim followed her, hoping all was well in the North and elsewhere.

TWENTY-SIX

Simultaneously, Jack Tomleson kept pace along a hundred-year-old fieldstone wall. He ran his hands along the cool moss that told of the wall's years. Soon, though, the cool, moist tactility was replaced by the wooden side of a home, or a tavern possibly. Jack rounded the corner, but his father palmed his chest, stopping him in place.

"Careful, Son", he whispered, explaining how "this is the house of [his] grandfather, and that [the man] wakes easily."

"It is cold. Can we not go inside for warmth?" Jack asked

"Just maybe; you could, I imagine. But I," Syd Tomleson admitted, "I could never….". Shame broiled in his voice.

"What do you mean, father?"

"Oh it's quite the tale, Son. And it's almost morning. We've 'gotta hide. So go inside, tell my Father about yourself. He will help you. But if he is sleeping, don't wake him. Sleep on the couch. I'll find a place for myself and return at dusk tomorrow."

"Goodbye, Son," Mr. Tomleson said. "Get some sleep." With that, he ventured into the town of Homverd.

Jack thought to follow his father down those barrel-fire-lit alleyways, but he opted not to do so. He was left unsure of why it was necessary to hide from the sunlit hours. He was left at grandpa's door, on which he knocked softly. Nobody answered the door. So, slowly, he rotated the knob and entered the living room. It was dark but for the lamplight of downtown Homverd slipping through the shades. Outside, life was doing as life does. People meandered around, some up to good, others not, some shopping, some drinking; some fooling, others not, others thieving or selling. It was peaceful inside. Jack went to sleep safely behind thick stone walls and an iron door.

Shortly later, Grandfather was up and about for his morning. He came over cloudy-eyed to stock the stove. He put his mug down on top of the stove. Some coffee drops hit the metal and they fizzled and hissed.

"Still warm. Good," he said.

The saying of those words triggered a reflex in Jack that made him murmur, "Nnnnmm what was that, Delilah?"

Grandfather Tomleson gasped at the familiar voice sounding from his couch. He gasped and he asked "Is that you Winnifer?" But it wasn't. So Grandpa was confused. Genuinely regretful for waking Jack, Grandpa apologized to the stranger who had been sleeping harmlessly on his couch, "I'm sorry. I thought you were...—Oh, I'm sorry, go back to sleep. I'll stoke the fire."

"No." Jack said. "No, wait!" He rushed to his feet, towering over the old man and startling him. Although Jack was sincere in his efforts to be calming, the reality was that he was a large, intimidating stranger in an elderly man's home. As such, he received a blow to the head.

"Jesus!!" Grandfather Tomleson hadn't had time to think. Now the strange invader began to stand up again, and the old man cowered.

Jack put up his hands, as to say "I come in peace."

The old man wound up to swing, but he didn't. "Oh fuck," he said, "Oh, fuck. who are you?"

The old man was thick and strong like his son. Of course he had worn out over the years. So on this day he was a harmless hunchback with harmless mannerisms. He embodied this wonderful flamboyance. His muscles were loose. He was mobile, despite having a hunchback. And equally agile as his motions were his words. In their selection and their articulation, there was a life to them. Flamboyant and shifty, yet straight as an arrow in the larger scheme -- what a potent blend of a man...

Jack tried introducing himself. "Hi. I... I'm Ja—————". But Grandpa cut in.

"Oh Jesus... Jesus, you scared the shit outa me, all big and tall and scary like that.. on my couch!! What are you doing buddy? Who are you? You're my grand son aren't you Jeeeeesuss"

"It appears I am, sir." Jack admitted, referencing the lump on his head.

"Ohhhhhh I ammm no sir. Call me gran-paaa! Come 'eer bud! 'Gimme a hug."

Jack leaned in despite some hesitance. Grandpa burrowed deep into his arms, eager to embrace his newly-discovered family. He held Jack so tightly, so graciously, and he kissed his chin. Still, he needed to ask:

"Wait... so, which of my son's kid are you? And where is your dad?"

Jack said, "my Father is your Sydney." And Grandpa backed away from this statement.

"That slime-ball. You aren't like him, are you?"
"Wait. Don't answer that. I won't punish you for your father's woes."

"Come 'ere! Gimme a hug!" Grandpa embraced Jack again. He told his grandson that he was welcome to stay as long as he needed to or wanted to, no questions asked. And he admitted that he doesn't gossip. "So there will be no talk of your father," he said. "Now you'll have to excuse me, I'm off to walk the neighbor's dogs. Are you staying here?"

Jack explained that he hadn't slept in days, and how he was exhausted.

Grandpa told him "oh yes of course. Sleep, sleep away. Sleep in my bed if you'd like."

"No that's okay grandpa. The couch will do."

"Okay sonny, yea, the couch is fine. I'll be off then. Will you be here when I get back?"

"I will."

"Oh wonderful! Maybe we can have some quality time this afternoon. Ya know, get to know each other??"

"I'd enjoy that, Grandpa."

"Oh great! Off I go then!"

The man slid out, a half-dozen dog leashes tucked into the back of his pants.

With Grandpa gone, Jack slept where his father had slept one day, and where countless bums and travelers had slept since.

TWENTY-SEVEN

For an eternity, Little One stared into the tangled scriptures. He stared through rain and drought, and most oddly, day and night. Normally night never comes in the forest of Galagna, nor does day. It is always the same. The water flows sometimes narrower, sometimes wider, but it inevitably modulates to one speed -- and the trees, they grow; their roots thicken. The trees let in light when it is too dark, and vice versa when it is too light. But with Father Galagna devoured by the forest and the other Galagna disciples nowhere to be found, the waters rose and fell and overflowed and went dry. The growing roots lost their form. Soon it was evident to Little One: he would soon be consumed by the forest.

Little One took this passing thought, he recognized its presence, and he allowed it to pass.

As with the passing canoe-men, more thoughts followed, each somehow a continuation of the previous, but each from a unique source. In his head, a storm of knot-chained chaos swirled, twisting and interweaving and engulfing itself, churning turning inside and out. At first Little One strained to work with the knots. But soon such conscious effort was no longer necessary, because the chaos in his head became less than the chaos of the outside. He was comfortable in that lessor chaos. So comfortable, he felt no reason to consider the outside world. He was sustainable and satisfied in his own universe. So he did not worry of the Galagna roots which encroached upon him and the eternity stone. He did not try and escape, because the roots did nothing but chain him to where he most desired to be.

This all faded, fainted away. The boy, he slept through thunder and scattering thunderbolts. He dreamed of gaseous churning flames, then mere whirlpools, and eventually it all collapsed down to decomposed layers of waves, and a simple, graspable intuition.

So, in the voice of Father Galagna, Little One echoed the tribal doctrine:

"We have defragmented our lives, devoting everything to the preservation of the elements. We've tended to them. In exchange, they have fed us and provided us drink. We have reduced our lives to this atomic purpose, and we ourselves have become primitive forms, unable to decompose further. We are elements of the world, my tribesmen, in their most basic form.

Devote your lives to regulating the waters, and to protecting the waters, and to protecting the trees. Devote your life in this way and you will live forever."

The rain stopped. In its place a haze sagged in. Little One laid on his back. Locked into place, he watched the clouds swirl and churn.

TWENTY-EIGHT

Mr. Tomleson ducked around the town of Homverd, his face hidden behind a round hat that he'd found. Homverd was a small but dense town, made mostly of stone, and with narrow alleyways acting as bum-ridden highways to everywhere. It was a lively place on weekends, with music and drinking in the taverns, and during the week, with work and business trotting along. This was a weekday. So it was imperative that Mr. Tomleson not be seen. So he made his way through a bookshop and behind the church-turned-courthouse. Around a corner was where he found the Unitarian Church. It was open at all times for all reasons. It had been in the past, but it hadn't been a long while. Anyways, Tomleson pulled open the door, which was heavy but well-oiled. Inside he found the candle-lit altar room. It was weirdly exactly as he remembered it.

It seemed that nobody was inside the church. Syd Tomleson looked around and whistled to be sure. Receiving no response, he went about his business, passing by the confessions booth and the altar and the crucified Jesus. He didn't deal out more than a glance. Because his purpose was downstairs, through the dark, demonic stairwell of a thousand cobblestones, of mossy walls, of brown sludge seeping through the sinking floors, and of a thousand ghosts loitering, procrastinating purgatory. Mr. Tomleson felt his way down this stairwell.

At the bottom, he peeked through the cracks of the old, wooden door to the cemetery. Just as he'd hoped, things were as he remembered. With a boot, he sent the hinges turning, and he made his way out into the gated churchyard. He followed a pathway through shadows and gravestones. Some light shimmered from between the raised winter tombs. From that direction, chatter could be heard.

He walked down a gravel path laced with shadows of gravestones, sometimes seemingly-moving shadows. The moon shined low, large, and yellow. Paranoid he was of finding some junky cornered up against a gravestone -- a ghostly white animal near to death but not ready to die. Eventually, though, he made his way around the tombs to the other side, where he found a wholesome mix of bums, druggies, and regular townies scattered around a barrel fire.

He remembered his buddy Bill showing him this place in the old days. They were kids. After school one day, there was supposed to be a hoo-rah. The gang Tomleson thought himself a part of didn't feel so appealing to him at that time. For his reasons, he stayed back, said he had things to do. Bill had a moment of his own and the both of 'em wound up lonely that night, not knowing the other was lonely too. It got late. Somehow they wound up walking through town, talking to bums, bumming cigarettes from bums, giving cigarettes to bums, bartering for nothing meaningful. Then it was time to head home. But as they went, Bill saw the shimmering lights in the cemetery. He got wildly excited about the lights for some reason.

"Common Syd," he said, "You most absolutely will want to see this. I thought it was a myth."

And so they went and got drunk with the bums who were relieved to know these kids were kids and not police officers. Next time they brought friends, only the good ones. They traded sandwiches for booze and they had an enjoyable time. This became culture - the towniest of townies hanging with bums around a fire and tombstones.

Now it had been years since anyone had heard from Sydney Tomleson. He'd been off doing his doings. Meanwhile, a new generation of bums and townies came up in his place.

Syd made his entrance smiling gently, pleased with the opportunity to surprise upon old buddies in this environment of his youth. He didn't recognize anyone, though. And all the faces, one-by-one, turned in towards him in an unwelcoming fashion that he had once displayed to others himself.

That was until a familiar voice called out "Ayyyyyyyyy Syd!! My man!!! Is that you?.." thereby causing the whole crowd of weary bums and townies to turn toward Tommy Jacobs, the townie among townies, who reassured them "he's cool, fellas."

This Tommy Jacobs, thin and enthused as ever, jogged over to his old half-buddy half-middleman, put an arm around him, faced the crowd, and said, "This place is cold. Wind comes through here like a flock of hornets. And the ground's too hard to sleep. But this here, fellas, is the fella that warmed me up to the cemetery."

Tommy's voucher comforted a lot of guys into getting on with their conversations and doings. Only a few cared to pay attention past the question of who it was invading their place of comfort. Knowing that Syd wasn't a threat, what did they care?

Pretty quickly, Syd got acclimated. It was a nostalgic scene with people laying about all over place. Little humble conversations went on. Kids scoured measly amounts of pot. Dads sipped drink periodically, hanging by the fire. One bum went on preaching about aliens and intergalactic Darwinism as the kids listened, and as the townies followed his lecture only passively. Some bums were rambling ears-closed to each other. Everyone was talking over everyone. One bum sat oblivious to everything, reading some book with a torn cover. Laying on his belly, he had a blanket over his back. You could see his feet hanging out, rubbing against one another for warmth. He was fighting to cover as many holes in his socks at once as he could. It was a hopeless fight, though.

Tommy asked, "Syd, want a drink?" Mr. Tomleson said "ah no thanks, not anymore." But saying that made for a feeling of separation, so he said, "ahh fuck it, gimme a beer." And in a snap they were back in old days: hooting, hollering, talking about girls. Tommy's wife had been depressed lately, Tommy mentioned. "She wasn't happy about 'nothin." She didn't want him out with the guys when he went out with the guys, but when he stayed home, she didn't want him around. "So here I am," he said.

There was a third wheel -- a long haired fella who had been more focused on his beer, it seemed, and the mesmerizing flames, than Sydney Tomleson and what our man had to say. This tagger-along turned out to have been listening the whole time. Because when he sat up from his spot in the grass, he said, "Hi Syd. Tommy, we've 'gotta have Syd meet my boy. You'd love him, man. He'll remind you of us when we were turds."

"Yeah, let's go," Tommy Jacobs said. So they went over behind the biggest tomb around, headed by an engraving

"Swartz", and surrounded by footstone graves each housing other Swartz's caskets, and they circled around to a smaller barrel fire where some kids were sitting on gravestones. One of them passed a ball to a fat kid. The next pass brought the ball to a long-haired little knot of energy who up and launched the thing into the barren ocean of shadows and gravestones. One kid got angry, saying "what'd you do that for?" Others laughed. A slobbering bulldog chased after the ball. The boys got on talking and Tommy introduced the long-haired kid to Mr. Tomleson as the long-haired man's son. "This is my boy," the guy said, putting his arm around his reluctant, squirming son. "I love him. I love him more than the moon." He smiled so wholesomely.

In that moment, Mr. Tomleson realized exactly who the long-haired fella was. And he rejoiced watching his old buddy break out into a song expressing his love for his boy:

> *I love him, as wind blows*
> *I love him more than I love life*
> *I love him, as echoes go*
> *I love him, My child: Moe.*

"This apple here. It is ripe," this long-haired fellow said, patting his embarrassed kid's head. "He's so smart, just like you. You'll love him, Syd. I love him."

Dad gave his barely-tolerant son a smooch, and that was that. The guy pushed the kid back to his business, and the kid took off like a race horse. The dog brought the ball back. And the kid, Moe, crow-hopped into a toss that sent the dog chasing the ball halfway across town. Then Moe said to his chubby friend, "C'mon Joe, let's hit the docks."

The long-haired fella explained, "When we were kids, we came here 'cuz it was spooky, you know. Now we come here 'cuz we don't got no place else. We've got 'nothin left to find 'cept for death."

"Yea," Tommy said, "But, you know, when the wife won't

let me in bed, I feel like shit. I drink by myself and I stay up half-awake all night. Alone. I feel terrible. But you know what I realize? I realize I'm always welcome here. Knowing that makes everything a bit better. I think about it when I'm working sometimes."

The long-haired fella admitted, "Yessir. There's a place for everyone in the graveyard. Everyone's welcome. (Well, most everyone)."

Then he talked about his kid who he said he would give everything for, but for whom he had nothing to give.

"Every kid believes his dad is the man for a while, and most kids get over that. But my boy.. I just thought I'd last a bit longer until he realized I was a bum. That's all."

Sydney Tomleson begrudgingly put an arm around his old friend. He had nothing to say, but he gave his friend the arm. Fairly quickly, Guy Long-hair declared it was time for bed and slothed out into the darkness.

That left Tommy Jacobs and Syd. The crowd was mostly nodding off at this point. Some people went home. Some slept where they were. Even Tommy looked tired, but he was there for Mr. Tomleson, offering him a place to stay.

"Tommy, I really appreciate it, but I've 'gotta lay low. I can't have your wife or anyone seeing me around. No offense, of course," Syd Tomleson said.

"You sure buddy?" Tommy asked.

"Yeah, I suppose I am." Tomleson admitted reluctantly, feeling cold air crawling across his neck.

"Okay, I understand. Well, that's it for me then. I'll catch you around?"

"I doubt it, but hopefully."

"Alright buddy. I hope so too. Well, you know where I live."

"By Sancho's place? Near the meat shop?"

"Yessir," Tommy said. "The meat shop is different now, though. It's a fucking book shop now."

"You're serious?"

"Yessir, but it's in the same place. Find me anytime."

"Will do, Tommy."

Tommy raised his hand for a shake, which he pulled in for a hug. Then he was off heading toward home, and that was that. "You're always welcome at my place. Just don't bring Dirtball over there. He's got a good heart but we've already got one too many dogs in the house."

"See you 'round Tommy. Good to see 'yuh."

"You too, Syd."

The two saluted each other; finally, that was truly that. The sun would rise soon; it was time for sleep. So Mr. Tomleson found a raised tomb, knowing tombs are always left unlocked in Homverd, always. It had been protocol to leave the doors unlocked since long ago, when a live man was mistaken to be dead and left to starve in his chamber. Creepy, sure, but Tomleson had an enduring stomach. He would sleep in the tomb of Bonnie Russel, a girl he had gone to school with. She'd cheered him on during the one football game he'd ever played. Bonnie's brother, his friend, Martin, had broken his leg during the week prior. Syd agreed to fill in, and he wound up scoring the winning touchdown. Everyone cheered, but Bonny cheered especially loud. They'd grown up together. Now she was gone. "Looks like we'll be spending one last night together, Bonnie," Syd muttered. Once inside, he climbed atop the casket to sleep. He knocked on the thing, but Bonny was quiet. "Hope you don't mind," he whispered, "'cuz I'm real tired." He said, then he slept a good sleep.

TWENTY-NINE

Grandpa Tomleson slid back inside his home. His dog leashes' metal rings clanked against the door on his way in, and this woke up Jack. "Ohhh heyy," Grandpa said. "I'm sorry. Forgot you were herre. Ai'm so sorryyy. Just bringing in some groceries. Ohhhh it's cold. Could you get a fire going?"

"Sure Grandfather, I can do that."

"Ohhh that's great. That's great. I'll be right back."

Jack had slept through most of the day. Now that he was well rested and curious, he gathered some paper and kindling. It was quite cold. So he sparked a match to some kindling before going outside to find some thicker wood. Grandpa said that there was a stack outside. What Jack found was a not a mere stack, but a magnificently symmetrical beehive-like structure composed of stacked firewood. Jack regretfully took an armful of logs. Coming back inside, he unloaded a few into the stove. The excess, he put adjacent to the kindling bin.

Then he sat back on the couch twiddling his fingers. Some clanging came from the kitchen. Grandpa was making supper: beef, bread and soda, plus carrots.

"Need a hand Grandpa?" Jack asked, looking for an opportunity to talk.

"Ohh yea suurre; do you cook?"

"Well, I can be of assistance somehow I'm sure. But Julia usually fixes supper."

"Oooooo who's Juliaaaaa?"

"She was my wife. She is the mother of my child."

"Whoaaa theree.. Oh sure! How about you chop some onions."

"I can do that."

Grandpa Tomleson put a bent-up knife on the countertop. Then he put half an onion in front of Jack. "What happened to this?" Jack asked, referring to the knife.

"Nothing! That's how it was originally. Ha! Haha!"

Grandpa explained how he'd made the knife himself. "I'm a hobby blacksmith," he said. "Looks ugly but it's sharp." He reached over and squeezed his two fingers on sides of the tip of the blade. He lifted the tip, forming a fulcrum with the handle and the countertop. When he let the blade lower down, gravity was enough pull it smoothly through the onion. "See," Grandpa snickered. "Oh I'm so proud of that thing. You try!" Jack did and Grandpa went "Oh yay! I love seeing people use it. Anyhow, let's get rolling ayy?"

Before long, Grandpa suggested that "that's probaahbly good," pointing to the home-blacksmithed metal bowl in which they'd been tossing onions and lettuce and potatoes. It was half full. After Grandpa sliced some meat, he said "I'll meetcha in the livin'room. I've 'gotta add the secret ingredient!" "Go.go.go! shew!" he urged, as Jack stood smiling not realizing at first that, beneath this man's jokingly wayabouts, the secret was real and indeed something the old man intended to keep secret.

From the kitchen, Grandpa yelled asking "you wan'anything to drink?" Jack said he would have something, but he didn't say what. "Well what do you want. Oh, you probably don't care. I'll get you something." Grandpa came in saying "I hope milk is alright. It's a little warm. Hopefully it's alright. It'll be alright." Jack nodded, sipping the milk to show it was okay.

For a while, the two sat by the fire. They ate from the same bowl. It sat between them on the couch. Each of them scrapped at it with their hands. And they talked; they talked of Jack's wife and her not wanting to be tied down, her love for Jack, her love for her child, but her love for the woods, and her love for others. They talked of Grandpa's broads -- they loved him, and he loved them, but only for a few nights at a time. Life would turn wild, but it would return to normal not too long thereafter. In short order, Grandpa liked to be walking Homverd's dogs and waving to the widows on their front-porches. Then he'd come home and make knives. He'd eat and smoke opium, and he'd sleep with his iron front door completely unlocked. He said "it's good to have a tonic note to come back to, but I'll never lock my doors."

They talked of all sorts of things: music, the broken piano decaying under the once-divine-but-now-leaking skylight, and anything but Jack's Father. Even after they'd finished eating, they kept on talking on the couch. Grandpa sat in awe as Jack described his beautiful daughter. "She's so smart, Grandpa. When Julia and I were having our troubles, it was her who.. she's so untainted by our adult nonsense. She just asks 'why can't mommy just live here only when she wants to?' God, and we just melted. We'd been fighting for days, because she didn't want to be anyone's wife. Then my daughter Delilah comes along with her brown eyes; she waves her wand, and poof, we love each other again."

Grandpa could barely speak.. "oooooo I wish I could meet her"

"Ohh I'm sorry for interrupting," he said. "Go-on, go on, please oh please". His soul ached for his beautiful granddaughter. Jack could see this, so he went on describing Delilah, telling stories about her and her friend Edie playing with dolls in the sand by the river-round. "She has the most wonderful, sweet imagination," Jack said.

Then suddenly Jack stopped talking. Grandpa fell forward in anticipation. Quickly it became apparent why Jack had stopped. It was because the estranged son, Mr. Tomleson, had peeked his head in the door. "Alright Jack, it's time to go," he said, only to realize that Grandfather Tomleson was in the room — sitting beside Jack, nursing a cut on the young man's leg, and talking to him while doing so.

"It's late," Mr. Tomleson said. "I thought you'd be alseep."

Suddenly all good congeniality went to shit.

Grandpa told his son, "Get out of my house," and he pointed to the door.

Father looked at son. Father looked at son. Son at Father. Son at Father's father. After Mr. Tomleson went outside, Grandpa joked, "People come in some nights and theyyy.. they just sleep. It's amazing, I trust them more than my own son." Then Grandpa sulked out of the room. He came back only briefly to finish his work with the gauze on Jack's leg. Once the job was complete, he disappeared into the kitchen.

Jack met his father outside.

THIRTY

Mrs. Greenlock boomed. She shrieked at her cowering husband, "I commanded you to keep the gates down! Yet you raise them! And you allow my people to drown!" Fuming from the ears, she grew wretched, vascular bat wings and swarming snake tentacles. Leo Greenlock lost all power over the Daughter of Elsedorwn, who shrieked and howled and invaded his library, tossing his books then ripping boards from the walls with her command of the elements, then dislodging the shelves from the walls, tearing them to bits, and swirling them into a hurricane of loose boards, nails, loose-leaf papers and books.

Leo Greenlock pleaded, "My love, I swear, I did so only because I saw no other way.."

Due to the lack of a male in her siblings, Mrs. Greenlock inherited the throne. Her husband found his place through marriage. Time passed, and Mrs. Greenlock forgot her place in the world. She became more of a spouse than a leader of the farm. But her very husband, her elected captor, had re-conjured memories of her grandmother and the knowledge of her power. Mr. Greenlock, the marriage-raised obelisk of Greenlock Farm, he who took the reins when they were passed to him... he climbed himself into a high place. But ultimately he is to serve under the true lord —— she who towered over her infertile mate, palming his head to the floor, pushing him to his knees.

"You are a plagued dying carnation, doomed to decompose and infect the lands.., seeding, sprouting, reproducing through me and my heavens, disgustingly displacing the world as it should be."

"My love, please," Leo Greenlock begged. His wife

floating high and mighty at the peak of the library ceiling. Dilated, the room was a hundred feet tall. So far above her mate, the Daughter of Elsedorwn retained no emotional connection. Leo could see this: the devil in her eyes. Her eyes, they wandered maniacally, swooshing worldly material with each of their movements.

Once more, Leo pleaded. "I remember our wedding, Hwen. I remember you in your beautiful dress. My mother toiled for weeks, stitching that dress. And you were so beautiful. Your mother and I, we melted watching you walk the isle. She was so happy for us, your mother ———

"DOOOO NOT SPEAK OF MY MOTHER!!!".

Momentarily, Mrs. Greenlock's craze broke, and she made contact with her beloved husband's eyes.

Leo said, referencing Mrs. Greenlock's mother, "she didn't speak for weeks, unable to do so through that smile of hers so pure that words couldn't pass through. Do you remember?"

It was true. Hwen Greenlock remembered how her mother glowed, and how she had been glowing herself, and how the world had blossomed big and whole on the day that she became a Greenlock. The sun shined nicer in those times. But she wished not to remember. So, promptly, she snapped back from her husband's worldly trap and she lopped off his head. Leo Greenlock became but ashes in an urn after she made him as such —— burned with the books from his own library. To ashes, to ashes.. to ashes.

THIRTY-ONE

The clouds blasted into the horizon; henceforth, the sun burned unimpeded. Mrs. Greenlock connived, hidden away atop her private rooftop courtyard. With each flick of her brow, she churned the air in the sky. She swayed trees when she licked her lips. "Today," she said, "marks the dawn of a new time." It was on this day when the farm's greenery roasted alongside the will of the people, for after many days of long hours and shadow figures prowling the fields, circling in upon those who worked with excessive leisure, whipping farmhands with teathery painful whips - and after a particularly excruciating day, during which a boy was whipped into picking cotton despite his fingertips being scraped to the bone by a meat grinder, and a day during which Daughter of Elsedorwn said to Sherri, daughter of Earnie, that she would be hers one day soon, as her father was Elsedorwn's, "sexually, for labor, housekeeping, and in every which way." The girl's skin crawled at the thought. Worse it was, when the farm's lady prowled over Sherri like a mantis does its mate, who'll inevitably be ravished and put to death. Telling her father of this later, Sherri explained "the mantis, it devours the head of its mate after intercourse."

The people congregated in their usual congregation spot. They marched to the front steps of Greenlock and demanded to be seen, but they went answerless. They yelled. They chanted. Eventually they made a ruckus enough to disrupt the Daughter of Elsedorwn's afternoon slumber. So she lifted her head from her rooftop futon. Disgusted, she sent her servant to manage the nuisance.

Squeamish and tense, Earnie emerged from the double doors. He slammed the doors on the men who tried squeezing in. "Back," he commanded, peering through the mail slit. "To the bottom of the stepway, or we won't speak until another day." People scrapping on the outside of the door drew him to pound, with all his might, from the inside, yelling "DAMNIT. DAMNIT! MAKE WAY!"

One of the fellas pleaded with Earnie through the mail slit.

Outside, people were chanting, "*Earnie, the widow, weak like a minnow. Weak and pathetic, why doesn't he just end it?*" referencing Earnie's misery that had been the victim of since the death of his wife. In her absence, he became a housewife, caring for Sherri and her older brothers during. That was, during his hours away from the mines. It was years ago since mines had since dried.

Tears filled his eyes. "Find me my daughter. Please. She is in danger."

Immediately the fellas, macho as ever, turned against their own. For the good of Earnie's daughter, they blunted the crowd, rearing it down the steps. Pushing. Shoving. Yelling over yelling.

"LET THE MAN SPEAK," one of them yelled. "Let him find his daughter!"

"I've had enough of The Man," Gerald whined, marching the steps, pushing farmhands out of his way. One of the fellas grabbed at him a half-hearted grab which Gerald slipped easily. Gerald kept on marching up the steps. But, with a single blow, an old man knocked Gerald on his side. It was the old man, the old fella named Gabriel, who Yofim and the Girl had overheard telling stories by the barn. Now he was nursing his fist.

Old man Gabriel said, "Let Earnie says what he needs 'tah say."

Some people helped Gerald up and propped him up affront the crowd. From there, his demented lip, alongside the unfortunate boy's bandaged fingers and a myriad of other farmhands with their respective torments — this all stood evidence of the atrocity that was the day's work.

Earnie peeped his head from between the heavy doors. "Okay, everyone," he said while scanning the crowd. "I know you're angry. I'll do what I can. But first, please, find my daughter. Tell her she is not safe. Tell her to run as I should have. Tell her not to be sturdy, not to finesse. Just run... run and never return ——"

Suddenly a force pulled Earnie back inside. From behind slammed doors, he screamed agonizing screams. Sherri's voice surfaced from the crowd. "Father!" she cried, hearing his pain. "Father!" She ran up and pounded on the door. It opened, and a musky, wretched-smelling but entrancing gaseousness fluttered out, its viscosity masking the Daughter of Elsedorwn, as she slithered out and around her prey, caressing her, enticing her, and lopping off the arm of Gabriel as he tried to rescue the girl.

The fellas were left bruised and exhausted from being pressed against the doors by the crowd. Gabriel had led the charge. He was left crushed and without an arm. And the boy, whining in pain, his broken fingers exposed bone and flesh which ached at contact with the gas. The gas entranced all these persons of the farm into becoming farm animals themselves. They flailed in mosh-pit of beings who pressed each other against the front doors and clawed at their wood, doing anything and everything to satisfy their desire for The Daughter of Elsedorwn -- her smell, her sound. Wanting to murder her. Wanting to embrace her. Wanting to make love to her. The screams and moans from inside fueled their desires.

All these crazed farmhands awoke some time later. The people laid like pieces of firewood thrown every which way atop one another. Yofim woke to find an upended boot resting on his face. He lifted it off, shifting the leg that the foot belonged to as well. But the movement caused a limp arm to come flopping down onto his chest. This startled the fat one. So he jumped, only to find his leg chained to the arm man himself. He foolishly tried to jump up and run again. Doing this, he pulled at the arm-man's leg and twisted it in a painful manner that caused the arm-man to wake up and shiver. He pulled at the chain and thereby pulled at Yofim and another man who had been chained to Yofim's other leg.

This other man told Yofim to hush. "Stay still, boy, and be quiet." It was the old, armless man, Gabriel. Gabriel played the waterbug in a sanctuary puddle of blood. Yofim himself was covered in blood. The old man said, "During times a'comin', one best keep quiet." He said this. Then he closed his eyes and died.

As morning wafted in, tan-colored, eastern-styled robes prowled the area. They moved as though they hovered just above the ground.

These robed entities segmented the farmhands into a dozen

or so chained-together lines of farmhands. By and large, the farmhands in these chains were dilapidated and delirious. Enormously confused. Nearly everyone complied due to their confusion and an overarching feeling of helplessness.

A few of these chains of farmhands were led meandering out into the fields and toward various destinations.

Not all chains had departed yet. Yofim's chain remained sitting on the steps of Greenlock House. It was tangled with two other chains. Some of the mysterious robe-wearing figures worked to untangle all this and move along.

A shadowy robed figure approached Yofim. It slithered toward him, and toward his eyes, then under his chin. It savored Yofim's aura of weakness — Yofim's soft-tissue throat, and his fear bubbling from inside. The creature made a grotesque glottal noise. It slurped its scathing saliva-dripping tongue across Yofim's adam's apple. Then it pressed down with its molars on Yofim's neck, gradually with more pressure, more suspense.. He could feel his jugular being squeezed. He could feel his neck skin stretch. A horrible death seemed imminent. But just when one more once of pressure would have broken flesh,, the creature pulled away and clapped its jaws shut.

Yofim shivered as he felt the creature's nose, prickly and raw, scape across his baby-butt-textured cheek. The smell of the creature, it was atrocious.

The creature sniffed and snorted and coughed a deathly cough. Doing this, he spewed gunk on Yofim's face. Yofim irked. "Shhhhhhhh", the creature hissed. "say a word, boy, and I'll have young instead of old."

It went on to chew on Gabriel's grub-infested stump. Yofim cried. The demented thing slobbered, chewing to the bone from the shadows of his robe's hood. He stopped only when a boot to his ass knocked him face-first into Gabriel's pool of blood. The creature's hood fell back in the process, exposing its hideous blistering bubbling burns caused by contact with blood and hot broiling sunlight. It scrambled to cover its face. But its superior who had kicked him originally kicked him again. This superior stomped his boot down across its subordinate's neck, pinning the creature's pained face and hand in the blood and own. The boot, Yofim noticed, was cylindrical. Certainly it was meant for no human foot. Its wearer, the superior, hissed in a language unknown to Yofim, before dragging its decrepit man-eater subordinate to his feet, kicking him in his ass again, and hissing something fierce.

This maintainer of order towered over the other robed creatures. They feared him.

He came and unlatched Gabriel's chains, and clicked the cuffs together. He tossed the body aside, then signaled Yofim to rise. The farmhands rose with Yofim.

In English, the maintainer of order commanded, "do as you are meant to do, and be free. Or try escaping from these chains, and become dirt."

The alpha-creature hissed again at his mangled subordinate who knuckled Yofim's shoulder as he moved toward the chain's head. At the helm, this creature wrapped his whip around one of the fella's necks. The fella croaked, and the creature hissed and pulled at the fella's throat. Soon, they moved along as the other chains had — as a chain of men, and some boys, moving toward one place or another, led by a monster, trailed by a troll.

They walked.. and they walked... and they walked.... and when rounding the barn corner, the second fella cut hard into the barn alley, where he'd once spoken to the now-diseased Gabriel. He darted into that familiar place, craving remembrance of the man. But as a result the leading creature whistled; and his troll snatched up the tormented boy who's finger tips had been ground to the bone. The boy screamed as the troll squeezed his head so forcefully it seemed it would burst. Now with the attention of the group, the creature explained that he was "known by the sounds: Kah-ff-mahh-n." That was his name: Kahfmahhn.

"That is my.. umm... my 'dog'," he said, pointing to the troll.

"Disobey and my dog will squash your boy's head. I will

devour his limbs." The creature licked his lips while saying this

THIRTY-TWO

Jack asked his father, "What happened between you and your father?"

Despite hearing this question from his son, Sydney Tomleson maintained pace quietly. He refused to even turn his head.

"He's a sweet man," Jack argued. "Until you came back, we had been enjoying each other's company."

Still, Syd Tomleson trudged on. It was dark, and it was silent but for the sound of feet crunching leaves. Jack hustled to avoid falling behind in this strange place.

THIRTY-THREE

In the marshes, Tomph found himself staring into the waters. He was delirious from days without food or water. He was seeing things in the water. The patterns of marsh weeds shimmering with the light, scattered and distorted by the currents, spurred all sorts of imaginings. A round women emerged into the boy's vision. This was the kind of woman so caring for others, her own health often suffered. She smiled at her child. She held his hand. Only after her boy kissed her cheek did she allow him to run off to the playground and ultimately to the swing-set. The nervous women watched from afar. She was so horribly nervous, watching the boy swing on the swings. It seemed as though her heart could fail at any moment.

She turned to Tomph and soliloquized:

"Often I find myself on a plateau between protecting my baby and allowing him to breath. I sit worrying and worrying, and I do him no good. My love for him is destroying me…
Will you watch over him, for me? I can go on no longer. My heart, it is worn. Please, Tomph, take care of my boy. Let him breath. But be careful; he's small; he's vulnerable. He'll choke on warm milk if you don't warn him that it is warm, or if he's too excited."

The women coughed and fell to her knees. She looked to her boy who was swinging nerve-rackingly high on those swings. On the swing beside the boy, an elderly, hairy fellow was swinging albeit less energetically. The two swung next each other and they talked, perfectly at ease. So perfectly at ease, a vessel burst in this women's heart. She reached her hand out as her body, deprived of nutrients, failed her. Spitting up blood, she fought to say, from a distance, "I love you, son." Into ashes, she burned until there was nothing left of her.

The boy thought that he'd heard something. Reality glitched and suddenly he was eye to eye with Tomph.

Tomph outreached his palm. The younger boy did as well. And like two glass-separated children would, they aligned each other's palms, but did not touch.

Instantly the boy was back on the swings, looking at Tomph from a distance, unsure why. He looked away as one does after making eye contact during an awkward time. Soon he talked again with the man on the swings. Tomph wandered off while keeping the boy in sight. Our Tomph circumnavigated the playground, and he circled in on a two-hundred-year-old oak tree. Then an opening in the fence caught his eye. The fence separated a playground area from the forest. There it was: The Forest Avenue wetlands, a familiar sight. In he went, to the piano in the swamp. He played a toon, and he sang:

"Meandering through the forest way,
Me and my friend Yofim play.
He runs, he laughs;
I yell, I scream.
Slow down fat one;
    I've got ice cream.

He runs, he hides.
I yell, I scream.
Where are you daft one?
I'm alone; I'm scared.

    Me and my friend Yofim played.
    Now I'm gone and he stayed.
    Where are you my friend?
    Darkening is the day's end.

I wish you'd come,
And you'd bring
Tunes for us to sing.

    I wish you'd come,
    And you'd bring
    Tunes for us to sing.

I wish you'd come,
And you'd bring
My eyes to the swings:
    empty, dangling;
    void of the vulnerable;
    tempting wisdom gone,
    along with prey, the vulnerable."

SPLASH!

Tomph swallowed dirty, cranberry tainted flood water. He found that his direction had been chosen for him. Frantic at first, splashing, he soon calmed. In these waters, he was powerless but also without responsibility. A tremendous peacefulness lulled him into a sleep during which he dreamed of a mountain-top valley, with a green, rolling field, and a tree at its edge. It was the only tree above the clouds, and from its biggest branch, a swing extended far off into open space, above the clouds. A sole horse scampered about the field, chasing a bug, losing sight of it, then being calm. The horse would do as horses do: eating grass for long periods of time. Then another or the same bug would come along and the horse would be off snapping its teeth, chasing the bug again. Meanwhile, that swing swung Tomph out over the perilous cliffside, then back to safety, and then out again, and then back, and so on. On the swing, Tomph took bites from a peach. Each bite opened a mouth hole from which the peach spoke. With each bite, a speaking voice popped up with tone proportional to bite size. With each bite, one grotesque bodily cavity overlapped another. The peach grew growingly grotesque. And from all of its bite wholes, the peach (in many voices simultaneously) told the following story, which garbled and hastened as it went.

"Hey, sonny boy. Have you ever thought about the ultimate ideal of life?

During one period of my life, I thought insanity to be the greatest of freedoms. Because when you go insane, you can do anything. I'm talking about the kind of insanity in which you stare into the sun, and despite feeling extreme pain, you continue staring, knowing that this pain is nothing but a hallucination, or a seemingly engulfing experience, or rather, tunnel vision at work. And knowing somehow that in hindsight you will look back and feel silly about being so afraid of something as worldly as pain. I realized what deception was, what it is, and what it can be, and how, when I'm thinking of myself going off the deep end, rolling on the ground, staring at the sun, turning my eyes to raisins and laughing about it, and I'm thinking of my dad looking down at the pathetic animal that I'd become, my father himself could be the face of deception. His care for me, and the obligation I feel to not destroy him by destroying myself. That is true deception, the kind of coercion truly indistinguishable from genuine love and shame. These extraordinarily complex, roundabout means of inducing compliance, they are nothing but God-level deceit tactics, employed by Satan, God, or someone else. Love can be deception, you see, the purest kind.

Understanding this, I thought, was freedom. But now I realize it is not freedom: because it is. With absolute freedom comes an unbearable, inescapable emptiness. You cannot simply forget. AHAHAHAHAHAHA, foolish boy, you are ruined!!!"

The peach screamed a hundred screams simultaneously, then a million. It sweated and yelled "YOU CANNOT UN-KNOW," while glitching in and out of reality. The mouths yelled at Tomph and at each other, and at themselves. The mouth that was product of Tomph's first bite was the biggest. During an upswing, it chomped down on Tomph's thumb. Tomph's reflex was to launch the self-imploding peach into the clouds. He watched it convulse, alternating between mania and apology, as it fell hopelessly into the cliffside fog.

SPLAT.

In his hobbit home, the gnarly man stood from his rocking chair in order to smack Little One across the face. "Be careful where you tread!" he told the boy. And with Little One cowering on the floor, tending to stinging pain, the man and his beard circled, lecturing, "there are forces in this world best left be." He circled and fidgeted with his hands, saying "I understand you are curious, but you wish to remain breathing, do you not?"

And again, SPLAT.

A clump of mud thrown by Omnious himself smacked Tomph's face.

From the high ground, Omnious yelled, "Swim, Boy! You mustn't go through the locks! You'll be torn to pieces!!"

Tomph wiped his eyes, thinking of the peach, the rocking

chair man, and Omnious, and his friend Yofim, and the farm. There were tremendous rapids ahead. Normally the locks were modulated such that boats could transfer from one higher body of water to a lower one or vice versa via the pumping of water. But now what lied ahead was an uncontrolled, crazed overflow, fractured wooden beams, and a world of pain. The imminence blinded Tomph. And with his eyes closed, he listened intently, as the knarly man sat back down in his chair and explained, "We shouldn't have built the walls, but we did. And we gave the trees, like water, a container to accumulate within. To pull the walls now would be to drown ourselves with rainwater that we collected in our vat."

SPLAT.

Another mud clump caught Tomph's attention, smacking his face. Thom had thrown this particular clump. And it was Thom who cried "Where's my boyyy? Where is Little One?"
Tomph scrambled for fresh air. He fought the current with reinvigorated purpose. Where was the boy? "Where am I? Oh, yes. Oh yes." The shore conscripted Tomph. It demanded that he explain to Omnious and to Thom what had happened. It demanded that he wrap his arms around the two after they helped him upon the bank. He did. Thom dropped to his knees. Omnious embraced Tomph.
"I was worried," Omnious said. "I'm glad you're safe."
"My Boy.." Thom said. "so young, so vulnerable. What happened to him, Tomph?"
Tomph admitted to falling asleep due to having been stranded for so long, pruned and hungry. He explained that the boy had disappeared during his slumber. It was during the crisis of scanning the horizon for Little One when a monstrous wind knocked Tomph into the waters and led him to where he was now.
At this explanation, Thom dug his hands into the muck. He reminisced "I loved that boy....." Meanwhile Omnious tended to Tomph's wounds. There was a deep cut on his leg which

Omnious dressed with cranberry, mud, and dirt.

"This isn't nearly as deep," Tomph said, drawing attention to a different wound on his forearm which Omnious began to dress in short order.

Tomph asked how long the wounds would take to heal.

"They will take time," Omnious said. "But we have nothing but time. That's why you might as well learn to care of yourself. Pay close attention, Tomph," Omnious said as he dressed this smaller wound precisely by the books. Tomph noticed, at the same time, that Omnious himself was in pain.

"I see you're injured as well. What happened?" Tomph asked.

"I've set the bone. It will heal. I am fine, is what I mean. Now, replace your dressing twice a day to avoid The Green."

THIRTY-FOUR

The barn smelled of death. Throat cut, left to bleed, the stubborn bastard Tom laid there dead. His caretaker sat cross-legged beside him, playing with her puzzle, singing:

> *"This piece here, that piece there.*
> *Tall scary men, every which where.*
> *How do I get back home?,*
> *When I'm here all alone?*
>
> *Tom ohh Tom, I wish you...*
> *You've really let yourself go.*
> *What a shame, what a shame.*
>
> *I'm stuck, shouldn't have came.*
> *Now I'm stuck, playing games*
> *in a barn full of no-names."*

She played with her puzzle, singing:

> *"Tom, my man, what has happened?*
> *You're helpless as Albany is short.*
> *My my, the horse who couldn't grow.*
> *Oh, the horse who'd only ever snort."*

But the Girl grew paranoid suddenly. So she peeked out from her stall. Realizing the coast was clear, she walked into the main barn where she peeled a mirror shard from its place. She climbed. Then, using this mirror shard, she peeked stealthily from the cupola in order to assure herself that those demons with their chains and whips were safely in the distance. They were, but ohh!!! the terrible acts -- Mystery Girl witnessed beatings beatings and beatings. The slaves carried corpses. And when the occasional poor soul fell to his knees out of exhaustion, he would be whipped, disconnected from the chain, and carried like any other corpse.

> *"I can't take this any longer.*
> *I must I must I must...*
> *Get out from this evil place,*
> *Bust out somehow from heeeere.*
>
> *Yofim, where are you?*
> *Dig me a hole to crawl through.*
> *I'll begin it myself.*
> *When you come, you help!*
> *Until then I'll dig away*
> *Please try and last the day;*
> *then together, we'll escape!"*

The Girl found a shovel that she hadn't noticed earlier. It leaned against the wall beside the 1st floor ladder. "Curious," she said, before beginning to dig.

THIRTY-FIVE

Thom rushed to his feet. "Okay," he said. "We 'gotta go. We 'gotta go."

"What, why, where?" Tomph asked.

"We 'gotta go. We 'gotta go now," Thom said, already limping into the distance.

Tomph looked to Omnious, who said, "I trust Thom. You trust me, do you not?"

"Of course, yes," Tomph acknowledged, "but you mustn't leave me --"

"Come along then. Quickly." Thom led frenetically. Omnious struggled behind him. Then somehow Tomph was the slowest despite having the most intact skeleton.

THIRTY-SIX

On a path that passed through a line of trees between two hay fields, Jack stopped under some lamplight.

"Father," he said.

"What is it, Jack." Syd Tomleson was tired and irritated by his son's persistent poking and prodding. They'd been going for quite a while. So Syd urged, "We have to capitalize on this darkness."

"Father," Jack pointed out. "It's the drawings."

Mr. Tomleson turned and saw his son stopped under the moonlight, looking at the drawings and letters that Master Greenlock had given them. "Oh, give me that," Mr. Tomleson said. "And stay out of the light, you fool." He pointed to distant ranch houses through the windows of which lights could be seen.

But when Syd Tomleson pulled at the papers, Jack resisted and said, "Listen to me, Father. I'm going to force you to listen to me. For once in your life, listen to me." Saying this, he locked his father's hand between his mits.

Syd Tomleson, being the man he was, could have easily popped his son in the nose, or tossed him to the dirt and explained to him exactly how serious their predicament was. However, he did no such thing. Instead, he looked into his son's eyes, and he said:

"Okay, Son. Alright. Alright."

"It's these drawings, Father. I remember them."

"You should remember ———"

Jack put up his hand, as to say "Wait. Listen. Hear my words, Father. Remember Hamza? On many occasions, I'd go to his workshop. Mother would drop me there when she had errands. Hamza built cabinets and things. I would help how I could. And when my assistance wasn't required, I'd pound nails into blocks of wood. While Hamza was working, we would talk."

"What did you talk about?"

"It was enjoyable, Father, really. No need to worry."

"That man was a nut and a---," Mr. Tomleson went to say, but Jack cut him off.

"Mother and I trusted him."

"Jack, that man tried running off with Tomph. He bashed the kid with a broomstick, grabbed him by the pelt, and ran for the boats. If it weren't for Omnious....".

"Jesus. Father, show some respect. The man had a good heart. And mind you, he was in part a Father of mine in your absence," Jack said.

Mr. Tomleson gestured that he was sorry and that Jack should go on. And so Jack went on, explaining "Hamza had his gardening hobbies. I didn't realize then, but I realize now. We talked about a map many times over. I asked to see this supposed map many times. Over and over, Hamza told me: *'when the time comes, when the time comes, I will show it to you'*. He would go on journeys following this map. After the first two journeys, I remember him returning to the shop, drunk and frustrated, breaking cabinets like a madman. Upon the third journey, however, came a new kind of madness. He came home in a mania obsessing over these horrible drawings. From that day onward, he'd go each week on these journeys. Soon it became a daily endeavor. I was young. I didn't realize... Mother forbid me from entering the woodshop. She understood he was dangerous, but she loved him, Father. You know that, don't you?"

"I do," Mr. Tomleson admitted.

"She wouldn't tell anyone what happened... But even after Hamza stopped fulfilling his woodworking orders, he spent 20 out of 24 hours in a day going on his trips and coming back and drawing what he claimed to have seen during the journey. He said I'd understand someday. Soon he started disappearing for days at a time. Customers came pounding at his door. Soonafter was when he took Tomph."

"So what's your point, boy?"

"Patience Father. These are his drawings. Now, on the map -- trace your finger along any of these lines", Jack told him, referencing the dozens of colored, meandering pathways that were sometimes solid or dotted or dashed, which looped in various ways from Hamza's place toward one common destination, then back to Hamza's again.

Jack asked, "Where do they meet?" pointing to one of the pathways.

Mr. Tomleson looked up, realizing that he stood precisely on the intersection point. Flabbergasted, he asked "what does this mean?"

Jack led his father off the side of the trail where he dropped to a knee and did to the deep grass what one does to a wardrop in order to reveal one's most treasured and hidden items. Kneeling, he scooped a handful of dirt and moss. Syd Tomleson followed attentively as Jack picked through some miscellaneous fungi.

"What is it?" Mr. Tomleson asked.

Jack explained, "Every time I asked Hamza for proof of his journey, he'd say that he would explain everything on a particular day, but he refused to set a date. As a kid, I had nightmares because the anticipation of this day was so great. But one day, Hamza's plans fell through by Omnious's doing. That gave me a profound sense of relief. Now I understand, though. What have here is A-grade psilocybin."

"Jesus," said Mr. Tomleson, examining the fresh mushrooms.

"So all this and Leo, it's a shame!" Jack said excitedly. "We can go home! We can help rebuild."

"That would be the case, wouldn't it." Mr. Tomleson said, "IF," he conceded, "that silly drawing had anything to do with the true reason why the Master sent us in this direction."

"Why are we here, then?" Jack asked.

"Come on, Son. Let us talk while we walk. I've got explaining to do, I suppose."

"It seems that you do," Jack said.

THIRTY-SEVEN

For three hours, Jack and his dad traversed mushroom way. They spoke earnestly, though not completely, and they walked. Mr. Tomleson explained why he'd been absent during so much of Jack's childhood.

"From the beginning, we were the caretakers -- Omnious and I. It had always been that way. Even before I got with your mother, we'd do our rounds. Once in a while we'd have gin together."

"Omnious doesn't drink," Jack said.

"Not anymore he doesn't. Anyways. The farm got bigger. It

got tough I remember once: Leo brought us in his library. He poured drinks for us. There was a slur in his voice. That was explained by the bottle being half-empty when we got there. He told Omnious he knew things were difficult, but that we didn't have a choice."

"What was he talking about?" Jack asked.

"That was the night he sent Omnious to the North. Right away, Omnious went home to prepare, and he prepared all night long." Mr. Tomleson explained this. Then he noticed how his son was kicking his feet, leaving upturned moss and mushrooms scattered atop the grass and mixed in on the gravel path.

"What are you doing that for, kid?" Mr. Tomleson asked.

Jack realized that what he was doing was dumb, so he stopped.

"Son. Omnious is a good man, but Leo was right in doing what he did."

"How so? He stranded the man in the marshes!" Jack exclaimed.

"Look. Leo and I were real close. So he felt an obligation, I think, to explain himself to me. One day, he was real drunk. He said to me, 'Syd, there's something you have that Omnious lacks.' I asked him what's that, and he told me 'you can put on a face.'"

"You certainly can," Jack admitted after pondering this for a moment.

THIRTY-EIGHT

Meanwhile, in the marshes, Thom trudged on, trailed by Omnious and Tomph, heading toward some somewhere. Tomph was but a burden because of his injuries and his exhaustion and his lack of athleticism to begin with. As such,

Thom suggested he "wait in de marshes".

Tomph argued, "There's nothing but mud here. If I don't starve, I'll turn into a prune. Then, when the waters go dry, I'll become a raisin."

Thom explained, "'Thats isn't true, boy. Build a mud hut like I's did. Makes a pile 'a sand. Cover 'et with muck. In the 'mornin, you pull the sand out, and you got a nice little house, ay? Good enough for Thom, good enough for you."

When Tomph doubted him, Thom turned heel, grumbling and tossing sand — showing that indeed, a hut could be built. He tossed a dilapidated salad of leaves and sticks and mud and sand. Then he muttered, "not pretty, can't protect anything.. perfect for you,". He said this, then he rushed to catch up with Omnious, who walked onward as Tomph stood paralyzed remembering the Galagna whispers that once lulled him into a daze.

Omnious spoke softly, "Thom, go easy on the boy. I know his heart. He is a good boy."

"Good for 'nothin!" Thom said.

"Easy, Thom. We'll find Little One," Omnious said.

"He went willingly!!", Tomph interjected, speaking of Little One, and lighting a fire under Thom.

"What's did you say, boy?" Thom asked.

"Thom, please, we must hurry," Omnious pleaded. "Forget Tomph. You know he is not at fault, and I know he is the cure."

Thom struggled internally for a moment. Then he cut towards the waters. Omnious retraced some steps. He put Tomph on his shoulders.

Tomph asked "where! are we going?"

And Omnious pointed to the sky. "Watch the birds, Tomph. They tend towards safety always, knowing that they will always have their wings."

Tomph's thin arms struggled to keep hold of Omnious's shoulders.

The crazed hyena Thom sprinted across hardening mud, shielding his eyes from the blinding sun, stumbling through puddles easily-circumnavigate able, fighting upstream with respect to the waters and the birds.

Omnious stopped. "The birds do as they do, but we cannot fly, Tomph. Now wait here," he said, placing Tomph down in the mud. "Make a hut as Thom suggested. I will return back for you."

Still pondering the birds and flight, Tomph was left alone watching Thom and Omnious scale the wall that separated the farm from the parasitic tree people.

THIRTY-NINE

The Daughter of Elsedorwn, atop her widow's walk, breathed in clouds and she exhaled ghastly poison. The slavers and slaves of her camp pounding iron below, while she and her lengthy claws spanned a mile-wide radius, plucking trees from the earth, fighting off mutant insects with her grandmother's sword. These trees, she shaved them with her razor teeth. Then she laid them perpendicular to blueprinted train tracks.

The creatures whipped Yofim and the other farmhands without mercy. Everyone was yelling these cryptic commands and responses. Even the farmhands took part, uttering pain-learned sequences of phonetics corresponding to certain things. Straighten the cross-logs. Run iron rails atop them. Dig mass graves for rebel insect carcasses and disobedient farmhands alike.

A mighty retaliation of the bugs, whose homes had been destroyed, drove Yofim's group and another group into the barn, where a poignant smell of death pervaded. Kahfmahhn's dog convulsed at the smell. Something about horse decomposition destroyed him. Kahfmahhn cried, "aahhhhh". He tried to tolerate the smell himself, but in getting closer to the grotesque midget horse, its throat cut, its innards partially eaten, he too found the smell unbearable. It was Yofim, then, who Kahfmahhn unchained and sent to deal with the odor. First, he was to dispose of Albany. Next, it would be Tom.

But Kahfmahhn grunted, "big dog first. Taste worse." So Yofim changed his direction. It would be Tom first, then Albany. Kahfmahhn kicked his Achilles when he moved too slowly. Then he barked at his dog, a dumb monstrous version of his self. Kahfmahhn bit the dog's thigh for its whining about the smell. On they went, locking slaves in horse stalls two per cell.

"Easy fella," one of the fellas said to Kahfmahhn when Kahfmahhn was too rough with the chains. "I'll do it myself."

Kahfmahhn growled and flexed his long, thin, menacing teeth. All you could see was his teeth.

The other fella, the first fella's cell-mate, stepped up and said to Kahfmahhn, "You know, fella, you're all terrifying and that, but we're brothers."

"Yea, we're brothers!" the other fella said.

The two stepped forward together, cornering the quailing insect. "Let's see who's behind the hood, ay, brother?" The fellas pressed Kahfmahhn against the boards, wrestling with him for his whip.

"Making a mistake," Kahfmahhn grumbled. To no avail he called for his dog. He was weak, powerful only in camaraderie and jaws. Now he was alone -- his mouth held shut like an alligator's.

One could hear Mrs. Greenlock howling at the skies from her rooftop.

Joe-fella remarked, "that conniving wench -- I knew she was up to no good."

And the other, Tom-fella, called her a "green-palmed wench," in the process, loosening his grip about Kahfmahhn's neck.

Kahfmahhn lunged for Tom-fella's throat. But Joe-fella slammed him against the wall with force enough to cause a coughing fit. Catching his breath, Kahfmahhn let out an ear-shattering roar. A fella threw a punch, and that led to

Kahfmahhn to stretch his long tongue in order to lick said fella's cheek.

"God-damn," the fella said, "it's burns, Joe! It burns!" Meanwhile Joe held the jaw of Kahfmahhn, who grinned there maniacally, as to say, "I dare you." When Joe backed down, Kahfmahhn circled in and feasted on their fear. The fellas back up against the stall-side. Soon Kahfmahhn's dog came rushing in in response to Kahfmahhn's roar. Some cryptic commands left the dog with the responsibility of dealing with the fellas, who no longer dared to resist.

Kahfmahhn wiped his purple, blue-oozing lip while exiting the stall. It seemed his dog had finished chaining the farmhands minus the fellas (who it was dealing with now). So, assuming everything was under control but for boy Yofim, Kahfmahhn followed the dastardliest of smells to Tom's stall. What he found was a partially buried carcass, ass sticking out the hole, and a half-finished puzzle at its side. No boy to be found. Kahfmahhn stomped the puzzle into the dirt when he realized the boy wasn't there. Then he hurried to escape the wretched smell.

Yofim and Mystery Girl hid under Tom's Carcass while, outside, Kahfmahhn howled "BOY!"... "BOY, SHOW YOURSELF!!!" Kahfmahhn himself growled like a dog. Yofim was mortified -- and made further so by the girl's giggling. Hush, girl. It's important that we are quiet. But she kept on giggling.

"What's so funny?" Yofim whispered, unable to keep himself from smiling despite blood oozing down his shoulder. The girl laughed and she laughed.

"It's just that... Tom! Finally! Finally, he's been put good use." Yofim laughed, and she covered his mouth

"We must be quiet," she said, before kissing his cheek.

Sensing Kahfmahhn's roars distancing, these two kids were put at ease.

FORTY

"Look, Jack, look!" Mr. Tomleson was so excited. There were lights and dancers and hula-hoopers, and there was a wild lion-like red-headed man frolicking about, breathing theatrically and throwing fire! Getting closer, it could be seen that this man was entirely nude. The others were as well, though some did equip loin-cloths. The others were smaller, darker in skin tone, but equally naked. The gathering was centered between clusters of wigwams. And the music, it was to the likes of a love supreme, but orchestral. The whole village took part, and it seemed not a soul had a clue what they were doing, yet somehow the collective in whole was jazz.

"We're here, Jack. We're here!" Mr. Tomleson was enthused like normally only a child can be. Jack wasn't so sure, so he did his best with the map to triangulate their off-trail walking with their time in Homverd and the length along the mushroom path. It was strange; according to the map, this place was nothing but barren wasteland (as cartographed by Hamza). But Jack noticed one straggly stray line in particular that did cross the spot Jack and his Father were approaching. It was the spot that Hamza, during his final journey, passed through before going to the place from which he never returned.

"Jack, why must you ponder now, out of all the possible times to ponder?"

"I'm trying to figure out where we are, Father. Patience."

"We're here, Jack! You must understand. We've never been more here! Tear that into pieces. Come, follow me! You're 'gonna love it."

In that moment, Syd Tomleson's inner child caught a glimpse of the world, hopped out from his cage, and broke into a trot. Getting closer, the groove pervaded. Syd's strides swung as jazz swings. Then the red-headed lion Redman noticed Syd. His subjects noticed Syd as well. Without missing a beat, Redman tossed an imaginary lasso, and he swayed his hips to the rhythm, pulling an arm's length on each third beat, syncopating his feat, janking bells strapped to his waist. Syd played along until Redman had reeled him fully in, at which point the two engaged in a ceremonial forehead kiss. Tomleson knew the tradition. Their interaction called for a steadying of the music, a calm in the storm. Primarily small, brown-skinned villagers gathered around. They kept silent. But one woman in particular whispered "white man in the brown coat!.. white man in the brown coat!.. white man in the brown coat!." She upped her volume gradually, and she quickened pace. This hardened, crazed women repeated herself.. Meanwhile, Syd wrapped his arms around Redman. The two embraced as the women up-tempoed her chant. Still, the women whispered, just more loudly, more quickly. Likewise the drums and throat sounds quickened, but in the volume there was restraint. A brewing was in the air.

Redman raised his arms, giving rise to an explosion of drumming and chanting. The woman yelled, at the top of her lungs now, "WHITE MAN IN THE BROWN COAT. WHITE MAN IN THE BROWN COAT". There was a brief misstep. But quickly Syd found the key and he jumped around on the stage with Redman in a cathartic cleanse.

Meanwhile, the chanting lady chanted:

"WHITE MAN IN THE BROWN COAT;
TIGHT MAN LOOSE, HE GAINS HOPE."

She allowed herself to foam at the mouth like a dog, her tongue hanging, and the citizens of the world echoed her words despite having very little understanding of their meaning. They loved it all the same. What a blend of tribal chanting people shouting chaotically by the scope of the individual but jazz on the whole scale. Gradually the drummers and chanters showed restraint, building tension. Again the whispering rhythms quickened. Then a downscale marimba cued the chanting lady, who, at the top of her lungs, yelled.

> *"RED MAN GOOD; WHITE MAN RED.*
> *WHITE MAN GOOD; RED MAN DEAD."*

At this, the Redman's body stiffened mid-stride. He fell to the hardwood, performing a theatrical death. Torch out, the chanters mourned. Each torch-wielding dancer and fire-breathing dragon ashed their flame. So it was dark when an elder struck a match, drawing all attention to her ragged gray hair shimmering, encasing her bark-like, sweat-dewed wrinkles. A small boy joined her in the light, and she set fire his torch. Solemnly, the boy climbed the stage. He circled around to Redman's feet. From there, he performed a prayer, rubbing his hands together and bowing. Afterwards, he turned away. A few times he looked back, working to align his shadow with Redman's corpse. Once proper, he spoke at first nervously, but soon, excitedly:

> *"RED MAN DEAD HIT HIS HEAD*
> *MAKE HIM BETTER*
> *MAKE HIM RIGHT*
> *HELP HIM SEE YET*
> *A NOTHER NIGHT"*

The elder women made her way to the boy to stand beside him. Together they raised the torch, and they chanted in unison:

> *"RED MAN DEAD, HE HIT HIS HEAD*
> *PEOPLE OF ROUND TOWN*
> *FEED HIM BREAD*
> *PEOPLE OF ROUND TOWN*
> *HEAL HIS HEAD"*

Villagers circled in. Each removed a loaf of bread from his side-pouch or her backpack. Each one of them dropped a fragment of break ceremonially atop Redman's belly. There were a hundred of them, each eager to give a parcel of their personal wealth to their beloved Redman in need.

"RED MAN DEAD, LET HIM BE", the elder woman said.

And the boy yelled, "BREAD IS GOOD, LET HIM SEE!"

The villagers returned to their places, kneeling now and bowing their heads. A loud silence pervaded as Elder Woman and the ring-bearing boy made their way to Syd Tomleson. They circled around and around. They handed Syd the all-important torch. Then, as they hurried back to safety beside their kin, they excitedly nervously curiously waited to see what the strange man would do. Jack watched from a distance. He had been watching. He wondered too, how his father would respond. Surely the torch-holder himself wondered also.

All eyes on him, the weathered whiteman who swung the torch slowly, investigatively, feeling the air, growing confident in the fire's ability to endure.

When he jumped, the people ooo'ed. They ah'ed when he spun and pranced. The villagers were as fascinated with Mr. Tomleson as they'd been fascinated with anything in their entire lives. They were always being fascinated as they'd ever been. The white man tested different movements. Soon he realized that there was nothing to fear. And so he embarked on a journey of relieved inhibitions which transformed the village into a zoo of wild beasts, hoo-hooing and growling and eventually converging into chant and rhythm. The whiteman ran with these rhythms, and the rhythms ran with him. What emerged was a gorilla-inspired stuttering excitement dance that made even the grungiest of village people jump up and down.

One villager laughed and ooo-aaahed, making monkey sounds to his buddy, who mimicked Syd Tomleson's style.

Everyone laughed. Even Jack did from afar. Syd laughed. He laughed at everyone laughing at his self, and he laughed at his own laughing but dancing away regardless.

Elder Woman left her boy with an Ethiopian midget man.

"Keep watch of him," she said. "There are strangers in the woods."

The midget man heeded her warning, keeping hold of the boy by his belt loop and scanning the tree line. The boy smiled understandingly as Elder Woman jumped to the stage. And as she growled and lowered her stance. A bulky woman. She was a bulky woman. Mr. Tomleson took notice, and he stared at her bulk. A territorial gorilla dance ensued. She would stomp forward. Syd, rearing back, would counter sideways, wrap around, and chase her back, roaring his arms. They circled each other thrice. Soon a misstep led them head-to-head. A collision! It brought great tension.

Things worsened when she scowled, "It's been many years, Sydney," and he solemnly admitted,

"I couldn't tell you how many years it has been."

The Women caressed Syd's cheek in a staunch, motherly way. She smiled. He was nervous. But she told him, "Dance with me!" She was already pulling at his arms. So he said "Okay," awaiting her first move.

Her first move was to reach out her arms stiff, and to cup her hands. "Well get on with it," she said.

Syd locked his hands with hers; and she, being bulky as she was, threw him around like a doll. This low-set, burly woman's unshakable roughness flustered Mr. Tomleson at first. But he caught on, and he pushed back. He was a powerful frame himself. But the woman had the low ground. But he was larger, younger, and absurdly strong. He pushed back hard, soon pushing her to the stage's edge.

On the brink of the abyss that was the stage's edge, Elder Woman whispered to Syd, "You are strong."

Syd laughed and pressed the woman closer to the edge. Her subjects prepared a soft landing for her for if she were to fall.

"You made me this way," Mr. Tomleson said.

But Elder Woman shook her head. She winked at Syd Tomleson. And she commanded something foreign:

"OOhh Woggie GarnFF!!!"

Out with the lights! That was her command. So: out went the lights. From the shock of it, Mr. Tomleson's hands slipped. Before he realized what had happened, he found himself center-stage lying on his back. Elder Woman stood over him, torch in hand. She leaned over the metaphorical turned table and jabbered:

"You are strong, Sydney, but I am wise. Now get up. We haven't yet finished."

What ensued was a more playful dance than the last, and it drove the village ever wilder. The former dance was the Gorilla Waltz. This was something new. Syd and Elder Woman jumped up and wiggled and shuffled and they'd drop down and jump up again.

Jack burst laughing at the scene. But his doing this attracted attention from Midget Watchman, with whom he locked eyes. The midget shielded the village boy behind his robe. He flashed his teeth to Jack. They were white as ghosts, contrasting with his blackness, and they'd been sharpened sharp with a file.

Without warning, blind yells washed away all rhythm and rhyme. Something had happened.

The Elder Woman halted her dance. She told Mr. Tomleson, "Get their attention, Syd."

He looked at her, as to ask "how?"

"Wave your torch, yell at the top of your lungs. They will listen to you."

He did, and she was right; the frantic villagers quieted down and calmed. Gently, then, Elder Woman eased into another chant:

"RED MAN NUDE; RED MAN CRUDE.
RED MAN LOVE; RED MAN MOVE!"

Redman leaped up growling like a lion. Now he and Elder

Woman and Syd all danced together. The whole village joined in. Now it was a celebration of their new friend. Elder Woman fetched the Ring-bearer Boy from the Negro Midget, who informed her that he'd scared off a prowler in the woods. She thanked him for keeping his eyes peeled, and she asked him to keep watch until things seemed safe. Then she re-integrated with the celebration. She and the others danced for a while longer.

They danced until lights bright, smoke thick. A huge explosion blinded the village! The flash illuminated clusters of heptagonal dome-like structures that surrounded the celebration area. Near-nude villagers, still disoriented from the blast, scrambled towards these huts. They were frantic but not scared. It was almost a theatrical frantic-ness that leads me to suspect that they understand something I don't. Redman, the boy, the midget, and Elder Woman had all disappeared. As a result Mr. Tomleson found himself an outsider with nowhere to go and noone to confide in. As such, he ventured away from the few remaining torches.

"Jack," he whispered. "Jack!" Mr. Tomleson peered through lanes between the trees, searching for his son.

"I'm here, Father!"

"Where? Come out. Dance with me son!"

"I'm going home, Father."

"What... we've only just arrived! C'mon Jack, where are you?" Mr. Tomleson begged.

"I'll be in my meadow shortly."

"You know Jack, I can put on a mask. But when I do, when anyone does, what's underneath is smothered. What's inside needs air, every so often, or I'll asphyxiate."

"I understand, Father."

"That's why I couldn't be around, Son. When you were young... I did love you, you understand that, don't you? And your Mother, I loved her too. I love you, Son."

"I love you as well Father. But understand, as you differed from Omnious, I differ from you," Jack explained.

It was then Syd pinpointed his Son's shadow in the trees.

Unfortunately the grown boy was distant and distancing, hopeless fast and hopelessly stubborn.

"No, Son!" Syd Tomleson called out. "The farm is not well."

"Nor is Delilah. She needs her Father. I am not meant to be here."

To a hand on his shoulder, Mr. Tomleson turned. It was the Elder Woman, that boy by her side. She hushed him and whispered, "Stay with us, Syd. Come inside. Your boy is a man now, as you were when... you remember."

From a distance, Syd Tomleson followed his son's silhouette through and through the trees until he lost it. His only remaining connection became the faint and fading sound of footsteps in the brush.

"He doesn't know the way," Syd worried.

"He'll find the way," Elder Woman assured him, one hand on his shoulder, the other in his crotch. "He is of the breed."

Elder Woman's saying this comforted Syd. So he followed her when she went strolled past the sleeping heptagonal sleeping quarters, and past a depressed amphitheater in which, as Elder Woman explained, the village would perform for outsiders in exchange for pay. Syd followed Elder Woman over a narrow bridge past a creek. It was a tour of sorts.

The village boy explained "must be quiet.. almost there." and Elder Woman appeared very proud. In silence Mr. Tomleson thought of Grandpa Tomleson. He thought of what he had done to be looked at with such disgust by his own Dad. He decided that under no circumstances would he react in such a way to his own son.

A small field separated them from the forestry. They crossed this without time as a consideration. The village boy pointed to a soaring night-bird. Then he pointed to his torch. Wielding it, he illuminated the bird's apparent curiosity, as it ventured near and then strayed and then flew near again.

The boy explained. "Those who fly are not to be trusted." The Elder Woman agreed, affirming that "with the flying types, there is always something they have seen that you have not."

The boy and Elder Woman ashed their torch, from then on, feeling their way through the trees. They had come upon a stealthy defined path that passed through thick brush and short, thick trees. The long, windy, dark passageway soon opened to a bon-fire lit meadow. From darkness, there was light. Around the flames sat three figures: on the left, Redman; on the right, the Ethiopian Midget Man; and in the center, a human the average of his neighbors. In height, skin tone, even temperament, it seemed, this man was steady in the middle.

Redman awed at Syd's presence; he showed a wonderment which in short time blossomed into a wide, wide smile prefacing a jump to his feet that brought him and Syd face to face. He held Syd's hands. He raised them to his own ears, then to Syd's ears, and he pressed his forehead against his friend's, savoring their togetherness.

Elder Woman introduced the middle fellow. This man, Maryon, tipped his round-top hat. The dark-colored midget glared at Syd as he had Syd's son. The dark-colored midget was expecting his introduction to come next. So he went ahead and introduced himself. "I'm Harlumn," he said. "I met eyes with your son. Now I look into your eyes."

"What do you see?" Mr. Tomleson inquired while still thinking of his son and his father, and wondering how this demonic stranger might have influenced Jack's leaving.

For a while Harlumn sat frozen in his wincing muse. He leaned in, possibly to look closer, possibly to smell the scent of his subject. And abruptly, but hinderedly, he admitted, "I am unsure," before retreating to his stump-carved seat, puzzled and sullen.

Elder Woman whispered to Syd, "Be careful with that one. He is the shadows." Then she patted his back and took her seat. The boy came. Giving a bow, he introduced himself: "I am Yawn-nah-theen." He had placed down a wicker chair, carefully sinking the legs into the soil for stability. The boy encouraged Syd to sit. Then, rushedly, he tended to the fire. "Please," he said to Syd, after dealing with the fire. "Sit."

GREENLOCK FARM

Mr. Tomleson sat, and he took note of the boy's name: "Yawn-nah-theen." On came a debacle with Redman scrambling and smiling about the grass. He laid on the ground, listening to the earth. It was dark.

Mr. Tomleson asked Redman "what are you looking for, Granger?" And Granger looked like a deer in the lamplight. Harlumn was worse.

Elder Woman corrected, "He is Redman now." That was that.

Now Redman, excited, skipped back to his chair. The impetus of this all, Syd learned, was a mallet, which Redman pounded rapidly on his armrest. The big child sat back and pulled his knees to his chest, anticipating something ---- looking to Harlumn, who looked both ways twice and again before declaring:

"Redman, Maryon, Harlumn, Golma, Yonathon, Harlumn, and the Stranger. Welcome. Hereby begins the 847th meeting of the council."

A maniac with his eyes closed, Redman pounded his Gavel wildly until Golma muffled his arm to ease him. He opened his eyes and smiled while awaiting further briefing. Harlumn stood up. He did a thing where he turned 360 degrees. This caused the bottoms of his trench coat to fling as a ballerina's whatever would. Redman clapped. Harlumn was not amused. It seemed that this trick was merely obligatory to him.

Harlumn acknowledged: "Our first order of business, today, is the jarring and selling of water to the townspeople."

But Redman was not amused.

Fortunately Harlumn interjected, "However! It is not yet business time. From a young friend of our community, we have been gifted many breads and pastries."

Harlumn's saying this rendered Redman jumping up and down, dancing a rain dance palms to the heavens as to say "Thank you." In the process, he made his way to Harlumn, who'd been reaching under his chair. Redman kneeled, bowed his head, and put out his arms. Harlumn smiled a venerable smile. Then he placed, as a ring-bearer would, a crate of gifts into Redman's arms. Redman toured these around the circumference of the flames. One for you! One for you. One for you! Everyone got one. But there was a puzzling extra pistachio muffin.

Redman looked at this extra muffin. He was unsure what to do with it at first. But promptly, it went into the flames. Having relieved himself of a troublesome burden, he smiled.

Everyone sat down. Redman raised his chosen pastry. He pointed something urgent at Harlumn, and when Harlumn complained, "I cannot understand," Redman directed his pointing to Yonathon, who, being sharp as he was, recognized quickly what the nude giant was hinting at. A few words and a toast; that was it. So Yonathon, in a quieter voice, chanted:

> *Thank you to the rivers.*
> *Thank you to the timbers.*
> *Thank you to the heavens and earth!*
> *And thank you, Mother Limber!*

Harlumn squinted at the boy for overshadowing him.

Redman smiled and gave the boy a nod of gratefulness and encouragement.

Elder Woman whispered to Syd, "smart boy. Reminds me of a certain such and such. Do you remember?"

Syd said, "I remember."

Then everyone ate their muffins and pastries. Redman savored each bite as though it was the greatest in the world. He bit and bit until there were no bites left. Suddenly, he was sad.

Promptly, Harlumn spoke. "Okay. To business now."

Maryon passed a wooden tablet to Harlumn. Harlumn pulled it close to his face. Carefully, he turned the tablet clockwise once. A pause. Counter-clockwise three times. A pause. After a series of turns and flips and so on, he announced, "the water is pure." Redman tossed his thumb upwards at the tale.

"The fruit is plump." Redman licked his lips theatrically.

"And the love is strong." Redman wrapped his arms around himself, leaned, and flopped over the back of his chair. Harlumn and Yonathon smiled at the sight. Then Harlumn concluded "that is the state of the Earth," and Redman raised tossed his arms in the air. Bliss.

Elder Woman leaned toward Syd's ear. She remarked, "He's loony as ever."

"I see," Syd said.

"But they love him for it."

FORTY-ONE

All alone, Jack weaved through trees. He skirted buildings as a centipede in the shadows. He was one with the shadows. During his trip, he was hungry. He worried of his kids. He relived his interaction with Harlumn, remembering those teeth, so big and bright for a small, dark man. Outside of the shadows, there was movement of various kinds. Jack couldn't remember what the demon had said, or if he had spoken at all.

Jack remembered Harlumn lip-speaking "leave. There is a fire coming. Leave. There is a fire. Leave," incessantly.

In the dark, Jack ran. Jack ran. Jack ran. Running made him scared. Running faster, images of brown loin-cloth people appeared in the trees, poking out their heads, peering in on him like owls of the night. He ran faster, so fast, the patterns of the trees made grids, and if he squinted his eyes, the moonlight passing between leaves would converge to magnificent but perplexing Mandelbrot fractals. The owl figures stretched proportional to Jack's acceleration until the they were not owls anymore but snakes. Run... run.. run!!! ....
On came a vision of Hamza pounding away at nothing --

hitting his hammer off various posts and beams randomly and uselessly but in precisely chosen locations. Each hit was critical to some ridiculous master plan. Each hammer which required perfect placement and velocity. Yet the pattern -- it was unbeknownst to Jack.

FORTY-TWO

In his bedroom, Grandpa Tomleson knelt on his bed. His sheets were amuck. Wanting only slightly to tidy up, he folded some sheets here, some there. He pulled one sheet out from its entanglement with another, all in all making for more bearable sleeping quarters. After doing this, he noticed what seemed like a raindrop that splattered on his hardwood floor. But this was absurd; his roof had never leaked. His own son had shingled it. Perplexed, Grandpa Tomleson looked up. It turned out that his rickety roof was indeed still strong. Certainly it was not the source of the liquid.

Grandpa Tomleson soon learned, rather, that it was his head as the cause. From his forehead, he wiped viscous sweat, and he remarked "sheeeesh, I'm tired." But a noise came. Grandpa called to his frequent guest, "Charlie baby I'm 'getting old. Don't scare me like that," but there was no response. So while sitting on his bedside, he grumbled frustratedly. On a nightstand, there were grayscale portraits of this Grandpa Tomleson, a square-faced woman named "Raundis," and each of his kids: both Sydney and Holverson. The frames were hand-widdled and rough. Each had a name carved into its base.

The disheartened old man reached for his nightstand drawer. He fished through some things. Hidden away was another widdled frame, this one unfinished and framing a portrait that was also unfinished. Grandpa fetched his quill and ink. However, he put these aside and opted for his pocket knife, which had been lying on the carpet, instead. This knife was his treasure. The way he opened it was the way a mother spoon-feeds her todd. Carefully, with this fragile thing, Grandpa Tomleson carved the letters JACK.

Meanwhile Jack stumbled upon a river crossing between Redman's village and Homverd. It was a river crossing big enough to challenge his destination and train of thought and everything. On one side, there was his Father, Redman, and the demonic Harlumn. On the other was his beautiful hidden Grandfather, and his home, and his child. Between was the most beautiful, pure, patternful water he had ever seen. It was as though the framework of reality itself surfaced there. And the fish, swimming, seemed to so symbiotically ride the waves of the universe. There was also the great blue heron flapping powerfully into the distance.

A horrible crash thundered from the kitchen. At this, Grandpa yelled, "Who's there!?" In blew a powerful gust, swinging in his bedroom door and blowing out his lamp. "Who's out there????" Grandpa begged for someone to answer. He'd fallen to his knees while searching for his precious knife, which he had dropped. In the pitch black and knifeless, Grandpa cowered under an intruding figure who glowed a gorling green color, standing above him, drooling.

Jack wanted so bad to swim with the fishes. Likewise his Grandfather squirmed with desire to find his pocket-knife and jab this monstrous intruder's throat. But neither of these desired were fulfilled.

From a passing wagon, a giant plucked jack from his feat, tucking him away inside under an inescapably large, heavy pile of blankets and clothes. Simultaneously, the towering figure in Grandpa Tomleson's house wrapped his callused iron fingers around the feeble old man's neck, clenching down with such furiousity the man hadn't a chance to scream. The two of them drowned simultaneously -- Jack in tranquilizing, calming captivity; and Grandpa, in death.

FORTY-THREE

In the barn, Yofim jabbed his shovel into the dirt. But it barely crossed the surface because a stone impeded its path. Vibrations invaded the boy's arm. Then the girl punched him in the arm for moving too slowly. She grabbed the shovel and kicked it further into the dirt with her heels herself, but it was not enough.

So she said, "Give me your hand," to Yofim.

And the couple pried back the shovel together. Success. Yofim dumped the dirt and the small troublesome stone behind him.

The girl pointed at the rock. She explained, "you have to go around those. Scoop them like ice cream."

The Girl and Yofim went on, doing this, and they talked.

"Where are we going?" Yofim asked.

"I think the East, perhaps," the girl said. "Or West."

Yofim remembered the bodies floating log-like in the river. And he remembered Kahfmahhn leading he and the others foot-blisteringly far into the East. It was desolate in that direction -- with bodies strewn about, and dogs like Kahfmahhn's dog prowling, devouring the less rotting carcasses, and then ordering Yofim and his neighbors to manage the rest. The dogs had the farmhands rebuilding bridges and reinforcing them. Boards atop boards redundantly.

At one point Joe-fella complained at Kahfmahhn, "this bridge is strong enough now ain't it?"

Tom-fella remarked, "This thing could hold a house!"

Kahfmahhn had been walking up and down the lines on his monitoring runs. Now he stopped affront the two fellas. Yofim was nearby. From his pocket, Kahfmahhn removed a dark, bronze-engraved cube, so dark, it seemed to reverberate scripture from the hellfires. He lifted this alien cube to eye level; then he let it fall. Now this was a small object, but it was extraordinarily dense. So, when it fell, it fell like a mammoth. It pulverized the bridge to ruble. What the farmhands had been toiling on for days became a mess. And the cube plunged deep into the earth's surface, and it gravitated, pulling the crushed boards and dirt down into the earth. The ground shook. The dirt was loose. Kahfmahhn watched his subjects struggle to resist tumbling into the hole created by the cube. Kahfmahhn grinned at this destruction.

In short time, a more dominant robed creature approached. He was a supervisor of sorts. This was the same supervisor who had reprimanded Kahfmahhn in front of Greenlock House. As commandant, this heartless thing breathed into Kahfmahhn's eyes, drooled onto his lips, burning them, and spoke foreign words that prompted Kahfmahhn to turn to the chain's rear. There stood Amelio, the small, tortured boy. Kahfmahhn ordered him to his knees and raised his whip.

Yofim remembered all this, but he realized it would be useless to explain to the Girl. So he told her, "The East is destroyed."

As though it made no difference to her, the girl said, "West, then."

She turned her body 180 degrees and begun digging in that direction instead of the previous. They dug for a while, until Yofim thought of what had become of everything. Everyone who'd ever cared for him had been killed or turned into an animal. He observed that, on those chains, everyone became animals, kicking and snarling at even the slightest causes of discomfort. Growling at friends, biting at foes. There was nobody in the world for Yofim. So he complained, "I don't know my mother's name."

The girl responded "That is sad indeed, Yofim." But she didn't feel what he felt. Instead, she thought out loud, saying/thinking: "we ought to find a bucket or something."

"Yeah... indeed," Yofim admitted.

The girl suggested, "If I slip out from underneath of Tom, I could make my way to Albany, Yofim." The girl exclaimed, "outside, just outside; I know where there are some buckets!"

Briefly she looked to Yofim. But realizing, past his distant glaze, that he would not be giving her a confirmation of any sort, she opted to climb out from under Tom. She went outside of his cell, crawled, and saw many broken-down people locked away in cells. She stopped outside an the stall of an older man who was looking at his palms with a puzzled, shameful expression on his face. He used them to massage his sore kneecaps. Then he looked at them again.

The girl eventually snapped out of her time-wasting daze. Pretty soon, she was back by Yofim's side.

She explained, "I saw this man... He looked so tired. He was sitting still, but still, he was in so much pain."

"Who was it?" Yofim asked. While the girl explained, he listened only passively. His focus was on taking the 5-gallon drum that the girl had retrieved, and filling it with dirt.

"An older man," she said. "He kept looking at his palms.."

"Oh no.." Yofim said.

"What?" she asked. "Why was he doing that?"

Yofim carried the bucket out of the hole, and he dumped it in Tom's cell. He kicked the dirt around, distributing it as evenly as he could. Then he climbed back down in the hole under Tom's carcass.

The girl asked again, then, "Yofim why was he doing that, the old man? He was in a trance."

Yofim explained, "I know that man. We call him Almond. He is the bread-maker. He was looking at his hands because does not believe what they have been made to do.... We must dig, so I am not forced do those things myself."

"Yes. Let us dig," the girl said. "On with it then."

FORTY-FOUR

Wading in the canals in the forest, Omnious explained the following to Thom.

"When I was here last, it was busier, noisier. It became as it is now only later. I was to meet together with Grandfather Galagna to discuss various things -- the farm, our interactions. I had my hammer in hand. They escorted me down these streams in one of their boats. I kept my head down, avoiding seeing what ought not be seen, and hearing what ought not be heard. I advise you do the same."

Thom cut to the point. "Promise you'll bring me to my boy, Omnious, and I'll do whatever you ask."

"Okay. Yes," Omnious said. "Swim then, Thom. Keep your head down. Let the current be your eyes."

They swam. And in their wake, Tomph built his hut. There were bugs and rats and beached urchins and crabs scattered across the mud flats. These creatures were easy prey for the death birds that riddled the skies, flying in from the North, circling, finding a meal for the road, and continuing Southward. Tomph navigated around nature's litterings. Tomph licked his lips toying with the thought that perhaps, when he got settled in, he would roast a crab.

Tomph harvested fine gravel from the outside corner of the riverbank. It was necessary that he carry this gravel back in shirt fulls to the nearest dry ground because this gravel was to be used in the construction of his hut. It was going to be the removable fill around which the mold would be formed. Many trips... many trips. He took many nauseating trips. The birds were darting in and out like locusts or angels stealing or saving bits of struggling consciousness from the earth.

Omnious ran his head into Thom.

"Open your eyes," Thom said. Omnious did. And there it was: a Galagna boat, sideways, blocking the canal.

"It's abandoned," Thom suggested, and he went to peer over its hull.

Omnious stopped him. "The Galagna do not abandon their boats."

Thom opened his arms and said, "Nor their trees, I see?" referencing sarcastically the empty forest around them.

"Shush your mouth, Thom. Swim under the boat."

"I'm sorry... I don't mean to be this way," Thom sincerely said. "Good 'ol Thom," he said, looking in on himself. He now opened his arms to the man he revered deeply, and he said, "You're a father to me, Omnious, even though I am older."

"I know Thom. Let's swim."

"Right," Thom said. And they swam.

Tomph worked to build his shelter. He formed a border of clay. Then, inside of this border, he poured sand and mud. This gave him his floor. Atop his floor, he formed a shell of clay around a mound of sand.

The birds if anything had intensified during this time. The sun had passed its prime height. But the outside world remained warm, cloudless, and the air was dry. The mud was drying quickly, which was good. What was not good, however, were the drying carcasses from which a pungent smell of death was emitted. The birds wished not to squander their opportunity by letting these carcasses spoil and go to the worms. So they swarmed from the skies. But when Tomph's hut had hardened, and when Tomph pulled his bark-rigged release valve, thereby releasing sand and hollowing out the inside of his hut, it was like a great kingdom of good knights had been sent out from their castle drawbridge, charging out, fertilizing the world with their goodness, causing the hell-spawn birds to disperse, and causing a wave of water to wash the death and parasites from sight, and allowing a touch of lightning to ignite Tomph's campfire, which he used to further dry his hut and to spark a delicious crab feast.

This was because, in the swamps, Omnious and Thom had

made their way to the Grandfather Tree. Grandfather Galagna remained encased in this tree. Of all of his parts, only one of his hands was exposed. Omnious grabbed hold of this hand. It was a powerful hold. And a shockwave shook the trees and the waters, and Daughter of Elsedorwn, grown giant commanding the locusts from her widows walk, fell to her knees. She looked to the North, and she saw the leaves shake.

Grandfather Galagna caressed Omnious's hand with his old-skinned fingers, which had grown bark-like over the years. Jittering from Parkinson's, these fingers felt their way in and around Omnious's palm. Lining wrinkles, the tree's fingers found their place with a thumb at the base of Omnious's palm. There, the tree pressed down dry and cool. Thom caught interest in the centered stone Obelisk that was two feet suspended from the dirt. Broken roots all around. Thom followed with his eyes as the foreign scripture led him round and round and round again, converging towards the unreachable singularity in the center. Approaching this center point, Thom's eyes widened. Something in his spine straightened him. And he read outloud words that reverberated through the canals and through all world's waters.

> *"As the waters rise, and the waters low,*
> *The air turns dry, and the clouds grow.*
> *Fires burn hot as only charcoal knows.*
> *But the children sob, and their mothers tense.*
> *The mothers frog; the offspring make mends.*
> *Ashes bring green feed for our hens.*
> *Galagna is neither good nor bad. It merely is."*

The spirits of memories navigated from far and wide to their destination: their father, The Grandfather Galagna, who, a connection to Simanru in hand, and scripture in the waters, was provided with the necessary means to re-establish order -- to calm the waters, to return the clouds, to grow the crops, to calm the angry, to unleash the dogs, and to give the calming words necessary to convince scared people to have some faith, and to set fire to Gerald's triple deck carriage that was ordered by Mrs Greenlock and which was never meant to be, and to take the oil-burning, winged demon carrying slaughtering killing machine off its tracks.

Just for one moment, Grandfather Galagna regained control. What ensued was a slaughter of the ages. Kahfmahhn's dog pinned down subjects, one by one, beginning with the fellas, Kahfmahhn drooled self-destructive euphoria. He commanded his dog, "AHWwmPH GawUm LORE", and the dog pressed all its weight upon Tom-fella's ribs, emptying his lungs of air and causing him to whimper and cough.

Joe-fella was being held down by the powerful beast's free arm. Tears slid down his cheeks as he struggled saying "brother, be strong. Don't give him the pleasure of seeing you cry."

"Sanchoe to you, Joe."

Kahfmahhn snatched Tom-fella's hand. Meanwhile the winged demons, having been tossed to the dirt, stood up and reformed their lines. Their commanders rode up and down the lines on tongue seizuring, yellow bulging-eyed hellhounds, rooing and rahing. Inciting murderous blood-hungry cries. The leaders were in process of organizing a dagger charge. They prepared their ranks. And by their ranks, I refer to a particularly mangled embodiment. A cigar-smoking devil, who was an amputee, sharpened swords on a squealing, warpig-driven sharpening wheel. Other hell spawns would approach this sword-sharpener -- they would exchange obscenities with him and he would sharpen their swords or spears. Another creature strapped spikes onto the knees and elbows of his men. Their most charismatic beast riled the band of murderous creatures.

Kahfmahhn became uneasy while watching this from afar. Many of Kahfmahhn's terrified brethren broke running in the direction of the birds. Kahfmahhn did not retreat, for he had business to attend to. On Tom-fella's hand, with a terrible curved blade, he engraved a symbol '¥¥'. At the same time his commandant yelled "HerUhn Gunm mAIG", or in English,

"Extinguish yourselves," then "Do not etch. Do not run. Extinguish yourselves resolutely."

Some of the Kahfmahhn's brethren ran. Others impaled themselves and turned to ash. Despite orders from the Commandant, Kahfmahhn cut the symbol into Joe; he cut this symbol into the beer-bellied fat man who had because of hard labor thinned; and he cut this symbol into the palms of everyone other farmhand in sight.

But he noticed: a chained group was escaping. These farmhands ran for their lives, but Kahfmahhn sicked his dog on them; then he continued cutting into the palms of his subjects.

There were two other escaped chains. They were freed because the commandant had stopped, let out a prayer, and sunk his knife deep in his own belly. Dropping to his knees, he demanded Kahfmahhn follow suit. However Kahfmahhn disobeyed again and rushed to finish his final cutting: on the tortured boy who, when cut, did not cry, did not smile; but merely watched the skies, as one would watch the skies on any October night.

When it became immanently necessary, Kahfmahhn abandoned his prisoners and ran intercept the two converging chains. Left were the fellas, the beer-bellied man, the tortured boy, and many more tortured souls, not bothering to stand or run; for, if they did, where would they go?

FORTY-FIVE

Sherri sat in the Greenlock House library. She had spent hours repairing the shelves, sorting books, finding furniture to replace broken furniture, and sweeping the floor. She was reading a book in Mr. Greenlock's chair when in hovered Mrs. Greenlock, well-dressed and freshened up, tip-toing in with her hands clasped behind her waste like a schoolgirl.

"Hi Sherri... Oh! I like what you've done with the place. Very focused.. very wholesome."

"Good evening Mrs. Greenlock. Thank you. I.. I've taken care to get things sorted as they were before, and I archived the Master's work as best I could. He should be able to resume without hindrance once he returns."

"Oh, aren't you a doll, Sherri?"

"It is a grand library, Mrs. Greenlock," Sherri admitted.

Mrs. Greenlock circled around the Master's desk. It became apparent to Sherri that the woman's eye was blackened and that her lips were bloodied. In the shimmering lamp-light, something sinful reverberated from the widow's eyes.

"Indeed it is," Mrs. Greenlock said, absent-mindedly acknowledging the library's grandiosity. Meanwhile the Daughter of Elsedorwn rested her hands upon young Sherri's shoulders, and she said, "Especially with your grace at its helm."

Sherri winced at this touch of pure evil. But the massage deepened, and although this woman was as cringe-worthy as maggots eroding the stub of an amputated limb, the massage deepened, and with its associated pain came spine-contorting pleasure -- the kind so intoxicating, one's desire seems capable of fracturing bone. So, as Daughter of Elsedorwn eased her grip, Sherri craved the return of the deepness. She arched back as her cravings for ecstasy reverberated through years-conditioned ambivalence. Seeing this young girl swoon, the monster smiled.

Suddenly the monster stopped massaging Sherri's shoulders.

"Sherri," she said.

"Yes?"

"This morning I met with your Father. We cleaned dishes together, and he cut me firewood. I strolled past him as he was cutting firewood. I waved to him, and he said 'Oh! hello Mrs. Greenlock. Good morning!' It was so pleasant, the way he greeted me. Later, after circling the garden, I turned back to where he had been. Your father was still there, cutting firewood as he was before. I eased his axe. That confused him, but I smiled and I took his hand. We strolled the courtyard together. It was oh-so-pleasant."

In a pause, Mrs. Greenlock looked at her hands atop the young girl's shoulders. For a moment she seemed the slightest bit disgusted at herself for laying hands on the good, innocent Sherri. But in short time, the Daughter of Elsedorwn emerged to squeeze Sherri's shoulders ever so tightly, inciting the girl to squirm.

"That's nice, Mrs. Greenlock," Sherri struggled to say. On came that deep, painful, pleasurable massaging that Sherri craved so perplexingly so. The Daughter of Elsedorwn continued telling the tale of her interaction with Sherri's father.

"We swung on the swings together!" she explained. "It made me feel like a little girl again, just fooling about with my childhood crush, you know. But your father turned his head when I leaned in for a kiss, so I had him hung from the Maple tree."

Sherri's eyes opened so wide, but Daughter of Elsedorwn deepened her massage, and she kissed the girl's ear, then her cheek, and then her neck. What was there to worry of now?

"I've been eying you..., you know," Sherri said.

"Relax, Sherri. Just relax...."

FORTY-SIX

On his carriage, Gerald chased Kahfmahhn and the other murderous dogs. The carriage tore flesh as easily as grass. Harald pulled. All throughout, Gerald laughed like a madman, fighting off robed creatures and demons and locusts. He felled some two-dozen figures before his carriage overturned. But eventually, Gerald landed badly broken underneath the thing, and he cried. The fellas came to his aid.

"Please, fellas, help me!"

They did, and they told Gerald that they admired his fight.

"She hung Earnie," Gerald whined. "I'm next. 'Gotta go gotta gooo gotttaaaa goooooooooo."

After the fellas lifted the weight of the carriage off his back, Gerald limped back into the fight. The fellas, dragging their chain, proceeded to release Harald, who had been pulling the carriage, to run free.

"There, buddy, run," one of the fellas said.

"Why isn't he moving?"

"C'mon lad. Go on."

Harald stood up and looked around. With nothing of blessing to see in any direction, the horse opted to sit back down. All he did with his newfound freedom was reposition his legs more comfortably. Then he laid his head down and rested as chaos ensued around him.

FORTY-SEVEN

With Thom reciting scriptures, Omnious felt a tightening. First it was his chest. Then, his hand. The hand in the tree -- it was coming alive and becoming strong. It shivered and shook. Suddenly the forest went still, and through his subjects, Grandfather Galagna spoke, saying, "It wasn't meant to be this way. But now it is, and so it is."

Omnious asked, "Where is the boy, Galagna?"

But asking was of no use; for the tree repeated itself: "it is, and so it is, Omnious. I am sorry. I cannot aid you over my own, when I can barely aid my own at all."

Thom continued as the vehicle of scripture:

*"Galagna is neither good nor bad. It merely is.
As love is lovely or as a rainstorm is.
But things that are in time, with time go unknown.
If our time has come, let us go numb.
Let us be unknown,
    in the name of the mother allows her child to bloom."*

FORTY-EIGHT

It was a hedonistic scene on the widow's walk. A low-sitting loveseat sat shrubbatious and cloud-like, covert between rose-vined knee walls. Among flowers and thorns, the Daughter of Elsedorwn brought ecstasy to Sherri. Sherri reciprocating, the couple's moans echoed through ages and swirled purple and black into the skies. A fornicating sacrifice! It was impossible not to hear Sherri's moans and cries, even in midst of battle, when her benefactress sunk teeth deep into her thigh. The pain! The erotic galore!! Redness penetrated the sky in the way it does the water when a shark seeks its prey. And Daughter of Elsedorwn, so immersed in Sherri's reciprocation, shivered in a world-shaking orgasm that shattered a jar and allowed the Ghost of Leo Greenlock to escape. This ghost soared Northward through the sky, leaking green color into the reddening purple.

FORTY-NINE

A peculiarly colored memory fluttered from the South, romping and mushing, carried by butterfly dogs, ultimately circling the obelisk. It's meandering curiosity brought life to the swamp. As a result, Galagna fellows, tired and melancholy, came lumbering inward, wondering what had made them feel how they felt.

"You must go, Omnious," the Tree warned, "the Galagna are returning. None of us are welcome here, not even I."

"Galagna, where is the boy? I cannot leave.. ---"

As Omnious began to say this, the peculiarly-colored memory jumped to Grandfather Galagna's hand, and thereby to Omnious's. Suddenly the answers were there -- answers to all the questions, even to those that hadn't yet been asked.

"What is it Omnious?" Thom asked.

Omnious planned to answer him as best he could. But Thom fell into another trance.. Seemingly the whole forest caught this contagious trance as Thom chanted compounding with Grandfather Galagna and his disciples:

> *"It seemed time had come, for fires to mother next.*
> *It seemed time had come, for us to clean us hence.*
> *It seemed that ashes would be the past. But no.*
> *So release the water bribe; let back the roots grow.*
> *The bearers have lied; the clouds hadn't known.*
> *I am small a piece of the pence;*
> *Galagna is neither good nor bad. It merely is.*
> *And by a boy and his Acorn, what Is will continue to BE."*

Encroaching upon Tomph's sand hut, the crabs pinched and scratched eachother. They poked at Tomph Eventually they prodded him out. Outside, he found storm clouds in the West and East and South. The water had washed up crabs and urchins and deer all over the shore. However, one runway clear of carcasses formed a Northward path for him. So he walked in that direction. Hearing the screams of the Daughter of Elsedorwn, he ran. But the shaking of Galagna brought a hesitance in him which caused him to slip up, trip, and fall. The crabs came, though, sweeping Tomph's legs, burrowing underneath him, and lifting. A thousand marsh crabs carried our hero to the waters where an empty Galagna boat awaited him. This boat had been delivered for him and the crabs, who held no power in the sea. The crabs loaded Tomph into the boat. They climbed in themselves. Tomph paddled using colorful, inward-wafting memories as his guide. Then, after the through and through through the Galagna canals, and upon their eventual arrival, the crabs again rose, and they carried our injured hero to his caller.

Tomph said, "thank you, nature's crustaceans." Quickly, the crabs scurried back to the canals. Tomph was left alone at the feet of a Grandfather Galagna, who now stood tall and grand on his own feet. The tree had released him. The disciples gathered around.

The Tree said, "My boy, you are wondrous." Tomph could not speak. Paralyzing roots encased his feet.

The disciples read from their obelisk:

> *"Galagna is neither good nor bad. It merely is.*
> *With a successor, what IS will continue to BE."*

This caused Tomph to understand. It caused him to feel the memories of the world slothing up the roots and into his ankles before his legs. As they contacted him they interwove through his pours. Illuminated was his life path -- a glowing stream wandering from distant lands, to the farm, and everywhere by Yofim's side, then to the River Round and to the North, and to the marshes and eventually to here. Tomph remembered Yofim calling him a loon. And he remembered Master Greenlock, who sent him Northward. And he remembered Mr. Tomleson, who had sent him to the Master originally.

As the roots climbed to waist level, everything flashed before Tomph's eyes. He felt a pressure on his hip. Then he awoke with Little One in his arms.

"Tomph!" the boy cried. "Don't leave me!!!"

Thom yelled from the canopy, "My boy!" Not a moment later, vines from above and roots from below cooperated in the separating of Tomph from Little One. Once again, Little One found himself bound hopelessly to that sacred carved stone. Above, jailed in the canopy, Tomph and Omnious hung like stoic prisoners awaiting their imminent execution. Thom was distant from these two, but trapped in the canopy all the same.

Circling in, the Galagna disciples chanted:

> *"The earth gifts us a sprout.*
> *The skies give drink to the green.*
> *What comes of it all is Galagna.*
> *And Galagna, he brings*
> *seeds to the Earth.*
> *It was forgotten how*
> *A seed needs nurturing;*
> *A seed needs churning ---*
> *To sleep and grow, it craves weight on its chest."*

One disciple stepped forward. He looked over one of his shoulders, then the other, locking eyes with and receiving nods from each of his fellow disciples. Then he focused in on himself and the cane on which his weight rested. The cane, it was lively as a Galagna limb, charred green, bark-like with blisters the burdens of eternal consequentiality lining every crease. The cane, its wounds were raw and churning. But the beholding disciple, with one of his hands, performed a small finger ritual over each of the cane's open soars. Reacting, they swelled and blackened and closed.

The other disciples followed in this one's trail, sealing their respective canes' soars. Then one by one, they placed their canes atop Little One on the obelisk. Little One cried. Thom cried. The disciples, having placed down the weight of their canes, cherished the weightlessness of their palms. Each disciple touched his left thumb to his right. Each disciple felt an inward vacuum force pulling his palms together. This force led the disciples to bring their palms together and wrap fingers around fingers.

As canes piled heavy, Thom called to Omnious. "Omnious, help good 'ol Thom. Help my boy! Stop them..."

But Omnious said plainly, "it is of no use. I can be of no use."

Thom wailed. He struggled but could not escape the mighty forest. So the flow of Galagna continued with nature. Thom could do nothing when The Tree, released by his tree, commanded the disciples,

> *"Make way for my decaying soul —*
> *Tree Galagna, having lived old.*
> *Make way, my children, maintainers of the world.*
> *Make way, my flame bearers; make new from old."*

Solemnly, a disciple, from his stomach pouch, retrieved a transparent, spherical, dimpled flask in which a slate green liquid sloshed. The liquid contained charred bits reminiscent of Galagna skin blistering like boiled leather. There were oceans in this liquid. There was lonely tundra in the surrounding glass. Under an overturned boat in one of these oceans, there was a woman, pregnant and plump, who floated on her back in frigid water. Her fellow sailors had either drowned or perished by the teeth of sharks. This woman floated candidly, her hands insulating her baby-bearing belly which floated just above water level. She gazed at the stars through the very puncture whole that had sunken her boat.

Grandfather Galagna turned his back to Little One. A summoned man of Galagna tip-toed toward his towering Grandfather. This approacher kneeled on his two knees. He lowered his head and raised his arms, preparing to receive the ceremonial blade.

FIFTY

The cowering, chained farmhands limped toward cover in the barn. Kahfmahhn chased them. He was exhausted but crazed -- the last of his kind. The revitalizing of the Northern blade incited hallucinations in him. Uncontrollable visions of his past were thrust upon him -- his past, when he, kneeling affront the Grandfather Galagna of a prior era, opted to perform the blasphemous act of carving in his very palm the symbol which tarnishes the tribe and its ways, and which marks an exodus of the actor and his offspring and their offspring, trading Galagna-nature for freedom and chains.

These hallucinations and others plagued Kahfmahhn as he swung his ax and as he stomped his boots. Slashing at a woman, the laundry cleaner in Greenlock, he saw her eyes watering, and in said eye water, he envisioned forging his weaponry over the flames of burning scripture pages.

Kahfmahhn was sorounded.

At his back, crazed demons from hell, determined to butcher all that is good or evil, encroached upon him.

From his front, an impenetrable line of solemn Galagna disciples crawled toward him. They read hymns.

The directions left and right held nothing for Kahfmahhn. Neither did forward or back. So he remembered his wife, taller but thinner than he. He remembered her toiling in the blacksmith's quarters during day, then tending to the thorn-coated roses during night. How shameful he felt for forsaking her.

Between Kahfmahhn and the approaching wall of disciples, there were cowering, broken animals straining to shield themselves from the sun.

One growled at Kahfmahhn and said, "Lean in here, and I

will tear out your throat with my teeth!"

Kahfmahhn responded, "you are insect, not beast." And he swung his blade. Off with the animal farmhand's head and impeding hand. Next in line. Kahfmahhn executed ducks from the rear of a slow-moving, crippled flock of farmhands. Meanwhile forces from all sides closed in.

FIFTY-ONE

The chosen disciple touched the treasured blade. Touching it ushered memories of other disciples who had done so in the past. Most in this disciple's situation did as they were meant to, as Kahfmahhn was meant to, and as this disciple was meant to. When they didn't, they carved up their hands. In effect, Grandfather Galagna would fall backwards atop the obelisk, atop the totem. He would to go gray instead of black, yielding infertility and eons of chaotic imbalance -- tundra and flames.

The chosen disciple grappled with influxing memories of Galagna. He was pained by the burden of choice, until ultimately he did as he was destined. Instead of carving his own palm, he stuck the blade deep into Grandfather Galagna's belly. Then he dropped it onto the ground. Quickly, the tree's roots enveloped the blade. Grandfather Galagna lowered himself to the ground as gradually as could. Once his knees bent past a certain point, he crumpled into Little One's lap. A final hymn marked the end of his reign.

> *"I see darkness and nothing more,*
> *But I imagine the young one here —*
> *Tending oceans, tending trees,*
> *Mending potions, succeeding me.*
> *And bringing a balance to things…*
> *As I have done."*

FIFTY-TWO

With his blade, Kahfmahhn struck the miner called Rumly Frone. His blade broke upon Rumly's flesh not because the man-beast had uncuttable bones or impenetrable skin, but because of the straying chains, which had, in the meanwhile, unified and thereby shifted the world's demographics. Now Kahfmahhn cowered and searched for sanctuary, but there was no sanctuary because Greenlock House had burned.

Gerald went bonkers, "AhahahahahahahAHAAHAHAA HAAHA!" rattling like a circus monkey with his face covered in ash. He bestrode a carriage powered by neither man nor beast. It was a driven by an unexplainable force.

Gerald pushed foward the lever with both hands. The beastly machine tossed petrol, some bits burning, in every direction, and it accelerated. Gerald gargled and choked on his own spit and blood. Our poor chariot craftsman went entirely mad, not chasing after anybody in particular. Just chasing ghosts.

"I set out after nobody, sure!!" he yelled, "but if you interrupt my glorious ride," he shrugged and pretended to croak, "this monster and I together say, so be it! BahaHAhaHAHA!"

Kahfmahhn took for the trees. There! His dog squirmed, mortally injured. To help? Kahfmahhn opted not.

FIFTY-THREE

That was because Grandfather Galagna laid on Little One's lap, and the boy consoled him. Grandfather Galagna and Little One looked upon each other as they had done during their previous lives. It was grace. It was terrifying. It was beauty. A mighty inculcation of matrowsity. The disciples made their way inward humming hymns wordless. Little One supported the tiring tree's head, which weighed too much for the Tree's atrophying neck. Galagna closed allowed his eyelids to rest. The disciples poured the contents of their flasks upon the stow. Liquid matted Grandfather Galagna's hair, and it flowed down his neck, onto Little One's hand.

Grandfather Galagna whispered to Little One. "Be solemn, young one. To cry out now would be to disrupt nature's way."

"What is this?" the boy asked, referencing the liquid and everything.

"This is geo'f-tangue water. This is Galagna."

"Who am I?" asked the boy.

"You are a boy. You are Galagna." explained the Tree.

"Who are you?" asked the boy.

"I am a tired old tree."

The disciples set fire to this gelatinous liquid, and thereby, to the boy and his Tree and all the walking sticks piled upon them. Young hope and old wisdom together burned into ashes.

Simultaneously, all that was erotic atop Greenlock house was no longer. Sherri, her lust stunted by the flames, hurled herself down a million stories to a peaceful death, leaving Daughter of Elsedorwn, viciously tearing apart locusts, to burn and cry high-pitched piercing cries across all the lands.

The winged demons and their troop, surrounded by Galagna, cowered in upon themselves. Those of Galagna pushed further and further still, tightening their grasp on the soul-less, the God-less, pressing them against their overturned creation: the massive, oil-spewing train. Some demons fought despite mortal having wounds. But effortlessly, the disciples parried blows and delivered belly dags. By ones then dozens then in whole, the demons laid down their arms. for as Galagna said to the boy while the two burned:

> *"Live for the individual and you will grow strong.*
> *Live for the society and you will live long.*
> *Live for the everything and you will be forever.*
> *The godless are strong while being blind shields them from the light.*
> *But no-one is blind forever, boy."*

Gerald swept Westward on his oil-powered carriage suspension-less but with speed never before fathomable. Bouncing, breathing, coughing up blood… passing the fellas, he called to them: "A scythe, boys!"

From the demolished cornfield, Tom-fella lifted a blade of massive proportions and one of a particular particularity. It was Granger's old scythe, made from Redwood and covered in pictographs designed for the intuition. Tom-fella lofted it up, floating it for Gerald to catch in stride. With this scythe, the madman proceeded to lop off Kahfmahhn's head. Then he exploded babbling laughing at what he'd done, "jeeee-zusss BaHaHahaHaaaaaaa! You're not so tough without your head, ay?"

Gerald swung the scythe wildly without regard for his direction. He had let go completely of the steering mechanism. So the oil machine barreled onward. It jeered left. It jeered right. By the grace of God, it passed safely through the Gauntlet of Galagna Disciples that worked to entrap the robed figures and the winged demons. The disciples made two groups. One went leftward. The other went rightward. They conspired to join as a circle around all of their foes. But Gerald was allowed through unhindered. And he, in his hijacked oil-spewing death carriage, barreled onward into the winged-demon mothership. What resulted was a tremendous explosion the likes of which no farmhand had ever seen. The flames extended toward the skies, but Galagna contained them with a torrent of rain.

After this, the winged demons were no more. And their luciferian vehicles were no more.

The Daughter of Elsedorwn was no more, as evidenced by her atrophying screeching.

FIFTY-FOUR

Out sprouted, from thin dirt atop the obelisk, the seedling of a Tall Tree. This newborn piece of greenery was lanky but thick in in knees.

Every third disciple stepped forward. Each of them crouched down. One sunk his fingers into the part of the earth that brimmed the obelisk. He reached his fingers underneath the obelisk. Then another disciple followed suit beside the first. Then another beside the next. Then another, and another, and so on until the obelisk had been surrounded. Together, the disciples lifted the obelisk and Little One, the seedling, and the surrounding dirt that now sprouted thick, white-flowered moss. Together, they transplanted the seedling, the casket, and the urn, to the footstep of the drying, dying Grandfather Tree, whose aged bark ground to sand when he moved.

From the canopy, Thom observed the disciples care for and solidify the new growth's root connections, and he watched them take turns patting down the dirt.

FIFTY-FIVE

The remainder of Greenlock House smoldered in its foundation. Just nearby, the lost chains of farmhands gathered and connected. One hand held the other. Only then did Galagna connect the group. A representative disciple emerged from the solemn wall of long silhouettes. Thunder brewed as this figure approached. Mercifully, he and the thunder halted at a non-threatening distance, but a distance over which their presence could be felt with certainty. Words were spoken in a language these people of Greenlock had never known. Yet, somehow, they understood:

> *"The disciples of Galagna apologize,*
> *For the sun fierce and all your cries,*
> *For the wells dry, and the floods.*
> *We have seen the end's beginning.*
> *So we will harm you no longer.*
> *In our eternal balance ponder,*
> *We will not rebuild your city;*
> *We will not kindle your love.*
> *People of the farm: we are returning home.*
> *May we, in new days, fit as hand-in-glove."*

The representative disciple walked backwards with his head bowed. Once he rejoined his kin, the disciples made way their Northward, carrying with them the remains of Kahfmahhn, Kahfmahhn's dog, and all of members of Kahfmahhn kind. Kahfmahhn's dog was mortally injured, snarling ferociously at anyone who ventured near. However, this dog went silent in the presence of sacred Galagna disciples.

Three regular Galagna boats waited in the canal beside

Greenlock house (still burning). There was also a fourth boat: a larger carrier vessel. The disciple who had spoken with the farmhands boarded the front-most boat. Doing so, he hovered the gap between land and boat. Then he sat facing ever straightly toward the rear, eying the farm. Next, those disciples carrying injured or dead loaded their carryings into the carrier vessel. Then they boarded themselves, and they trailed the leading pirogue with destination the heart of Galagna. The representative disciple stared back toward the farm until his lantern blended into the horizon.

The remaining people of Greenlock found their chains evaporating into swamp moths which circled, scurried, and figure-eighted on the trail behind the distancing trees. Distancing, these moths begun to blend with the horizon. but they transformed collectively into the moon.

Joe-fella embraced his friend, his brother, Tom-fella, he said, "I'm gone-ah go checkup on me mum," and he made his way. In his absence, brother Tom grew independent. As such, he wandered the ruins as an individual, no longer a trailing carrier vessel but a pirogue, carved from a single age-old trunk. Scattered fires pulled at Tom's peripherals. It was instinct to stomp them out. But he realized that bugs would be better burned than squashed. So instead of stomping the flames, he booted them and the bugs toward one central pile. The flames caught on. Soon, locust cries were compounding on each other in the most dreadful ways.

Tom dragged a burning, life-strung locust by its whiskers toward the flames. It was then he heard a whimpering. Most people of Greenlock had dispersed. Even the wounded had been carried off by this point. But behind Tom, there was a whimpering distinct from the locust cries. It turned out to be the boy tortured most by all this. He sat cross-legged in the mud crying every tear he had. Tom walked toward him. The boy's hand was sitting in a puddle of reddened, watery mud.

To the backdrop of the dilapidated cornfield and Gerald going mad, Tom sent a probing "hello" to the boy.

For a good while, there was nothing. The boy sat as he was

for a while without even turning his head.

Eventually, he said, "I have nowhere to go."

"Where is your mother?" Tom asked.

"I dun no."

"Where is your father?" Tom asked.

"I dun no. Harry is curled, Tom. I 'dun know where to go."

Tom-fella scanned the horizon. What he saw changed something in him. It marked his realization of something that he had inside of him that he hadn't before realized that he had. So he asked the boy, "What are you called?" And, given the boy's name, he said, "You can come with me, Henry."

"I can?" Henry asked, with those pained, watery eyes in full view.

"Of course," Tom said, proceeding to lift the boy up upon his shoulders.

The boy let out in pain when Tom, trying to lift him, accidentally ravished the deep wounds on his back.

"What is it, Henry?"

"He whipped me raw, Tom," Henry explained.

"Let me hold you by your arms, then."

"Okay."

They situated themselves with Henry on Tom's shoulders and Tom holding Henry's hands. Then they proceeded toward the aftermath of the day. The boy hung on as tightly as he could. He was so comforted having someone to hold on to.

Tom raked locusts into the fire. And he piled downed cornstalks to be collected later. And he growled at starved monsters looking for a leg to chew on. Henry smiled slightly at the growling, for it was comical to him. They observed it all. The scene. The despair.

They stumbled upon Gerald who was rambling off his rocker. His eyes were entirely white (pupil, iris, and all). Yet he stared with wild intensity toward whatever sounds he heard.

"I see God," the carriage-maker claimed. Looking to the skies, he was horrified and excited by the power of the all-mighty. He was mortally wounded. His leg, through his hip, was completely obliterated. And he had blistering burns all

GREENLOCK FARM

over him, across his face, across everywhere.

"I fear God!" he said, and he pleaded for mercy. "I have never feared something so wholesomely to the bone, and inescapably. The POWER.... LORD, SPARE ME OF MY SINS, I COMMAND you!" He hesitated, then he shook his head. "Jeesus, does it work that way? LORD, please, I feel your multitudinous grip; I hadn't felt it before. I do now. Relieve me of my pain!!"

Hearing his own words, and realizing, after a moment, how hopeless he was, being blind and stranded in the mud... Gerald was ashamed. "Ahhh what a joke," he said, splashing his hands in the muck. It was not his desire to splash himself with intrepid earth guts, but that is what happened. When he dropped his hands into the puddle, he splashed putrid battle and juice into his on mouth. Thereby infuriating himself further, making him yack, and making him wipe his tongue with his hand.

Tom-fella revealed his presence. "Gerald," he said. "It's Tom."

"Tom, where is your Joe? My friend, Joe. Oh hey Tom! How'd you fare today? I rode a marvelous machine on this day, did you know?"

"You're going mad, Gerald," Tom said.

Gerald admitted, "I know. Yes," -- afterwards, transitioning into a period of introspective thought.

Tom allowed Gerald to savor his unexpected period of calm, for a while. Then, when it seemed all was had that could be gained from it, he asked, "Gerald, would you like a hand?"

But Gerald declined. He said. "No.. No thanks. I'll stay right here." Clearly he was mortified. A kind of petrifying fear of everything bound him to his exact rigid position. Any movement, any sound would somehow bring back the demons and the flames.

"I must be still," Gerald whispered.

Tom whispered back, "Are you certain?"

And Gerald said, "Yes."

"Okay, then," Tom said. He and Henry made their way,

continuing as they were.

Quickly Gerald got to yelling at and about God again, splashing in the mud, foaming at the mouth. He was so angry. But in an instant, he would revert to apologetic mourning, and a moment later, he'd be explaining himself. Then he'd bellow at whoever or whatever he saw or thought he saw, "You arrogant FUCK. LISTEN to me!!! I am Gerald, crafter of the finest carriages in the land." Suddenly he was saddened, realizing the newfound lack of truth in what he'd claimed. And he cried. And he called to Tom. "Fella! Hey! The world is in ashes now, see! You are free! Things are going dark. ON comes freedom! I love you Cassie."

Tom thought of Gabriel, who'd told stories of the farm's early days. The stories had been interesting to Tom. They were beautiful myths of building something from nothing. Of giving lost souls a place to find and be found. Gabriel had explained this, and Tom had listened. Tom understood, but he didn't feel it in the way that Gabriel did. Now Tom could feel it in his veins. Beside his brothers, it was time to build; it was time to grow something of his own.

He explained to Henry, "There is much to look forward to. Your wounds will heal. We will plant vegetables together. We build ourselves a modest hut. Joe will join us for dinner on Thursdays. We will feast, Henry. Together."

"We will?" Henry asked.

"Yes, Henry. It will be nice."

"Thank you, Tom.", the boy said. Still, he was pained (tears dribbled his cheeks). Fighting through a piercing sensation so strong his eyelids pressed shut, he asked Tom, "are you my papa, Tom?" And Tom thought for a while at the question, remembering his own father. He looked to the skies, remembering when:

"He was walking downtown with his father on some sweaty, miserable day. There was work to be done. They were building a stone wall for the wealthy family in town, The Knowlsons, who owned a farm and a hundred steeds. On their way through town center, pops made a stop. And he said to Tom, "Tommy, I've got to see about a lady. You stay here; keep watch of the wagon."

Tom's father made his way inside the post office, a rolled newspaper hanging out his back pocket. The walls were thin enough and the windows were open enough for Tommy to hear a young woman post-office attendant ask his father, "what do you got for me today, 'ol Gruden?"

"A smile and, if you will, a drink?"

"Oh no, not today." The girl laughed. "Maybe another time. What else do you got for me?" she asked.

"Aww. Too bad. Well, at least I got to see that glowing smile of yours.", Gruden said.

The desk attendant chirped another giggle. Then she said, "Anytime, Gruden."

"Wonderful", Tom's dad said. "In that case, I have for you two letters: one for the President of the United States, and the other, for Mr. Elmhouser. I'm seeing about some business with the two. Oh! And this, this little bit of harmlessness, is for you."

"Oh, you shouldn't have, Gruden."

"Oh, but I wanted to, love."

"Okay. But you don't expect anything in return now, do you?" she asked, raising a brow.

"Of course not! Unless you insist...", Gruden winked, simultaneously grabbing a pen and scrap paper to scribble something down.

"Okay. Have a good one, you old bastard."

"Love you honey," Tom's pa-pa (Gruden) said as he returned to his son. Another man crossed his path. This man was run-down. So was Tom's father. But this man, he lacked any sense of humor for 'ol Gruden to cling to. And he complained, "my hands are worn to the bone, brother. Look into my eyes. I can't go on any longer."

"John," Gruden said. "Look at my fingers. They are broken. When I am building walls, I lift the stones with my wrist stumps."

John took a gander, and he winced. "Oooh," he said. "Gruden, that's horrendous. How do you get on?"

"Look outside. Look at my son. This is for him. Everything is for him now. John, you say you are dying. I am a dead."

John nodded his head and the two parted ways. "I'll see you around?" Gruden said. And John responded unenthusiastically, "yea. Maybe you will."

Then Gruden came out to his boy, smiling and gallanting, waving something in his hand.

"What is it, pa-pa?"

In Tommy's beloved father's hand was a note that read:

// Hey handsome.. lunch Friday?

// Meet me at Gloria's tavern. 11:00am, sharp!

and the two walked on to work on their Sunday, carrying their fishing poles, planning to cut out from work early and enjoy the day.

"She slipped it in my hand as I handed her the letters," ol' Gruden said. "Then she gave me a kiss on the cheek."

"That's garbage!" Tommy joked. "I don't believe anything that comes outa your mouth."

Gruden put his arm around his son. "I don't believe that!", he said."

From the skies, Tom looked to the Henry, who gazed with profound curiosity and a queer tranquility interrupted only for an instant when another shot of pain made him convulse. But the pain passed. And once without pain, all was tranquil.

"What is on you mind?" Henry asked. "I see that there is something."

"What do you see?"

"I 'don know, but there is something," Henry said.

"You're right. It's my pa-pa, Henry. I was remembering him."

The boy was intrigued. For a while he did nothing but sit on the idea that Tom had a father. The he said, "Wow."

Then Tom said, "There is something in you, as well."

"What do you see?"

"I see all kinds of things, unexplainable things. Powerful things."

"What do you mean, Tom?" Henry asked (from Tom's shoulders).

"Most importantly, I see that you need water. By golly you probably haven't eaten in a week. Let's make our way home for supper and milk."

Henry was again pained. When able, he agreed to go home. "Yes, that sounds terrific." And the two walked westward over one hill, through forest pathways, and towards a hut in one of many hut meadows there were on Greenlock Farm. It was modest but private and therefore safe -- peaceful. It was so very peaceful. Char-faced farmhands, bloodied, exhausted but relieved, straggled in from various directions. Many had their hearts set on home. The others traveled with buckets and, in one case, pulling a carriage carrying a bathtub filled with water.

They were fighting back against the current of flames at the heart of Greenback. Other farmhands wrangled the remaining orphaned locusts. One strange boy, Rich had a leash around a bug's neck. He struggled with the thing. It spit on him. He spit on it. The bug toothed his finger and scrambled away when Rich let the leash slip out of his hands. But the bug escaped only to be caught again and enslaved.

Everyone tried and succeeded and failed and tried again. It was all the same; these individual and collective struggles as many distinct keys blurring into chromaticism.

There were spores of tension here and some there that demanded one's eyes but that were too numerous to focus on all at once. For one, there was the basket-smuggling girl, affront the same hut where the Tomlesons had witnessed the Greenlocks romping about. It was a hedonistic hut, equipped with a stone chimney on the border of the stone bath, meant to provide heat to the bath via conduction but also via a cauldron hanging from a metal swivel that could be filled, heated, and dumped back into the tub. While most huts in this meadow (and most huts in Greenlock during these times) were stripped bare or had been bare from the beginning, improvised from this and that, this particular home was a grand monastery with gardens and stone creations including an out-door staircase that circled up from the basement library to the rooftop star-gazing observatory. A short split-railed fence lined the property. And white flowered fungus coated every rock face on the northern side.

The monastery-like home had thick walls, and an impenetrable door, which this girl pounded on with all her might, waling, "God-damnit. Let me in Elizabeth. Earnie, open up!"

Henry, atop Tom's shoulders, asked, "who is that, Tom?"

"I am unsure," Tom said, pushing on towards mother's hut.

But Henry pointed out, "she seems in distress" in such a pure, caring fashion that Tom couldn't help but yell to the girl "hey, Excuse me! Over here, yes. Are you alright?" Unfortunately, just as Tom caught her attention, this Elizabeth peeped out her door and slapped our young, frantic subject across her face. The door slammed. Then, rattled and crying, this girl ran off into the hut meadow.

"I hope she is okay," Henry said.

"I do as well, Henry."

With a few dozen strides came a familiar sight -- sunflowers too tall for their own good, bending and breaking; the family cat, too, too fat for his own good, slumped on the doorstep; and the pathetic 'door' made from two overlapping nailed boards leaned against the shack. This domicile was more boxy than the others. This is because the fellas, in their youth, had scavenged old cabinets and rectangular items of all kinds from the dump in Homverd. They carried them using one of Gerald's old carriages and a rented steed. The other hut-builders had taken comparatively leisurely routes gathering their materials.

Then there was Tom's neighbor, Paul. While the fellas were about thirty, this man, worn out but strong, was roughly 50. Now he carried a heavy load of garden hoses, various nozzles and things, along with an overflowing bucket of blood-stained water. It splashed and overflowed as he ran. He yelled to Tom.

"Tommy boy," he said. "Drop the kid at your mum's. Give me a hand. We're putting out the fires. It's all over, Tommy-boy. Time to rebuild! Like old times. Granger's coming home!"

"He is?" Tom asked.

"Ya, boy. C'mon! We want the fires out before dark."

Tom thought to put Henry down and go help. He looked to the boy, though, and ultimately Tom yelled back to his neighbor, "I'll meet you at Greenlock House. I've 'gotta check on me mum."

"Allll-right Tommy boy. Hey, and don't bother with the Master's place. Let it burn. Find someplace else to lend a hand."

"Okay, Paul. Watch your step out there."

"Oh, I will," Paul said, and he hobbled along carrying that heavy bucket of water. "Say hi to your mum for me."

Inside, Tom's mum rocked in her chair, unconcerned with

everything. It was odd, the way her son approached her without saying a word. Tom just walked toward her.

Henry said "hullo" fairly loudly.

But Tom explained, "she can't hear, Henry."

And boy muttered, "oh," pondering that concept. "I have never known a person who could not hear."

Tom lowered the boy down so that he could hug his mother. She prodded at Tom's shoulder. He was soar; she could tell. But the boy, he was the focus. Mrs. Fella made signs to him. She goochie goochie goo'ed him like a newborn. In a way, it was condescending considering all that Henry had been through. But Henry was amused. He smiled for the first time Tom had ever seen. Indeed this sign language interested him. So much so, he tried making signs of his own. He raised his hand, facing his palm down. Then he took his other hand and cupped it around the first, and with his hands like that, performed a swirling motion which concluded with the first hand, palm out, facing Tom's mother. The performance made him giggle and smile. Meanwhile Mrs. Fella watched confusedly, hunched over because of the way she'd been sitting for 30 years.

The woman's gaze locked onto Henry's palm. She was mute, but one could imagine her saying,

"Ohhhh lord, what is that? Tommy, what is that, on the boy's hand?

Ohhhh lord, on your hand too? What happened?"

Mrs. Fella rushed for water and soap. Waddling back, she waved her arms at Tom. She smiled at Henry. She washed their wounds with sharp, prickly soap. Amazingly, Henry showed no pain. Tom on the other hand winced at the stinging sensation. This confused Mrs. Fella, and she proceeded to sign to Tom:

"Who is this boy? He is made of stone."

Tom signed, ## "A special stone. Nothing can hurt him but the headaches."

"The headaches?"

"He is hungry, Mother. Thirsty too.".

The lovely woman rushed off for bread and apple juice.

Once the boy was eating and drinking, she could be seen signing this and that, catching up with her own child.

"This boy is beautiful," Tom said, "but he has nobody."

"I cannot care for him, Tom. I am old."

"It is my duty, Mother. Not yours."

"You love this boy?"

"Yes, mother."

"Okay. I love you, son."

She embraced her Tom, having not done so in too long a time. Henry ate his bread and toyed with some playing cards. It was curious. He would line them up and stare. Then he'd rearrange the cards and repeat endlessly and without boredom.

"I missed you," Mrs. Fella signed.

"I missed you as well Mother. Have you seen Joey?"

"Yes. He is outside. He is helping."

Smoke fluttered thickly between the trees. A gust of wind sent some sliding over outside of Tom's mother's kitchen window. People rushed to and fro. Tom could see them through this kitchen window. He looked toward the heart of the farm, imagining himself building post and beam structures with his own father and with Henry. He imagined tilling monumental fields, doing this and doing that, and transforming Greenlock into something of consequence. But he also looked to Henry, who sat at the kitchen table massaging his temples with two spoons.

Tom's mother asked, ## "Are you to find Joe?"

Tom replied, ## "No. I am not. I will take care of the boy."

Tom's mother smiled. Then she signed, ## "I love you, son," before returning to her chair and knitting herself to sleep.

The outside world yellowed with the lowering sun. Tom thought to step out and take a gander at the farm under the sunset, but he stopped, not wanting to give an impression of his departing. So he took to the sink window instead.

"Tom," Henry said. "What is out there?"

"Hmm?"

"What is outside?"

"Nothing," Tom said. "There is nothing. That is what's so strange."

"Tom," the boy said.

"What is it Henry?"

"I want to show you this some-thing."

"What is it?" Tom asked. But he was distracted by the window.

"I want to show you this some-thing Tom," Little One said.

"Oh, okay, yes." Tom peeled himself from the glass.

Henry had scrambled his entire deck of cards and played them out across the table. It was a square, tiled table, clean but for the cards. Henry had placed all of the other table items — the candle, the napkins, and the silverware — onto the floor beside his seat. He was excited.

"Look, Tom!" he said. "Look at the cards!"

"I am looking!"

"What is the code, Tom?"

"The code?"

"The formula! The pattern in the cards! The code! What is the code, Tom?"

Tom hadn't realized that there was a code. Henry was a boy. A special boy, undoubtedly. But what was he on about? What was the pattern?

The cards, Tom realized, were not randomly placed. They were arranged roughly into a spiral. There were four corners. Four interwoven curves, spiraling inward. On the outside, cards were precisely where they were meant to be. But on the inside, the order of things became increasingly hackneyed.

So Tom said "ahhh, I see. A cornucopia, like the one my mother gave me. On the mantle, there! You see. You are perceptive, Henry."

Henry smiled.

Tom continued. "My mother, she was sick. Ohhhh, she was sick. Her memories, they were fading. Then, one day, Joe was off courting a lady. I worked to prepare a roast. I am a cook,

Henry! I make good foods! Joe is the hunter. But on that day, my fire was low, Mother volunteered to gather some more wood. I told her it was not a smart idea to venture into the woods alone, but she nodded me off. She seemed alert enough, and I couldn't bear to allude to her condition. Before nighttime hours, she was typically alright anyways. So she wandered into the forest without her ears, her mouth, or her mind.

I began to worry after a while of her not coming home. When Joe returned, we searched for her. Two days past and she hadn't returned. We didn't know how to help; so Joe went again, carrying lantern, to see his Julie. And then, just after Joe made his way, I saw a shadow emerge from the trees. It was Mother, my lovely mother. Her cheek was bloodied, and her shoeless feet muddied, but she was smiling all the same. Do you understand, Henry? In her hands, she held that there cornucopia."

Henry had listened intently to Tom's story. Meanwhile, Tom had looked back and forth between the cornucopia and the window glass above the sink. Now Tom looked to Henry, and Henry couldn't help but smile; he smiled so widely, Tom grew suspicious.

He asked again, "do you understand?"

And Henry said, "Yes, it was a beautiful story. Your mother is a lovely woman, Tom. But…"

"But…?"

"But the cornucopia is not the code." Henry grinned.

Tom realized "there is more. Yes." He pointed. "Here, in this corner, we have the two of spades. And on this corner, the three of hearts. And here, the five of clubs. Finally, the seven. Now a four. Ah!. Traveling inward, they double or are multiplied by two."

"Oh, Tom, but sometimes they half."

"Yes, of course."

"And other times they do other things."

"They do?"

"Yes, Tom. The cards do all kinds of things, but what is the secret?"

Tom focused hard, following the spirals inward, looking for a pattern. Henry looked disappointed.

"I am no numbers man," Tom admitted.

"C'mon, Tom. What is the secret?"

Henry tilted his head and rubbed his chin, pretending to be thinking hard. "Think, Tom!" he said, and he scratched his ear theatrically. It was all theatrical.

Tom wanted to appease the boy, but he couldn't. He frustrated himself while trying to. And progress on the farm was rolling on, and he was sitting here thinking about playing cards. So he admitted. "I can't do the figuring, kid."

Henry sighed.

"What is it then?" Tom asked.

Henry sighed again. "A card deck contains 51 cards."

"You're one off, buddy. There are 52."

"But Tom, there are only 51 here."

As Tom began counting, Henry tapped his shoulder.

"Wait one moment," Henry said. "You have a some-thing behind your ear."

Tom was confused. Henry laughed, and there it was.

FIFTY-SIX

The mute mother of Tom was a knitting lady, filling every spare minute of her life with the craft. Over her years, though, she never produced a sweater or a mitten or a hat. People saw her toiling incessantly, and they wondered if she was obtuse. But they could not investigate further, because before leaving her rocking chair knitting quarters, she would lock away her progress in her green secret box.

Upon spare time from gardening and caring for her boys, she would take her key from her belt loop, and she would open her secret things box. From inside, she would retrieve a rectangular section to continue working on. Sometimes she would finish a section; in cases such as these, she would begin another.

What nobody realized was that, although a deaf-mute, Tom and Joe's mother was not a loon. She didn't stitch mittens or hats. Instead, she embroidered a grand tale into rectangular sections chronicling the history of the world.

Once Tom and Henry were dealt with, she hobbled over to her rocking chair and she continued her project. Thus far, the product of her knitting came only in the form of ordered rectangular sections. But as new days came (carrying new developments), she recorded the history as it happened on new rectangular sections. But she also begun knitting all of her sections together into a sweater. And in the center of this sweater, she embroidered a cornucopia.

On the first day hence, Tom mended Henry's wounds. They were deep, but the boy was strong. The cuts on his hands transformed into thick callus. On the outside, Tom's brother and the farmhands doused the fires which deposited ash everywhere from Greenlock House to the cliff-overlooking tree. The tree had deep roots, though, and so it did survive. It more than survived. Free from undergrowth and competition, there was abundant sunlight and rain and nutrients to be had. And in crisis, those deep, wrangly roots reached far, wide, for friends of all kinds to grab hold of and bring grain. The farm, likewise, had deep roots. So the farm and the tree alike grew tall and wide and balanced.

FIFTY-SEVEN

Tomph woke up in the barn. Realizing that it was daytime, he asked, "Yofim, what is the time?"

There were people out and about. The barn smelled of

death. The light and the sound and the smell… all things perceptual were a collective cringe. So Tomph covered his eyes and winced. Eyes covered, he called, "Yofim? It has been too long, I traveled too far." He sighed, "too far…"

"Yofim?" he called again.

The moment Tomph realized that there was no Yofim, the sun went down. But in this place of manure and death, Tomph smelled fresh air. He felt a cool breeze. Moonlight made the ash look like moon cheese, craters and all. It was dark, but light enough to see one's feet and a ways further; it was light enough to just one or two footprints in line of footprints ahead. Tomph followed these as though they were his guide, bordering large craters and hopping the small ones. Moving cautiously from one position in the unknown to another.

A familiar but froggy voice explained, "the unknown strikes fear in us, sure, but only when something is known."

Tomph walked onward, thinking little of the voice, thinking little of anything. He was vaguely reminded of something, but he couldn't make out what. He felt reminded — that was nearly all he felt. And he felt tranquil. Whenever a footprint ahead became illuminated ahead of him, Tomph's physicality was inclined to step forward. His feet would lift. Suddenly the footprint on which they stepped would become visible. But the ground was so dry. Each step would send a mushroom cloud up and outward. Then the cloud would drift back down. It would seem almost frozen in time. Eventually it would fall to the ground as a crater itself, perhaps inside of a larger crater. And the original footprint would be gone.

The phantom guru voice explained that, "with every footstep comes a footprint visible only until after you look upon yourself."

Looking onto himself, then behind his self, Tomph panicked at the idea that, by stepping forward, he turned precise history into something of lower definition.

"Look; see, history was, but history is no longer," the guru explained.

Tomph repeated this mantra aloud, "No longerrrrrr. Noo

longer. Nooooooo looooooonger," and an echo, a familiar kind, revolved upon him such that the "no"s and the "longer"s spliced and intermixed and overlapped.

The voice familiar but froggy explained, "No longer is this. No longer is that. This man stepped here. But his stepping said that he did not."

Somehow these words reverberated important and wholesome and clear over Tomph's mantra singing.

"How frightening it is," the guru admitted. "How frightening indeed."

Tomph walked upon many footprints, and he left craters in his wake. In his dream state, he didn't think that in order to preserve history, he could simply stop in his place. So, from one step came the next. He fretted over trampling yet again over a moment out of a person's tragically finite supply of moments. Tomph would nearly think to change something. But suddenly the next step was upon him, and he started from the beginning again because his frame of mind was narrower than the time between two steps. It was one moment. Then it was the next.

"It is frightening," the guru said. "But when nothing is known, one is most capable of considering oneself truly."

It was then Tomph pressed his hands against his heart. He felt nothing. For this reason, he panicked.

But the guru calmed him, explaining how, "acting in the way of the camel and not the horse, the heart has not a beat, but instead a continuous, perpetual circulation. Do not to worry, my camel."

Left was the matter of the overwritten histories. Tomph again found his eyes immersed in each successive destruction, each successive step. Each one ruined him sufficiently to distract him until the next destruction, the next step, which ruined him again. This inescapable cycle led him to become manic.

Until his guru reminded him that, "when one forgets all things, a certain kind of truth becomes most recognizable."

Tomph looked at himself to realize that he was wearing a

suit jacket and tie with ripped jeans and a top hat. And he realized that he was walking barefoot on the moon cheese. He wore no shoes, and so everything was okay. Looking up again, all that there was was a grand moon-lit moonscape. There were craters in every direction. Tomph walked forward, not worried about where he stepped or where he did not step. He walked this way for a ways.

Then the familiar but froggy voice returned. It said. "Okay, good camel: you have gone far enough. Look into your palms and learn what is the next step."

Revealed in Tomph's open hand was the talking peach — ravaged by many bites, cauterized by fire, and smashed by a fall. It existed in his open hand only long enough to be perceived. Then it was dust, having burst into a mushroom cloud above Tomph's head. Peach seeds wafted in said cloud, and fell to the ground. One seed sprouted immediately upon touching the dirt, into a grand peach tree! It was only a moment before this tree blossomed wholesome and full, supporting good and plump fruits.

Tomph stood no longer at the heart of the farm. He found himself teleported to the top of the mountain, level with the clouds.

The next step was to rushedly gather these seeds, and with them, to plant rows upon rows of peach trees. These rows produced echoing, reverberating growth.

At the base of the king tree, two ropes laid like snakes coiled on the ground. Each had a loop on one end and a knot on the other.

Tomph realized that he was not a moon man, but a man.

The king tree regressed. It stood just barely as a nub stump on the ground. But it TRIED to grow. Tomph could see how hard it tried. And so he gathered many peaches, one from each tree and he TRIED squeezing their water upon the tree. He TRIED and he TRIED. And GROWTH came. The tree continued growing, under the clouds in the sky which zoomed along as they did.

An Easter Island type of stone stood tall beside the rock

stairway entrance to the mountain top. The stone was matted in ash which Tomph swashed away with his hand. Doing this on the downhill side of the stone, he revealed engravings that read "Gobbler's Round: beware of the pull."

Past this stone, Tomph strolled down and around the windy mountain path that seemed to curl under itself like a round staircase, around and around itself, through layers of clouds and down towards reality. He strolled... he strolled. Down around the staircase path, which, on its steepest section, was made from almost unmanageably narrow stone steps and short stone rails. The situation was made worse by the darkness. For much of the journey, Tomph could not stroll; he crawled carefully. But eventually the steepness disapaited, and he strolled again.

It was a long way down the goat path. And it was such a treacherous way, Tomph moved at the pace of the moon's falling, and as well, the sun's rise. When he found himself upon level ground, it was morning. The birds chirped and flew, tending to their usual business of food and song. Morning dew coated the grassy mountain meadows and the forest greenery.

A windy path led Tomph to the forest. The path, it was so old, so worn. Moss grew over the stepping stones and the gravel packed in between them. And moss grew on the logs bordering the path that had had sunk into the dirt to the point of being level with the ground. Tomph had come to the section of path through the forest. The forest encroached upon and claimed man's work. Yet it allowed and nearly encouraged man's passage. The birds, the trees, and the life in general was preoccupied if not welcoming.

Then there was a flatland meadow, huts all around. A sudden and complete calmness brought closure to Tomph's journey home. A clothesline rattled gently with the breeze. It was empty but for garments stained pink and covered in mud. A shovel laid against the side of a tee-pee, innocuously as ever. The gardens appeared to have been harvested and tilled. Compost fires smoldered in various places. There was a compost fire in the center of each garden. They were unattended fires of dry flowers and dry cornstalks.

Our hero felt great resolution in this meadow village. Of all the places and meadows of Greenlock, this was where his journey led him? It was the first vague sense of home he had felt in a long time.

He resolved to nik the aforementioned shovel and enter the largest of the nearby gardens, apparently the village garden, in contrast with the smaller, hut-specific gardens. A short, rotten-posted chicken wire fence protected the garden. And while Tomph very could have stepped over it, he opted to unlatch the gate, step inside, and re-latch the gate behind him.

Our hero tended to the smoldering fires in the way an old shop owner might sweep his floor after a days work at the shop that doubles as his home. Tomph consolidated and tilled, and consolidated and tilled, and consolidated and tilled, even when all he was doing was shoveling dirt. He fed the flames with whatever sticks and cornstalks and abandoned t-shirts that he could find.

The sun remained low despite its rising.

To our hero wandered a man --- an exhausted man who at first appeared suspicious of Tomph's presence, but in reality was not suspicious at all, but instead, tired and stunned because of his brain's having been scrambled like an egg.

The man admitted, "I cannot sleep. I haven't in I can't remember how long."

And Tomph thought for a moment, and he looked at the man, and our hero said, "you've reminded me of sleep. I haven't slept in weeks."

This was a verbal handshake of sorts between the sleepless, fence-separated lads. Afterwards, the man made his way inside the gate in the same composed fashion Tomph had. He was sure to open and close the gate properly. Tomph observed and was comforted by this.

"Tending to the fires?" the man asked.

Tomph nodded.

"I'll give you a hand," the man said.

His hair was ruffled, his beard unshaven, his age high in the twenties. The man uncovered a shovel from the ash. With it, he raked the remains of locusts and broken cornstalks inwards. Meanwhile Tomph looked over the locusts, mistaking them for hallucinations. He chose to ignore them and instead focus on the cornstalks and the coals, piling them such that they would burn most thoroughly.

The man noticed Tomph's eyes stuck on one of the locusts. "Demonic things, aren't they?" he remarked.

"They are," Tomph admitted.

"I have seen terrible things. These are not the worst," the man said.

"What have you seen?" Tomph asked.

"Oh so many things. It feels as though this past week spanned years."

"I wonder if it has," Tomph said.

"I've seen the most beautiful of things, and the most evil of things. I've experienced curiosity of the child's kind. I've seen another world. But I've also tasted insanity. I've smelled my own death. I tasted a touch of the universe!"

"How did it taste?" Tomph asked.

"What?"

"How did the universe taste?"

"It brought me to speak with death. It made me feel fear so overwhelmingly that there wasn't time to think."

"I don't understand," Tomph said. At this point, the boy was shoveling on, conversing only passively. The man, however, was absorbed in his memories so completely, he did nothing but wave his arms and look to the sky, then the dirt, then the sky, with his shovel propped against his side.

"I was watching this magnificent girl. She was a woman. A mother! Pushing her child on some swings. 'Higher, higher', the child was begging. The mother pushed harder. She was only so strong, and the child whined more. That brought disappointment, so much disappointment on the mother's part. Exhausted, she trudged on. She was stepping into each push. Each push built on the previous. The boy swung high, but not high enough. So the mother ran, carrying herself under the boy as he swung upward, and thrusted her strong arms outward as far as the could go, pushing him to the sky. Building... building... Running back to catch his next swing, I saw: the mother smiled wide.. But I realized, on this particular swingup, that she would launch her son over the pivot of the swingset and inevitably toward pain and suffering. So I called out to her. But she was so beautiful, smiling.. I warned her so quietly. The mother put more strength into this push than she had for any of the previous. She even extended her fingertips and toes at the end of her throw, garnering all the power she could. The boy flew into the sky. And he transformed into a buzzing bee, good and fed; and his mother became a flower. The swing turned into scattering pollen particles in a garden of sunflowers. Do you believe that?"

"I don't know what to believe," Tomph said.

"But then, from the bee and his flower, came a bird buzzing around a tree. And eventually, it all became a tetherball flinging around its pole. But before that, I saw a million different worlds, each structurally the same, fundamentally, but so lively and individual nonetheless."

"That sounds incredible." Tomph admitted. "Things are very incredible on some occasions. Then they aren't. Then they are."

The boy looked to his shovel, which had stopped shoveling a while earlier. Its head was ashy and covered in dried mud. But there was a cleanly spot on it off which the rising sun reflected.

The man explained, "It all felt so instantaneous, between the first transformation and the last. The instant that buzzer bee left his mother's grasp, was when I opened my eyes."

"Golly," Tomph said.

"Then I was drowning in death. Horrible horrible horror! Innocence, goodness, plundered for cheap jewelry!! His neck cut and a candle stuck through the hole."

"Hey... hey!!" Tomph yelled. "What are you doing? You're staring into the sun!!" He slapped his companion on the shoulder, then the cheek, playfully, as he used to do to Yofim. Returning to reality, the man strained. He rubbed his eyes with his fists, in pain, letting his shovel fall to the ground. Tomph asked him, "can you see?"

"Jesus, I am not alright," the man said.

"You aren't. Don't do things like that. Because if you do, you will be hurt or made dead or made blind. Can you see? Let me help you as you have helped me."

Looking toward Tomph, the man saw blearily a rough looking boy but also an angel of pure goodness, light so bright only the truly good could bare to see it. The man looked away from the angelic figure who hovered above the treacherous ground, glowing, equipped with wings and a halo and all. At first, the man could not see. But Tomph's light grew gradually more bearable.

So the man answered, "yes, yes, I can see more clearly than I ever."

"Good," Tomph said. "I see that the sun is rising. Let us go for a walk."

"Let us step here and there and here again!" the man exclaimed.

"A walk will do, I think," Tomph said.

"No, it is more than that!"

"Sure it is," Tomph said.

"Yes!"

So Tomph and this man walked down a road toward no place in particular. The man talked. He talked and talked. The birds flew around chirping because they were alive. A horse rider came running against Tomph and the man's direction, toward the village. On his way, the rider, an older man, greeted them, "morning boys, I'm looking for Syd's meadow." And he asked, "Do you know where that is?"

Tomph didn't. His companion, however, did, and he proceeded to explain, "It's through this meadow here, this is Paul's meadow. Then you'll find two paths on the opposite side. Take the lower one. You'll find no uncertainties after that point. Just watch out for this and that and this and that, you know."

"This and that?" the rider asked confusedly.

"Yeah, this and that and that and this," the man reaffirmed.

Tomph interjected, "My companion hasn't had much sleep."

"Okay, son. Yes. He looks quite… quite fried. Quite fried indeed. But yes, thank you, son, and thank you as well, fried one. I'll be on my way. May this gorgeous day treat you good and proper."

"Indeed!! And you as well!!" The fried one emphatically said. He added an emphatic salute as well, mimicking the slight, satirical salute that the rider had thrown to him from his brimmed cap as he rode off. "Nice fellow," the fried one said.

"Indeed," Tomph confirmed, smiling, nodding his chin. "Indeed."

Off they went, to this place and to that place, two daybats romping the world. More and more, as the morning rose, things around them grew busier. First the lone rider. Not long after his passing, he passed again in the opposite direction, and he said that he would "return by the noon hour". Shortly after, a carriage approached from the original direction. A haggardly voice called from inside, "driver! That is far enough." The voice's woman peeped her head, first, through a small octagonal window; then she hobbled to the carriage front. Each of her steps made cracks and torsion creaks. It was almost like music.

So Tomph thought, "This reminds me of the Everything Man!".

"Yeah! Everything!" Our hero's companion agreed enthusiastically but somewhat emptily.

"Do you know the Everything Man?" Tomph asked.

"Of course! The man of everything! Everything!" Fried Man proclaimed, pretending to wrap his arms and eyes around the entire planet.

"You are a lune," Tomph told him.

"What do you mean?"

"I mean the Everything Man, the man from Homverd who

carries drums and bells and whistles. He uses his fingers and toes and arms and legs, his voice and everything. Everything is an instrument for him. Take any thing, and he'll play music from it."

"Oh…" fried man said. "I thought you were talking about the other Everything Man: The Everything Man!"

"My apologies, I was not."

The hag on the carriage now propped her fat leg out from behind the curtains on her enclosure. Her head followed suit. Then came the rest of her fat body capped with a sun hat with a ridiculous feather sticking out of it.

After taking some breaths and waving her hand fan at her face, she said, "Excuse me. Do you boys know where I could find Syd's Meadow?"

"Oh it's right that way, ma'am."

"Thank you, child. I sure do wish I could call you handsome, but I must admit that you two are looking quite unswell if I do say so myself. I do wish you the best now, as I go on my way."

"What's the occasion at Syd's meadow?" Fried Man asked. But the carriage had already begun moving.

The lady hadn't yet returned inside, though, and, waving her fan, scanning the horizon, she said, "We at Chazborough keep to ourselves. But when Greenlock (of all places) could use a hand, we put down our beers, and we bring all the hands we have. Expect the convoy shortly."

"Thank you, Ma'am."

"You are welcome, young man. Goodbye, now." She waved goodbye with her fan. Fried man waved back. Meanwhile Tomph held his hand still in the air. They were left alone on the forested dirt path. The dust had settled, and they walked along listening to the many sounds that nestled in from different directions.

"I here shovels, and a hammering," Tomph said.

"Yes, and I hear voices."

"Coming from where?"

Fried Man thought hard, then he pointed in the direction

they walked. But he also pointed backwards toward Paul's meadow, where Earnie lived and where the fellas live with their mother. Behind them, the sounds were loud but steady. In the forward direction, things were quieter, but loudening.

Tomph took a side road too narrow to be traveled by carriage.

"Why this way?" Fried Man asked.

"Because the convoy is coming, and we are loons. This road is no place for us."

"Buuuut the convoy is full of nice people! Good people. And probably, they have biscuits! I here that the convoy has the best biscuits!"

Fried Man protested but followed nonetheless when Tomph assured him "we'll find biscuits elsewhere" and strided forward. The trail, it followed near-parallel to the main road. At first only 10 meters or so of brush separated the two. So when segments of the convoy came passing by, carrying old friends who jibbered and jabbered, catching up with one another, Tomph had to restrain Fried Man to keep him from drawing attention.

"Quickly, behind here," Tomph said. At first Fried man was confused. Tomph pulled him back behind a tree. Some carriages would soon be passing.

Fried Man looked Tomph in the eye, as a dog would when wanting to ask, "what have I done wrong?"

"If we are seen, then we will be caught, and we cannot be caught. Not today," Tomph said.

"Oh, I understand," Fried man said (a bit too loudly). "We have to do the hiding dance now. Okay. Okay! Yes!"

He was excited so much so that, again, Tomph was forced to pull him behind a tree and hush him. But more carriages were nearing now. Tomph couldn't stop Fried man from peeping around the bark. So he hid with his eyes closed, hoping that, if Fried Man were discovered, he himself might be overlooked. Fortunately the convoy was preoccupied as they passed by. There were ladies jabbering and jabbering. One driver conversed with the next driver who was 15 meters or so behind him. A dozen men and boys worked to stabilize a far oversized trailer load of, among other things, a drum from which water splashed down atop one boy who played as boys play in the sprinkler. The men were less amused, soaked and uncomfortable. One man spoke of rice. Another mentioned mules.

Then there was quiet. Tomph opened his opened eyes to see Fried Man sneaking like an undercover operative along the road bank. He was in the woods just beside the trail. Crawling in the roadside ditch.

"C'mon, you, don't you want to see the most beautiful place in the world?" Tomph asked.

"I thought it was sneaking time. Y'know, covert activity." Fried Man winked.

"No, you loon. We can walk normally now."

Fried Man crouched now when before he had been prone. As if being hunched over would make up for his standing in plain sight for a mile each way. Again he stared confusedly like a dog. But in short order, he jumped to and led the way.

"Alright, then, my friend. Off we go!" he said.

"Yes, let's!" Tomph said, trailing behind.

"Oh, bollocks. Where is our destination?" Fried Man asked.

"Our destination is the final step in a sequence of increasingly significant destinations," Tomph explained. "Our first is that there stone, the painted stone, there, on the trail's horizon."

"Wonderful, lad! Rendezvous there. But wait! We must complete the briefing firstly."

"Of course," Tomph said.

"Brief me then. I desire to be briefed."

"Okay," Tomph said, kicking dirt about. "Bring me a utensil, Fried Man, and I will convey to you information in the optimal way."

"Of course," said Fried Man. "Yes!". Then he skipped into the woods muttering the mantra, "Yesterday I saw a pristine utensil, I knew you'd require. I saw a pristine utensil, I knew you'd require. I saw a pristine utensil, I knew you would require." The trees muffled the mantra as Fried Man made distance.

FIFTY-EIGHT

A horse rider came galloping by, casting sound over what could still be heard of Fried Man. When the rider passed, things became quiet again, and Fried Man could no longer be heard. Tomph called to Fried Man. But on came another slinking cluster of carriages, these ones struggling more than the last. As they neared, it became apparent that the carriages, but for the leading car, were pulled by mules in place of steeds. Likewise, these carriages, but for the first car, weren't meant for passengers. Instead they overflowed with barrels upon barrels upon containers of miscellaneous kinds. The leading horse pulled a small two-wheeled trailer, which towed a trailing rope which guided a pair of mules, who pulled a load of rice, which towed a trailing line, which guided another pair of mules, which pulled more rice and more mules and more rice. There were six rice carriages in total. Twelve mules.

Tomph observed the driver grumble and ache as his carriage hit bumps that caused him to be compressed and sprung. A lifetime of lumpy roads had ground his spine to rubble. Now he was more akin to pudding than man.

In the far rear of the convoy, hidden by larger carriages, was a small cart in which a boy sat facing backward with a horn strapped around his neck. He was being pulled along. Soon Tomph could see his face. It was not a his face, but a her face — a young girl. Scanning the horizon fearfully, whistling a tune, she was so beautiful, Tomph gasped, and he thought of Yofim sitting beside this girl, making jokes, making her smile. But soon the girl was a girl no longer. She fattened and wrinkled and grew hair on her arms. Simultaneously, her physicality dissolved into transparency, and in this transparency, a small boy illuminated into existence, occupying the same space as his withering mother. Tomph remembered them so clearly. At the wetlands playground, the mother had told him to watch over her boy. But now she was gone, living through her boy who now was more than a boy, older and probably less in need of watching than Tomph himself. He wore his mother's horn, and he watched out for bandits in the woods as his mother once had.

Tomph found himself at the painted stone. More than a stone, it was a monolith, painted in remembrance of a beloved someone. It was a portrait of a silhouette looking a sunset over cliffside. It was from the perspective of behind the silhouette. In the background (over the cliffside), there was an impossibly detailed portrayal of the farm, blessed with heavenly colors, with people all around doing things, drawing crop circles in corn and hay that read things like "remember him always" and "consider not only who you feel for, but who feels for you, when you contemplate him".

Rounding the monolith, Tomph found a set of keys atop an upright piano that was tucked into the underside of an overturned tree. He sat at the piano on one of two log-carved seats that were just sufficiently rotten to be comfortable. And he played, and he sung.

> *"Under the water but over the fish,*
> *Beside my pillowcase I make a wish.*
> *I breath, I breath.*
> *It strides, it bellows.*
> *I'm lonely, I need*
> *Yofim, good fellow.*
>
> *He runs, he hides.*
> *I yell, I scream.*
> *Where are you daft one?*
> *I'm alone; I'm scared.*

My wish, my blend. Yofim gave.
Now it's up-end; Yofim stayed.
Where are you my friend?
I am in need of amends.

I wish you'd come,
and you'd bring
tunes for us to sing.

I wish you'd come
and you'd bring Fried Man and we could walk around together."

Having finished, Tomph bowed his head and he allowed his hands to fall to his lap. His sounds continue reverberating in the woods, he deduced, because the sustain petal had rusted thickly down and because moss had grown atop it.

Quietly but loudeningly came a

DONGGG, BONG, TRUMMMM, HUMMMMMM
VRUMMMMMMMMMMMMMMMMMMM, HUMMMMM
TRMMMMMMMMMM BON VRRR HUMMMMM

Tomph looked left and there he was — Fried Man — sitting on the left stump, playing the low notes.

Fried Man asked Tomph, "Why have you stopped playing?"

Tomph looked to his own hands, then to Fried Man, then in the opposite direction. Far into the rightward, he could see a boy; it was Yofim! in the distance, waving, smiling, putting his thumb up. Tomph was made smile by his old friend who glistened like the cart-riding boy had, and as that boy's mother had when she was young.

To Fried Man's dissonant chords, Tomph improvised with one hand a schoolhouse melody of the intuition. Yofim grooved in the distance. But the sun rising and shining through the trees, made Yofim hard to see. Still, the jovial ghost grooved, and Tomph played. They smiled at each other.

When the time was right, Fried Man reached his right hand over Tomph toward the high notes. He made eye contact, as to say, "watch this." After showing Tomph a syncopated rhythm of chords consonant with the bass notes, Fried Man return to his side of the keys. His left, still playing the base chords. His right, improvising a glorious building accompaniment. And Tomph, continuing his melody while also syncopating it all, as Fried Man had showed him. It was so wholesome there, behind the monolith, that Yofim danced himself out of existence. The sun had risen.

The music playing dulled upon Yofim's fading. An overarching dissonance masked everything musical. So Tomph stood, stretched out his legs and wiped the dirt off his bottom. Again he was alone. But soon he found Fried Man sitting against the opposite side of the painted rock, eyes closed, resting.

"Fried Man?" Tomph said. "Are you sleeping?"

"I was, yes."

"Why?"

"Why, I suppose because this was our first destination of a series of increasingly significant destinations. It's been two and one half hours, if my sun reading skills have not forsaken me. We ought to proceed."

"Fair enough," Tomph admitted.

"What are we doing, anyway? Why am I following you?" Fried Man asked.

"I don't know."

"Because, of all the things I ought to be doing under these circumstances, I can't ponder anything of lower priority than running in circles with a child."

Tomph thought for a moment. He appeared angry, then worried, then resolved. And he said, "Shut up, Fried Man! Have you the utensil?" with such absolute resolve that Fried Man could not help but grin a maniacal grin and pull the utensil from his pocket and brandished. "Perfect, Tomph said."

"Time for briefing?" Fried Man asked.

"Time for briefing! Yes!" Tomph said, proceeding to draw in the dirt with the stick that Fried Man had retrieved.

"Alright, what have we here?" Fried Man asked.
"That is the barn."
"And here?", Fried Man asked.
"That is the garden."
"Which garden?" Fried Man asked.
"THE garden."
Alright, now this circle here?" Fried Man asked.
"That is where we stand."
"Of course, captain. How could I be so Foolish?"
"In the same way I was so foolish disappear, thinking you'd disappeared," Tomph said.
"Yes. Right. Exactly. Now, captain, what is the 'X'?"
Tomph smiled.
"What is it, my captain?"
"That is our coming destination!"
"Yes! I will lead you there."

Tomph said, "With haste, Fried Man!" And they were off darting through brush and trails. On trails. Off trials. Behind fieldstone walls bordering fields on which people and carriages gathered. Large bonfires burned. The farm smelt of pig. Silence was imperative.

The brush thinned and allowed Fried man to move faster. Tomph struggled to keep up.

But Fried Man called back, "Captain, with haste!"

Tomph, struggling to run, said, "Shut up, Fried Man!"

"Of course, yes," Fried Man said, and he continued on. Moments later, he circled around, allowing Tomph up front. Then he, Fried Man, accelerated tenfold. Like a horse, he scooped his rider, and together they embarked toward the countryside.

Fried Man admitted, "I have lost my way, captain."

But Tomph assured him. "Fried Man, my steed, worry not!"

"Of course! Yes! Yes!"

Field after field they past was burned, and many homes were nothing more. As such, when Fried Man requested direction, Tomph had his mind preoccupied. "Everything is burned," he said. "Why is everything burned."

Realizing the severity of the situation at hand, Fried Man asked, "Why? Why must you wallow in historical misfortune? You mustn't, my captain. We have destinations ahead of us that must be reached! Let us think forward!"

"You are right, Fried Man. My steed, I am sorry for requiring your psychological as well as your physical aid."

"Worry not, my caption. Let us run!"

"Let us! My. oh. my."

"At the coming fork, which will be my direction?" Fried Man asked.

"Leftward, my steed. Leftward here," Tomph said.

"Yes, my captain!"

"Now leftward again."

"Yes, my captain!"

"Finally, go rightward!"

"Yes, my captain!" Fried Man hollered as he darted between a shed and a fence, then through a gap in a boarded fence.

"Onward onward onward!!!" Tomph yelled. "Charge!!"

Suddenly they were in the open again, rushing toward these towering mounds about which Fried Man didn't ask. Galloping galloping galloping. Stumble. Balance lost. No. Balance returned.

"Stop. Stop! Halt, my steed!"

From his near fall, Fried Man skidded to zero affront a sign that read "EAST DEPOSITORY. Use permitted only by direct permission from Uncle Edward himself. All business otherwise, be gone."

Tomph unmounted. He led Fried Man, first, into a shack that stood just outside the depository fence. It was a trailer, this shack. And its door was unavoidably locked. Tomph entered and exited the window before Fried Man could think. When he exited and made his way toward the gate, Fried Man was in awe. Tomph fiddled with the lock for a moment. Then, with pride, he yelled, "Men, we are here!" He pushed the gates open wide.

"Genius!"

"Why thank you, Fried Man!"

Tomph proceeded into the depository, explaining to "heed warnings of this dog and that. They are nasty demon dogs. Not to be challenged." Fried Man followed closely behind, fearing these dogs for himself and for his captain, whom he had sworn to "protect, regardless of the circumstances."

"I appreciate your loyalty, my steed," Tomph said.

"We must push forward."

"Yes, you are right, my steed. But I must warn you, it is not me who will need protecting here. For the dogs are friends to me."

"Are they?"

"They stop at the licking of my face. From you, though, they will tear limbs and leave you as a sausage," Tomph said.

"An atrocious way to go, surely," Fried Man acknowledged.

"Yes."

"I will take utmost precaution, then."

"That would be wise, my steed."

"Indeed."

There were piles of metal. There were tangles of rope. There were kid's toys and yarn balls. There were cabinets and doors. Yes, cabinets — perfect; Tomph skidded to a halt. Quickly he scrambled through cabinets and cabinets, ripping off their doors and sizing them. Finally, he found a cabinet door that satisfied him enough. He showed it to Fried Man. "A noble taking, no?" he asked.

"Hold on, I must examine the thing," Fried Man said. He inspected every corner and crease, every warp and texture. Promptly, he put his thumb and forefinger to his chin. He was deliberating.

"What is it, Fried Man?"

"I am afraid to say."

"Please, do not be intimidated. I am a mere man, as any man is," Tomph said. "Speak as you are inclined; I will respond earnestly, graciously."

For a moment Fried Man contemplated this thought.

Promptly he said, "yes! Alright. Hold the board firm, captain."

Tomph did so.

With a swift blow, Fried Man busted a whole clean through the cabinet door.

Tomph shook his head. He was flabbergasted that Fried Man would demolish his treasured finding. After brief mourning, he admitted, "then that is that, I suppose," before becoming overwhelmed with sadness, so much so, he dropped to his knees and cried. Fried Man dropped to his knees as well, certainly not feeling what Tomph felt, but expressing a willingness to understand or to provide help of some kind.

"Why are you calm? Why must you grin such a maniacal grin?" Tomph asked.

"Because, my caption, I do not understand — I do not believe I ever could. But this wood is flimsy."

"Yes, so why must you grin? Our purpose is foiled. We are empty. I am empty. And in emptiness, my roads and cavities are vulnerable to be bloodied by sadness in its purest form."

"My captain. Please, compose yourself. That is exactly it! Our purpose! Mount my shoulders, this instant!"

Reluctantly, Tomph climbed onto Fried Man's back. Then Fried Man galloped onward yelling "yes, yes! Yes!", fleeing from the countryside. They made their way all the way back the direction from which they came, left then left then right, this way then that.

In the fields, people mingled and worked, unloading supplies from carriages. In the woods, the ghost of Yofim wandered in circles and caught toads. Behind the monolith, the motherless boy tapped a quiet melody with his one and sometimes two fingers. It was early afternoon. Greenlock felt alive again, though still somewhat groggy from sleep.

FIFTY-NINE

Henry navigated the crowded fields while holding onto Tom's hand. There were people of all shapes, all colors. And while many people of Greenlock chatted with their visitors — to some about old times and to others about today — Tom knew nobody and he found himself having little to say. Still he was sure to be cordial to anyone who looked upon him or Henry.

"Hello there, how do you do?" Tom would say.

And a concerned fellow would reply "Well enough. I hope for you the same, my friend." Crouching down, this onlooking fellow would clasp Henry's hand gently as one clasps a frog, and he would say "I express my deepest sympathy for your hardship, young one. It is my hope that our givings will stand you on your feet. It is my hope that our aid will make the community whole again."

Henry would smile somehow knowingly. He would say "Your givings will help the farm. I am certain.

The fellow would smile. And Henry would smile. And a glimpse of God would emit from their clasped hands. "Very well then," the fellow would say, smiling so wholesomely, and he would notice men smaller than him lifting heavy barrels of rice. And he would point with his eyes; "I must lend my hand," he would say. "Shall we re-unite upon Granger's coming?"

"Yes," Henry would exclaim. "Of course! We will dance!"

"We will dance as Granger himself did!" the fellow would exclaim. Then he would shake Tom's hand, looking him in the eyes and whispering so Henry couldn't hear, "Thank you for your service, my friend. Thank you. For serving this boy, you are the friend of many."

This fellow would go on his way. Then Tom, the patron

saint, would follow his boy Henry around as people worked and conversed. Many people stopped and smiled when given the opportunity to greet the boy. Farmhands and foreign friends of all kinds came to speak with the boy. Tom learned to say only what was asked of him. Henry was the spectacle, and in the spectacle, despite his youth, he shined wisdom and love and hope.

Once most people in the area had said their words to Henry and heard Henry's words, it was Tom's chance. So, in the forest of foreign hearts, Tom pulled Henry aside.

"There is a whole lot of unknown inside you, my boy, is there not?" he asked.

"What do you mean, Tom?"

"I mean, you are so serene when these fellows speak with you of this and of that. It as though you already know."

"We should all be serene, Tom. Should we not?"

For a while, Tom thought. He muttered, "after all this….", and he thought more, and he looked into the boy's eyes, which were so engulfing and calming, and he, Tom, said, "There is a whole world inside of you, boy. I would like to understand it someday."

"No you wouldn't, Tom."

For a while, Tom thought. He thought and he thought. Eventually, he acknowledged that Henry was right.

Henry did not wince, bat an eye, or express any bit of reaction to Tom's words. Upon their passing, he asked, calmly and unaffected as ever, but curiously: "How does Granger dance?"

Tom admitted, "I do not know. I'm sorry, Henry."

"It is okay," Henry said, still holding Tom's hand (but not because he himself needed his hand held).

Suddenly there was a ruckus. A rider had arrived. Farmhands and foreigners alike gathered to hear his message. The rider waited for people to finish gathering. Then he stood in his stirrups to proclaim, "A MESSAGE FROM THE SOUL HIMSELF, HAMZA, MODERNLY OF GRANGER'S VILLAGE!!"

When everyone gathered around the rider, the patron saint and his boy were left alone. In lonesome, Henry asked Tom, "Can we go home now, Tom?"

"Of course," Tom said. "But may I ask why?"

"Granger's arrival won't be for a while. I would like to see your mother before he comes."

"Okay. Yes. Okay. Let us walk this way. I know a path."

SIXTY

Fried Man, with Tomph on his shoulders, galloped down the same path that Tom was leading Henry toward. Tomph looked side to side. He focused through the middlebrush into the meadow where all those foreigners and farmhands had congregated. He tried listening to the message from Hamza, but it was hard to make out the rider's words from such distance. So Tomph's focus wandered, first looking here, then looking there. He caught eyes with Tom, who was leading the boy carefully through a short connecting path that led from the field to the main path. The boy trudged carefully with his eyes down, for the connector was overgrown. So Tomph never saw his face. With Tom, however, he locked eyes. Tom was lifting vines and pushing underbrush aside to aid Henry. Both Tomph and Tom were perplexed at the sight of eachother.

As Fried Man galloped onward, Tomph pivoted his head to keep eyes with Tom. The familiar face re-conjured in Tomph's mind a million connections to his past, a million random daily interactions and passings by on the Greenlock Farm.

But as quickly as their eyes met, the forestry came between them. Fried Man cut one way, then another. Soon they galloped beside the garden where they had met. Tomph was amazed by luscious new grow that had emerged from the garden ashes. But again, Fried Man cut this way and then in that direction. Tomph caught glimpses of huts of various kinds. He saw smoke rising from chimney pipes. Then he passed through a door. Then he found himself engulfed by finely finished carpentry. A keystone caught his eye. A fire burned below this in a finely crafted fireplace. The smell of bread wafted strongly.

"Mmmmm it smells so heavenly," Fried Man said. "It has been a long while since I've smelled this smell."

"Where are we?" Tomph asked. "It is familiar."

"My captain, we are at the house of Hamza! Do you know why it is familiar?"

"I'm unsure," Tomph said, still pondering.

"Likely because you were born here! The birthplace of the captain!! Think of that." Approaching the other room, approaching the smell of bread, Fried Man muttered, "The birthplace of everyone..."

"I'm unsure about that..." Tomph thought. But he found himself alone.

From the other room, Fried Man mmmmmm'ed and bragged. "Ohhhhh, this is so delicious, captain. You must have a taste. I mean it! I won't have another bite until you feast yourself on this buttery goodness. The captain eats first! Well, second... but first!!"

Tomph explored the million little knick-knacks and things in the quirky domicile. There were a million masterly crafted shelves and revolving doors, each and every one strong and beautiful. The wood, it was pine with a thick polyurethane coating that made it shine and that reminded Tomph of the upper floors in the barn. Also there were statues and figurines that shined their respective shines. But suddenly there was silence; Tomph suspected trouble. So he went into the other room to find Fried Man fried again and sitting on a rocking chair, buttery bread in one hand, a book in the other, a spoon full of butter resting on his tongue. He drooled dumb while staring into The Book which grasped him firmly. Tomph roundhouse kicked this book out of Fried Man's hand and to the shadowy corner of the room. Fried Man's spoon bounced on the hardwood, and Tomph's companion rubbed his eyes.

"Never read those words!" Tomph said.

"Of course, my captain!. I would never! But you must try this bread. Come here."

As the rocking chair rocked uninhabited, candles burned atop a hand-carved picnic table. Fried Man sat down. He waved for Tomph to do the same. When he did, Fried Man patted his captain on the shoulder. To Tomph he slid a plate on which there was bread and a knife. The butter was on a separate plate between captain and steed. Fried Man made eye contact as he buttered himself a slice. Tomph took this as a hint for him to do the same, and so he did. When Tomph sunk his teeth into the goodness, Fried Man smiled.

"Good, yes?"

"Mmmmmmmm, this is wonderful. I wonder where it came from," Tomph said.

"Well of course, it was me who fixed it for you caption."

"Oh, you did?"

"Of course!" Fried Man said.

"Why thank you, Fried Man. I must say, it is delicious. Thank you."

Under candle light, they sipped wine and took small, sophisticated bites of delicate bread. The crackling from the fireplace in the living room could be heard. And there was complete peace.

Soon Fried Man rose and said "that is enough for me." He asked Tomph if he was satisfied. Tomph said that he was. So, from within one of his many pockets, Fried Man retrieved a key ring. One particular key — a large, hand-forged iron key — became the spectacle. With this in mind, the two approached an especially large door covered with intricate engravings. It was a very important door; as such, it was endowed with a heavy iron lock. With some effort, Fried Man jimmied it open.

Fried Man and Tomph made their way into the dark room. They left the door open behind them. They'd left their plates and bread crumbs on the kitchen table. Fried Man rummaged around without explaining himself. Tomph could barely see him, but he did see Fried Man reach upwards to pull a string. This string rounded one pulley, and then it forked in two different directions. The two consequent strands wrapped around separate pulleys in order to pull from opposite directions the double doors of Hamza's grand skylight.

Amazing natural sunlight illuminated the room. Craftsman tools packed shelves from wall to wall. There were saws and planers and screws. Hinges and paints and stains. And on the center work table, directly below the skylight, there laid a violin that smelled fresh of polyurethane. It shined bright — so bright, Tomph was inclined raise the bow and play. Upon completion of a short tune, he found Fried Man on his knees, bowing to his captain.

"Oh my captain," he said. "Hamza would be so proud. He could never play as you played, with such grace. That was beautiful, my caption."

"Thank you, Fried Man."

Fried Man explained, "That is the house violin. When so many have moved in and out and in and out again, she has remained the house violin.

After a moment of silence, Fried Man moved her from the work table to a safer place. He disappeared for a moment after that. But he returned with a bucked log upon his shoulder. He put down on the work table. He gathered some big clamps to secure the log to the table. Tomph sat back looking at so many species of tools that he had never seen or imagined.

Fried Man disappeared again, around a corner, and he returned with a double-handled saw. Captain and steed cut with the grain of the log (at though they were cutting the tree top-to-bottom), flattening one side of the log like board. Fried Man loosened the clamps and tossed the excess wood aside. Now they had the shape of a soda can sliced in half vertically. Fried Man tightened the clamp again with the flat part of the log facing down. It was time to flatten the other side.

Tomph worked obnoxiously hard pushing and pulling the

saw. Quickly he began sweating profusely. He got all worked up. His nose splattered snot and his ears turned red. A vein on his forehead looked like it would soon rust.

"My Captain, you needn't be so ferocious," Fried Man said. "The blade is sharp."

Tomph went on anyway until, on the opposite side of the log, Tomph's end of the saw burst through and scraped hard against the metal clamp.

"Awwwww, look what you've done," Fried Man said. "You've ruined the blade."

"It's not ruined like a goat Mother, is it?" Tomph asked.

"It's ruined. You ruined it."

"Aww no I didn't. It's fine. See… Right? It's fine. Let me test it on some scrap wood," Tomph said, chomping at the bit.

"Calm down you maniac. This is Hamza's best saw. I'll need to sharpen it."

"But we must get on with it! C'mon, c'mon, c'mon!!!". Tomph begged, pulling the saw from Jack. They each had an end, but Jack was a young Fried Man. Tomph was a boy.

"Patience, boy!"

Finally Tomph calmed. He let go of his end, and he meditated for a moment. He pondered. Then his head rose and there was a glistening is his eye. Fried Man saw the glistening, and Tomph knew Fried Man had seen.

"Fried Man, my steed. It is imperative we have this board ready this instant."

"I believe you, my captain. My apologies! But I must ask: for what reason is it imperative!?"

"Because the instant after this, it will be imperative we are out that door," Tomph said, pointing to a shadowy door between a stack of five-gallon drums and a shelf housing many painted pots. "Because the instant after we are out that door, and a few instances later, it will be imperative that we are in a mystical place far from here."

"If for you it is imperative," Fried Man said, "it is imperative to me."

"It is imperative to us all! Indeed, everyone! Everything!"

Tomph said.

"So, my captain, I will fetch Hamza's second cutting saw."

"Do so, my steed, and I will prepare the clamp."

"That would be a respectable thing to do."

"Well. On with it then!" Tomph said, booting his Fried Man in his ass.

It was not too long before Fried Man returned to help Tomph figure out mechanism used to undo the clamp. Upon the re-clamping of the clamp, Tomph said, "curious! I hadn't thought of that. Thank you, Fried Man," and there was a shaking of the eyes.

"Thank you for thanking me! I was taught by the most curious of them all!"

"Hamza?"

"The curious!"

"Hamza, The Curious!" Tomph repeated the name to himself, treasuring it, hearing it echo a million times in a moment. "A man I hope to drink tea with some day," Tomph said.

"A man I wish to canoe with some day, upon a canoe carved by our very hands, with a tea kettle bigger than a watermelon in its center."

"Indeed," Tomph said. "Has he never shared a tea with you?"

"I so sadly must say that he has not," Fried Man said. "There was never time. And throughout the whole time, I was too young."

"Indeed," Tomph said.

Then Tomph realized that Fried Man had thrust upon him not a saw handle, but the raw end of a saw blade. Fried Man had wrapped a cloth around the last few inches of teeth. When Tomph complained that his end was "rather plebeian", Fried Man explained that it was "for the better, given the circumstances. Trust me, my captain. At least this once."

Tomph obliged, saying, "I trust you, my steed. I will always trust my Fried Man."

"Pleasant," Fried Man said, smiling. And they cut into the

log. They cut and they cut and they cut. Then, upon a fast deceleration of the blade, Tomph sliced his hand. Fried Man apologized before removing the very cloth that failed to protect Tomph's hand. and tying this cloth as a tourniquet for Tomph's deep wound.

Fried Man smiled. "See," he said. "You can trust me, always, to mend your wounds."

"Indeed," Tomph said, examining the medical work. "A tremendous fix!"

"Yes!"

"However!" Tomph said.

"Yes?"

"What you can't provide me, is time. We are never going to make it in time."

"I beg to differ, my captain. You must necessarily allow me to finish the cut myself. Now, if you will, please step outside; for only craftsmen may occupy the crafts room. Take your time that I am giving you, and we shall reunite shortly."

"I oblige," Tomph said. He stepped outside to find silence but for a distant roar. Fear of getting lost kept him from straying very far to investigate. Instead of finding a better view, he sat against Hamza's wall. Inside, Fried Man played a record — reggae jazz — to which the man hummed and whistled and jumped. Tomph heard the saw scraping back and forth. He unwrapped the dressing on his hand. The wound was so deep with blood so red, the world seemed gray.

Fried Man emerged with the board in his hands. It was perfectly cut, perfectly routed, perfectly sanded. It was pristine. His smile faded when he saw Tomph's open wound. He rushed to replace the bandages. "We must develop," he said. "No time for blood-letting! So many instants have passed…"

"You are right," Tomph admitted, reaching out his hand. "Help me up, and we shall chase what is ahead of us."

Fried Man went to help up his captain, but he hesitated. He remorse in saying, "I am so sorry, my captain. The blade was duller than I expected it to be. It was a slow cut, and against the grain."

"Worry not Fried Man. Give me your hand."

"I cannot. Raise yourself, my captain. Show me the way."

"Why can't you?" Tomph asked.

"These are not the proper circumstances, see," Fried Man said, pointing to Tomph's tracks which led left than right then to the place on the ground where Tomph sat.

"Alright then," Tomph said, propping himself up and walking leftward then rightward, searching for his bearings.

Fried Man remained in place still. "Show me your direction," he said, "and I will carry you in that way."

But Tomph could not find his way. There were so many potential ways. He knew there was a someplace where he desired to be, but he hadn't a clue where it was. So he floundered and floundered.

Fried Man told him, "Knock, when you are ready." Then he retreated inside.

Soon the reggae jazz could be heard again. Fried Man hopping around and dancing again. Outside, Tomph examined all the nearby huts. He searched everywhere for anything that could jar some memory inside him to remind him of where he was. He examined everything from walls to fences to the unique ways in which each individual hut or tee-pee was mangled together. He searched for some tiny detail that might conjure remnants of a grasp. But, out of a million details, not one lent him a hand. Worse so, he found himself lost; he could not find Hamza's house.

But then Little One was sitting on a blanket in the grass, sitting with his mother and with Mrs. Ruth's dog (each alive and doing well). They soaked up the sun's rays together. Little One's mum braided his hair. He petted the dog while she did.

He noticed Tomph. Tomph could not speak when the boy approached him — smiling, saying "I have seen you before, haven't I?", and continuing, realizing the circumstances of Tomph's being frozen. "It's okay if you cannot talk.", Little One said. "Sometimes people cannot."

Tomph wanted to ask where they were and where, from here, he was meant to go. But his vocal chords remained stale.

"Mother believes silence is a gift," Little one said. And he strutted away aloof and in some seemingly random direction. His mother followed him, paranoid of his interactions with strangers.

In that moment, Fried Man swept Tomph off his feet and galloped in the direction that Little One's ghost had implied. Soon they were bordering the fields at light speed, zooming unnoticed by the crowds of farmhands intermixed with foreigners from various neighboring villages and distant lands. The crowds hipped and hawed, dancing around small brown nudists who drummed and danced affront a grand wooden carriage (the grandest they had ever seen). It was glorious how so many miscellaneous carriages and chariots and people of various kinds scattered about the field like electrons zipping about their center mass. Time froze, they moved so fast.

Tomph gave Fried Man directional cues by pulling on his ears. "Leftward around this hut."

"Yessir, captain"

"Now rightward around this tree."

"Yessir, captain."

"Let us stop for a moment, Fried Man," Tomph said. "We are coming upon a familiar place. Coming up ahead is the ashy burned garden where we originally met."

"No can do, captain. There is no time," Fried Man said, keeping pace.

"Probably, you are right." Passing the garden, Tomph immersed his eyes in the luscious greens and spectacular yellows and blumescent blues that now overflowed from the once-barren garden area. Soon a stone entryway could be seen on the clearing's distant edge.

Fried Man asked, "why here? Why this way?"

"Not that way." Tomph corrected. "Cut right. See: the unmarked path!"

"Yes! Of course. Yes!" In stride, Fried Man leaped over the fieldstone wall bordering the meadow. He dodged overgrowth with Tomph on his shoulders. For a while, the path was like this: narrow, uneven, overgrown from the sides and above. A wild rush of things darted across the trail, worsening the visibility that was already bad. They were darts. No! Birds. Tiny birds darted across the trail, humming and chirping, and swooshing like Dolphins delving above and below branches.

Suddenly the woods opened to a small, pine-needled clearing. This place had a sacred calmness to it, and a certain feeling of security. There were no birds. There were no sudden movements or sudden sounds. Everything flowed like the breeze: smoothly and gently.

The sudden change in environment suggested a change in pace. So Fried Man lowered Tomph to the ground. The two of them stood on their own feet. They each turned in circles, inspecting the little world they had ventured upon. Listening very carefully, one could hear the birds whizzing around just outside the borders of the meditative place. But the sounds were muffled by the trees like ocean waves heard through glass or seashell.

Then there was a voice. It was Yofim's voice. It said, "The totem, Tomph, you were right. It was more than a nut. I'm sorry Tomph. I'm sorry I called you a loon and laughed. And I am sorry for the many times I have told the others that you are a loon. You are not a loon, Tomph. You are my friend."

Tomph turned to find his friend standing short, round, and sincere.

"Yofim!" he called directly to Yofim's face.

"You are not a loon, Tomph," Yofim repeated blankly, unresponsively. "Remember the shade overlooking the corn fields? Some day, we will meet there again."

"Yofim, wait!! Where are you going?"

"You are not a loon, Tomph."

"Yofim, come back!!"

"You are not a loon, Tomph," Yofim would say, walking into the trees. And he would repeat this over and still over again, all the while putting distance between himself and his friend, who teared up reaching his arm out, wanting more than anything to touch hands with his friend and know that he was real. Quickly, the mantra faded behind the muffled sounds of the birds. There was quiet again (but for Tomph's whimpering). For a moment it seemed Fried Man was no more.

Jack Tomleson asked, "are you alright, my friend?" But Tomph wanted nothing to do with his supposed friend. All he wanted was Yofim. So he turned away. He turned away and he made for the opposite end of the zen clearing. In that direction stood a tall, familiar rock that read something Tomph couldn't read before Fried Man erupted "yes!! yes!! yes!!!", shouting because of a turtle he described as "the most aquatic specimen he'd ever once seen."

"My captain, feast your eyes upon this beauty and the family it lives for, then together we will ascend the mountain path, and together we will know why life is to live for."

Tomph reluctantly turned away from the engraved stone and the mountain path. Fried Man was holding the very board they'd labored for. This piece of wood, it was all that they needed. But at the focus of Fried Man's eyes was a gangly wrinkled tortoise crawling along the meadow floor. On its back, it carried a helplessly small child turtle. Then a dozen more tortoise-turtle pairs followed straggling along behind the leading mother tortoise, who seemed a particular way.

Fried Man described her, saying, "She is ever so resolved to climb this treacherous mountain trail. She is perfectly relaxed — at one with the treacherous journey awaiting her!" Fried Man admitted, "I have never been so amazed at anything in the duration of my life."

Tomph grinned. He agreed that "It [was] amazing." Before, he had been fearful of becoming distracted. But he lightbulbed and rushedly grabbed Fried Man's attention. "We must help them!" he said.

"We must do what?" Fried Man asked.

"We must help them! We must help them! We must help them!!"

"Yes! Yes!! Yes!!"

"We must."

"But how?" Fried Man asked.

For a while Tomph and Fried Man deliberated.

"I've got it!" one of them would say. "We'll place them atop this board, then carry the board up the mountain!"

"I'm skeptical as to whether or not they will stay on the board once they are on it."

"They trust us, my captain. They know we wish to help."

"Possibly a netting of some sort. We could carry them in a bag."

"Or we could put a border around this board — a cage to keep them safe."

"Cages never keep people safe," Tomph said sadly, mourning Little One.

"You're right."

"Maybe we should just lift one, carry it 30 meters or so, then come back for another. We could inchworm the whole group at incredible speeds!!"

"Yes!! But maybe in pairs."

"Yes!! They seem to move in pairs, except for that lone fellow in the back."

"What lone fellow?"

"The lone fellow. He is small and without a partner, yet he crawls along…"

"I don't see him. Gosh, my captain, they're gone!!"

"What?" Tomph was astonished.

"They are gone. Nowhere to be found. Spoofed!!"

"Bollocks. Well, we've got to go then," Tomph supposed.

"Yes," Fried Man said. And he prepared his stirrups and his saddle. And he bit the wooden board between his teeth as his bridal. And he said, "Get on my back!"

"Mounting up!" Tomph said. As fast as he jumped on his friend's back, their journey had begun — up inclines increasingly steep, and on increasingly narrow, treacherous ground weakened by years of alternating heavy rain and dry drought. The periodic fires had burned holes in the vascularity, opening doors for rot. And the floods washed out important, stabilizing roots. Tomph and Fried man traveled the stone pathways and the long, seemingly self-rounding stairway, climbing through clouds, some of whom bursting with thunder, cutting with lighting, and pounding with rain.

"My steed, I see we are sliding," Tomph said.

"My most sincere apologies. This mountain wishes not to be climbed, but I will climb it regardless."

"I see you feel my weight. Place me down, Fried Man, and we can carry each other's weight."

"No can do, my captain."

"For what reason?" Tomph asked.

"This mountain wishes not to be climbed, but I will climb it regardless," Fried Man reaffirmed. Then he continued climbing. He struggled and he struggled and he climbed, sloshing through mud, falling, cracking his shins on the stone stairs. Holding Tomph as though there were nothing more worthy of being held, Fried Man sacrificed his body for Tomph's. He would catch himself with his shoulder or elbow or forehead, and he would make sure that Tomph never touched the mud.

Fried Man built momentum. Faster; faster; stronger, toward the skies. Then they burst suddenly through the clouds. And there was light! Ten steps further, and there it was: the eggstone, standing tall, reading, "Gobbler's Round: beware of the pull."

Past the eggstone, a field of verdant greens extended as far as the eye could see. There were grasses and bushes, berries and young peach trees. In a big theatrical movement, the left and the right sections of these greens parted like oceans, thereby revealing a grand tall tree at the edge of the world, and a carpeted pathway stretching the whole distance to said tree. It was as though Fried Man and Tomph had found themselves in the currents of a main artery sending its flow towards the heart of it all.

Fried Man smiled and said, "Well, then." Then he stepped from the stone patio on which he had been standing (still, with Tomph on his shoulders). His feet, being in the currents, began to step forward. A new energy came over him. He strode long strides. He muttered to himself, "incredible, how incredible, incredible, incredible, how incredible, incredible incredible, how incredible." Meanwhile a chant could be heard low and gentle, seemingly sung by the grass. It left one listener questioning whether what they heard was of the world or of their own mind.

> *"YOU CAN'T UN-KNOW.*
> *YOU CAN UN-THINK.*
> *BUT UN-THINK TOO HARD*
> *AND, YOU'LL BE*
> *ON, THE BRINK."*

This whispering voluminated proportionally to the wind's strength. Fried Man, with Tomph on his shoulder, continued onward across the field of greens. At the halfway point, though, he was splashed in the eye with peach juice from Tomph's peach, which Tomph had picked during their run.

Jack Tomleson remarked, "Less wind, and a person has their thoughts to think. More, and your ears become your brain."

"Yeah," Tomph said.

A full day went by during their walk to the edge of the world. For the final quarter, Tomph and Fried man flowed in a majestic pink river under a spectacle of nighttime sky. The beautiful Milky Way was in plain sight. You could see the whole damn galaxy, just by looking up. Approaching the edge, the river morphed into a deep blue.

Then they were overlooking a sky-scraping cliff with a view of Greenlock Farm. Looking down, it seemed as though the ground was further than the stars above. But two dozen naked, dancing brown men could be seen down there, in the distance. They danced with their arms and legs and every part they had, somehow balancing a magnificent casket on their heads at the same time. They were carrying the casket toward the inner corner of The River Round, where a huge crowd of farmhands and foreign visitors had gathered.

Tomph found the old ropes from the old swing. He worked to loop one of these to each end of the wooden board from Hamza's carpentry shop. Jack Tomleson, from the edge of the cliff, observed the music and dancing and fire-breathing.

Jack said solemnly, "My father spoke of festivals like this one. I don't remember a casket, though." Sadness could be seen in the fried man.

When Tomph gazed off the cliffside, he focused on Henry who might as well have been Little One, and the boy's guardian, Tom-fella, who might as well have been Thom. While holding his guardian's hand, the boy met eyes with Tomph. Tomph signaled to the boy, as to say, "watch me; watch this." Then he tossed up the ropes with hooks on their ends, trying to latch them to the grand branch hanging over the cliffside. Little One laughed when Tomph missed and had to try again.

On one of Tomph's launching attempts, the hooks clanged off the grand branch. Then they fell dangling down over the cliffside. When Tomph tried pulling them up, he learned that the hooks had tangled with some bonsai roots. So, ignoring the fried man's warnings, Tomph laid over the world's end, and he reached down over the edge. With his feet being held by the worrying fried man, he untangled the stray hooks from the all the roots and vines.

It was a dangerous task. But Little One cheered when Tomph succeeded. The boy was too distant to be heard, but his joy in that moment reverberated for miles. The Boy was alone among his peers while his peers focused on each other, the naked brown dancers, the casket, and the river's rapids. The Boy and Tomph, though so very distant from one another, were incredibly together during this time.

Fried Man touted some more. "That negro midget, he has intimidated me before. What is his business here?"

But Tomph succeeded in hooking the ropes and their attached board to the tree branch. And he flicked the ropes in order to spread them out a bit. The swing was perfectly arranged. So he focused on The Boy who inspired him to sit his bottom atop the board, far too thin, and who inspired him to swing out over the edge of the world. The Boy cheered and laughed so hard he keeled over.

Only when Jack yelled, "Christ, almighty!!" did Tomph attend the fried man's words. The tortoises, coming in pairs, walked stoically off the edge of the world. And when Jack stepped in their path, they circumnavigated his legs with complete resolve. Just the same, they would walk off the edge. A whole many of them, pair-by-pair, fell a long, long ways — into the fog clouds, through the fog clouds, and fluttering down towards the rapids.

"My grandfather said to me: 'let me tell you: in the River Round Rapids, there is no hope. If they don't get you on impact, they'll get you with time.'"

From these falling turtles, Tomph's gaze shifted outwards. He swung back and forth: inwards, over sturdy ground; and outwards, over the edge of the world —— in the process, seeing the mossy ground, then seeing the Boy, beside his Father, then seeing the stars, and then the boy again, and then the mossy ground again. With each glimpse of the stars, he found himself on his back, floating in water, seeing darkness but for a cluster of stars that smelled wretched.

A whimpering sound brought Tomph's attention to within the fog clouds. In them, he saw the pregnant women under her overturned boat. It was her whose whimpering it was. She laid on her back in the frigid water. Her stomach was plump, her skin pruned. And she cried. She cried and she cried. She tried speaking to the cluster of stars through the hole in her boat, but no words could escape her hyperventilating breaths. So suddenly, she exhaled all the air in her chest, closed her lips tight, and held her nose. Her tears, they infused with the blue water mellow and pink, as her airless dry-heaving self sunk deep into the ocean.

Then Tomph saw that The Boy was perplexed and scared. In this instant, the thin board cracked underneath Tomph's bottom, and our hero followed in wake of the turtles. He fluttered down into the fog. Through the duration of his fall, he kept eyes on the boy. The boy watched Tomph's falling. But nobody else bore witness. The festival funeral festivized on as it had been festivizing.

Chasing to catch his friend, Jack found himself skidding to a stop at the edge of the world, contemplating life and everything with a million memories flashing before his eyes.

As Tomph fluttered down through the air, the many turtles began completing their journeys, splattering one-by-one onto the rocks in the grand river. The fried man could not handle watching Tomph fulfill the same fate.

The peach trees chanted on as they had before:

> *"YOU CAN'T UN-KNOW.*
> *YOU CAN UN-THINK.*
> *BUT UN-THINK TOO HARD*
> *AND, YOU'LL BE*
> *ON, THE BRINK."*

Jack saw Henry acting frantically on the riverside. The Boy stepped to dive into the waters, wanting to save Tomph. But he was only a boy, and Tomph was certainly dead. Anyone going after him would be certainly dead as well. And for no reason. Especially a boy. Thank the lord, because Tom grabbed The Boy's lapel before he could jump.

"Christ, Tom!" Jack yelled, from way up on that infinitely high cliffside. The relief when the boy was saved, it was so incredible; Jack found his hand on his chest, composing his heart.

"Good 'ol Tom!" Tom yelled, giving a solute with his free arm and still dancing to the nudist music unphased. "Good 'ol Tom, saving the day!"

"Christ. Phew." Jack waved down to Tom and gave him a solute. When he did this, the dozens of farmhands and foreign strangers and brown people and even Harlumn noticed Fried Man waving from way up there on the Great Mountain. Even the Elder Woman Golma from Redman's village noticed. She stood beside Tom, holding the boy's left hand while Tom held his right. Excluding the boy, whose hands were tied, all these people waved and cheered to Fried Man as though he was the second coming of Jesus. Unbeknownst to them, Jack stood on the edge of the world, his chest tightening, his vision blurring, his eyes gazing upon the specs of turtle splatter on the rocks, and his thoughts wandering into dangerous places.

> *"YOU CAN'T UN-KNOW.*
> *YOU CAN UN-THINK.*
> *BUT UN-THINK TOO HARD,*
> *AND YOU'LL BE*
> *ON, THE BRINK."*

Fried Man looked to the waters that had washed his captain and the turtles away. He thought of all the destruction in the world. The horror. The confusion. The confounding, wild, inescapable beauty and power of things. He thought of the river, the universe, and how the river, despite its beauty, had now taken his only true friend from the world. The patternful flowing waters were no longer pure and soulful to him anymore.

Jack thought to leap off the edge of the world.

But then there was The Boy, calmed by Tom and Golma, who realized Fried Man's desire to jump. They were so sad. And there was the beauty; the whole damn festival went on so beautifully. There was Harlumn, who danced with the naked people while dinging his bronze triangle. This midget, despite having every reason to hate the world, was happy off his head. There was Jack's Father, Sydney Tomleson, who, after so many years of burdensome work, now danced uninhibited atop Redman's casket. And there were so many other wholesome souls enjoying the company of their neighbors.

It was then the dancing singing People of Bliss joined strength in order to toss the casket of their lovely leader into the River Round Rapids, Jack's father aboard. Immediately, the music stopped. Along with Redman's casket, Jack's father disappeared in the water. The festival went silent but for the brown people and their friends' theatrical cries (Henry's and Harlumn's heard most loudly).

Following his friend's and his father's fate, Jack edged the cliff. Doing so, he sent some pebbles and stones down bashing off rocks and roots and stumps, ultimately to be thrown, flailing, battered, into the rapids.

But his father reappeared on the shoreline. Harlumn gave the man a hand. And the festival erupted into chaotic samba jazz, Harlumn and Sydney Tomleson dancing at its helm. Jack stepped back from the edge of the world. He looked at everything. He looked to Tom. And beside Tom, he looked to The Boy. Henry kneeled on the ground, clenching his chest and hyperventilating. Beside Henry, Tom and his deaf mother smiled up at Jack. Tom's mother performed a weird series of signs. Golma raised her thumb. Then she waved Jack backwards and into safety.

Turning, Jack caught a glimpse of the broken swing where only a moment earlier his companion had swung. The two dangling halves of the broken board had already grown green moss that flowered with small, white buds.

When Jack's gaze continued around, he saw the sea of peach trees again parting ways. Like Tomph, he picked a peach to enjoy on his journey across. After night had passed, it was early morning. Jack found himself at the eggstone that read "Gobbler's Round: beware of the pull."

From behind the eggstone, a single lonely turtle emerged.

Jack said, "Hey little guy," and he offered the turtle a nibble of peach. Hesitant at first, the small creature circumnavigated Jack's legs and crawled onward. Jack found this curious at first. Then he pondered for a moment, and he became tremendously sad. Quickly, he snatched the turtle up from the path between parted seas. And he said "no, that is not your direction." Soon the turtle was thankful to be in someone's arms. And when Jack offered more peach to the turtle, it filled its empty stomach.

"Oh, you are hungry," Jack said. "You're shivering as well."

The turtle continued eating peach and huddling for Jack's warmth. It communicated all that it needed to. So, Jack said, "It's okay, Fried Man will take care of you." And Fried Man smiled and stepped onward past the eggstone, turtle in arms, making his gradual way down one uneven step after the other.

ABOUT THE AUTHOR

Dernberger Spengleton is an editor and columnist for The Surreal Times (surrealtimes.net). He is based in Amherst, MA., at the University of Massachusetts Amherst, where he studies Mathematics and Linguistics. This is his first book.

Updates on Dernberger can be found at spengleton.net, and he can be reached at spengleton@surrealtimes.net.

NOTE: This book is a golden ticket. If presented at the gates of Spengleton's Castle (once she stands), its beholder will be given entry and accommodations as are available.

Made in the USA
Middletown, DE
25 January 2017